01017548

CALGARY PUBLIC LIBRARY

NOV ·· 2015

The
Cook,
the Crook,
and
THE REAL ESTATE
TYCOON

The
Cook,
the Crook,
and
THE REAL ESTATE
TYCOON

A Novel of Contemporary China

Liu Zhenyun

**Translated by Howard Goldblatt
and Sylvia Li-chun Lin**

Arcade Publishing • New York

Copyright © 2007 by Liu Zhenyun
English-language translation copyright © 2015 by Howard Goldblatt and Sylvia
Li-chun Lin

All rights reserved. No part of this book may be reproduced in any manner without
the express written consent of the publisher, except in the case of brief excerpts in
critical reviews or articles. All inquiries should be addressed to Arcade Publishing,
307 West 36th Street, 11th Floor, New York, NY 10018.

FIRST ENGLISH-LANGUAGE EDITION

Arcade Publishing books may be purchased in bulk at special discounts for sales
promotion, corporate gifts, fund-raising, or educational purposes. Special editions can
also be created to specifications. For details, contact the Special Sales Department,
Arcade Publishing, 307 West 36th Street, 11th Floor, New York, NY 10018 or
arcade@skyhorsepublishing.com.

Arcade Publishing® is a registered trademark of Skyhorse Publishing, Inc.®, a
Delaware corporation.

Visit our website at www.arcadepub.com.

10 9 8 7 6 5 4 3 2 1

Library of Congress Cataloging-in-Publication Data

Liu, Zhenyun.
[Wo jiao Liu Yuejin. English]
The cook, the crook, and the real estate tycoon : a novel of contemporary China /
Liu Zhenyun ; translated by Howard Goldblatt and Sylvia Li-chun Lin.
pages cm
ISBN 978-1-62872-520-9 (hardback)
I. Goldblatt, Howard, 1939- translator. II. Lin, Sylvia Li-chun, translator. III. Title.
PL2879.C376W6313 2015
895.13'52—dc23
2015008545

Jacket design by Anthony Morais

Ebook ISBN: 978-1-62872-552-0

Printed in the United States of America

The
Cook,
the Crook,
and
THE REAL ESTATE
TYCOON

1

Yang Zhi

Yang Zhi first met Zhang Duanduan at Lao Gan's Xinzhou Restaurant.

Lao Gan had a throat problem that created a raspy voice; it was hard for him to talk, but that did not stop him from trying. After Yang polished off five flatbreads and a bowl of mutton soup, Lao Gan came up with the check and sat down to inform Yang what had happened the day before. A man had jumped from the Dahongmeng Bridge on Five-Ring road, an attempted suicide—he managed only to break a leg—that created a five-car pileup. A speeding Mercedes was turned sideways and sent flying by a Shanxi coal truck in the adjoining lane. When it landed, it smacked into a bridge pylon, breaking the pelvis of one of the passengers, a man, while the other passenger, a woman, died at the scene. There was more to the story: the dead woman, not the man's wife, was his mistress, a revelation that caused a commotion at the hospital before the accident was dealt with.

"You can't blame him for being careless," Lao Gan said. "It just goes to show you."

Too preoccupied to pay Lao Gan attention, Yang scooped up his fanny pack.

"That flour you used for the flatbreads, Lao Gan, it was rancid," he said.

"So you could tell. But it's not the flour, it's the sesame seeds. The vendor mixed last year's seeds into this year's. You can see a man's true colors in a tiny sesame seed.

"Have you found the man you were looking for?" he added.

Yang and Gan were both from Shanxi province, Yang from Jincheng and Gan from Xinzhou. One from the north, the other from the south. Yang often ate at Lao Gan's diner, not because they were from the same province, but because of the mutton soup. It was top of the line. Like everyone else, Lao Gan bought the carcasses in the local market, but for some reason his soup just came out better—fresher, richer, and more aromatic, which justified cutting corners with the flatbreads and other dishes, hot or cold.

That did not sit well with Yang, especially after he heard a rumor that Lao Gan put opium in the soup to improve the flavor and develop an addiction in his customers.

On the night of the twenty-fifth of the previous month, a thief had sneaked into Lao Gan's house while the family was asleep. It was clearly someone who had not cased the place beforehand and knew nothing about Lao Gan. Tables, chairs, and stools out front weren't worth stealing, and nothing but well used pots, pans, bowls, and utensils filled the kitchen. So the thief, hoping to find some money, went into the bedroom, where the family slept, with the belief that money must be hidden there. But Lao Gan never kept his money in the bedroom. Instead, each night after counting the day's take, he wrapped it in a plastic bag and buried it in the sesame seed vat. Seeds on top, money at the bottom, ensuring that his wife and children would not get to it. It was a thief-proof hiding place. The thief searched the room, opening the armoire and chest, even checking the clothes strewn around by the sleeping family and the edge of Lao Gan's pillow, but came up with only three and a half yuan. He squatted by the bed to contemplate what to do next, unaware that Lao Gan had woken up and was silently watching him. When he realized that the thief was baffled, he could not keep from laughing. Now, if he'd called out for help, that would have had little effect on the thief, who had encountered plenty of people doing that. But on this night, what the thief heard was raspy laughter, seemingly coming out of nowhere, which so unnerved him his hair stood on end and he ran out, yelling "Thief!" He did not leave empty-handed, however; as he sprinted through the diner, he swept up Lao Gan's jacket, which was hanging on the wall. There was no money in the jacket, which was faux leather, sort of like Lao Gan's diner, a tiny place with the grandiose name Xinzhou Restaurant. There was, however, a school kid's arithmetic exercise book in one of the pockets.

Many of the vendors from the market next to the diner, and migrant workers from the construction site just beyond it, ate at Lao Gan's Restaurant; they were there to fill their stomachs, not sample gourmet food, which was why it was possible for him to cut corners. Since these men did not always have enough to pay for their meals, he ran tabs. Lone diners rarely owed anything, since they would calculate how much they'd spend beforehand. It was groups of customers, with one picking up the tab, who came up short, because people tend to order more when someone else is paying. When the food and drink started running low, the host, wanting to display his generosity, ordered more. They would then run a tab and pay up the next time they came in. Lao Gan kept track of the tabs in the exercise book that had been in the jacket pocket that night. Prior to that, the book had hung on the wall next to the jacket.

One day, while a carcass seller from Inner Mongolia was waiting for his food, he took down the book and began merrily reading out customers' names and the amounts they owed. Afraid he'd offend his owing customers and that his business would suffer if diners spread the news, Lao Gan snatched the account book away and stuffed it into the jacket pocket. It was a spur of the moment decision that then became a habit—he put the book there after finishing the accounting each night. He could not have imagined that a thief would steal it one night. All the small amounts added up to over a thousand yuan. In fact, Lao Gan knew who owed how much, since he also kept the accounts in his head. But losing the book was more than bad luck, since he no longer had proof of who had run a tab. What if they denied owing him anything? He had to get it back.

Yang Zhi was a regular customer, and Lao Gan sensed from their conversations that he seemed to be on good terms with the thieving community. He never asked Yang what he did, and Yang volunteered no information, but the way Yang talked and carried himself gave Lao Gan that impression. So he asked Yang to help him find the thief.

"I don't care about the leather jacket. I'll even give him twenty yuan if he returns the book," he had told Yang.

Now he brought it up again with Yang, who spat on the floor and said:

"First you ask me to find someone for you, then you want me to pay for my food. You can tell a man's true colors in a single meal."

Money in hand, Lao Gan rasped:

"You're right. Here, take it back."

Ignoring him, Yang got up and walked to the door. On his way out, he picked up a napkin from a table to wipe his mouth and spotted a skinny girl at a table by the door, a bowl of noodles with sheep entrails in front of her. But she wasn't eating; she was just gazing out the window at passersby. Yang left the Xinzhou Restaurant, but about halfway to the subway stop he reached for a smoke and realized he'd left his cigarettes on the table. He thought about going back for them, but to save trouble, he bought a pack at a roadside stall. He opened it, took out a cigarette, and lit up. As he continued walking, he noticed the girl from the diner following him.

"Want a date, big brother?" She caught up with him.

Now he could see she was a working girl. He took a closer look— small bones and a small face, seventeen or eighteen at most. Another glance told him she was different from the regular streetwalkers, who sized up potential clients like a cat eyeing a mouse. This one acted like a mouse eyeing a cat, as her face reddened when she propositioned him. Yang was tempted, not by the fact that she was a hooker or that she was blushing, but by the rare sight of a blushing hooker. He hadn't been interested to begin with, but now he couldn't resist, so he nodded and fell in behind her.

"Where are you from?" Yang asked as they walked along.

"Gansu."

"How long have you been doing this?"

The girl glanced at him and lowered her head.

"You probably won't believe me, but I started yesterday. I came to Beijing to find my brother, but he's moved. I called his cell phone but it's no longer in service. I'm doing this for train fare home. You don't have to believe a word I say, of course."

Yang chuckled.

"We'll never see each other again after today," he said. "I lose nothing if you've been at it for a year and gain nothing if you started yesterday."

They walked on.

"How old are you?" Yang asked.

"Twenty-three."

That surprised him. Most girls in her line of work pretend to be younger, but this one, who looked to be in her late teens, wanted to be older. She struck him as someone who was candid and open.

"May I ask your name?"

"No need to be so polite. My family name is Zhang, but just call me Duanduan."

It had to be a phony name, he assumed, but she answered when he called her, so it became real. What difference could it make, anyway? By then, they'd passed two subways stops. He stopped.

"How far is it?"

"Not far." She pointed ahead. "Just up ahead."

Her "not far" took them past yet another subway stop before they turned into a dirty lane barely wide enough to walk side by side and overflowing with the liquid contents of three public toilets. With broken streetlights, he had to watch his step. At the end of the lane, they turned into another, even smaller, lane.

"Is it safe around here?" Yang sized up the place.

"We've walked this far, Big Brother, just to be safe."

Finally, at the end of the lane, they reached a dilapidated house with crisscrossing cracks in the wall. The door was a makeshift entrance made of a sheet of particleboard in a frame of three wooden slats nailed to the wall. After taking out a key, Duanduan bent down, unlocked the door, and stepped inside to turn on the light. Yang looked around and, reassured by the deserted lane, stepped inside. She locked the door while he took stock of the place. It was seven or eight square meters in size, with a bed along one wall and cookware on the floor.

"Light on or off?"

"Off," Yang said after some thought. "Safer that way."

They undressed after she turned off the light. Once they were in bed, Yang Zhi was finally convinced that Duanduan was indeed twenty-three years old, for she knew what she was doing. At first he took the lead, but once they got going, she took over. He did not want to be too rough with the scrawny girl, but before long, she was moving like a pro, a tip-off that you can neither judge people by their looks nor measure the ocean with a scoop. Now that she'd gotten him worked up, he began to enjoy himself. But just then the door was kicked open with a bang, and three brawny men, breathing hard and reeking of alcohol, stormed in, so scaring Yang that he broke out in a sweat. He thought at first they were cops, but their rough exterior and thick necks told him otherwise. Quickly realizing what was going on, he grabbed for his own clothes, which had already been snatched away, along with his fanny pack, by one of the men. The second one gave him a savage slap.

"How dare you come here and rape my wife, you dumb fuck!"

Yang was stark naked, so his hands went to cover his privates, no time for his face.

"This is all a misunderstanding."

He turned to look at Duanduan, who had become a different person, now sobbing with her hands covering her face.

"I was making dinner when he broke in and forced me with a knife." She pointed to the windowsill, where a straight razor lay. The third man picked up the razor and pointed it at Yang.

"Do we take care of this here or do we go to the police?"

Yang realized he'd been suckered, that Duanduan was the bait, which he'd carelessly risen to. The man holding Yang's clothes rummaged through them, taking out his cell phone and wallet, in which he found Yang's money and ATM cards. Then he picked up the fanny pack, which had a knotted strap, opened it and found a large wad of money. The last thing to come out was Yang's ID card.

"Liu Yuejin, it says here." He read the name on the card, then studied him. "Is that you? You're Liu Yuejin?"

Admitting defeat, Yang ignored him, but that did not bother the man, who was checking the photo on the card against the naked man standing in front of him. "Doesn't look like you."

Yang figured it out. Duanduan had been watching when he'd taken money out of his fanny pack to pay at the Xinzhou Restaurant.

2

Ren Baoliang

Everyone at the construction site knew that Liu Yuejin was a thief, but a different kind of thief. Thieves normally steal from people, but not Liu, who preferred to ply his trade at the site. Construction material didn't interest him, for he was a cook, and his thefts were of food, but at the market, not the kitchen. He rose early each morning to shop for supplies. At the market, prices for the leeks, radishes, cabbages, potatoes, onions, or meat were all clearly marked. But since he shopped for several hundred construction workers, he could drive a hard bargain when buying large quantities of onions and potatoes, and could save five fen for each jin of groceries purchased. That alone added up, and he received special treatment by buying from the same vendors all the time. The various cuts of pork—lean, marbled, necks—were priced differently and offered another opportunity to skim a little more off the top. People said that the workers at the site all grew thick necks because they seemed to be eating nothing but Liu Yuejin's pork necks. But a thief only becomes a thief when he's caught; since they never caught Liu Yuejin in the act, he didn't count as a thief, and that is what upset people.

"I've always thought the worst thief was the one you caught," Ren Baoliang, the foreman, complained. "But now I realize that the worst thief is the one you can't catch."

Liu and Ren had known each other for decades. Ren was from Cangzhou in Hebei, while Liu was from Luoshui in Henan. Sixteen years before they met, Ren had served two years in Luoshui Prison, where one of Liu's maternal uncles was a cook. The uncle, Niu Decao, had big eyes as bright as searchlights until he suffered from cataracts at the age of forty, and everything appeared as a blur. Before losing his sight, he had been a slow talker; after the onset of cataracts, he pounded his listeners with loud abuse.

"Don't think I can't see; my mind's eye is clear as can be."

Back when Niu could still see well, he virtually ignored Liu Yuejin when the boy came with his mother to visit. Yuejin was afraid of his uncle. He may have been a prison cook, but he was haughty— not because he worked in a kitchen, but because he worked in a *prison* kitchen. Cooks at regular diners prepare the best food they can, while cooks in prison offer the worse food they can manage. For one thing, they couldn't cook anything palatable for prisoners even if they wanted to, since they're given the same thing the year-round— pickled vegetables, gruel, and cornmeal buns. Diners curse a restaurant cook when the food is not up to standard; that's something convicts will never do. In fact, they treat cooks with humility. Restaurant cooks all looked down on Niu Decao, who in turn had nothing good to say about them.

"Shit," he'd trumpet, "all over the world you see cooks waiting on diners. Where else do you find diners waiting on cooks?"

Though he cursed them loudly, his coworkers and friends took advantage of his poor eyesight by bitch-slapping the back of his head when they met. "Swish," as their hands moved from his head down to his neck before they walked away, giving him no chance to figure out who they were. One winter, Liu Yuejin went with his mother to see his uncle in prison, so Niu took him along to buy pickled vegetables at the market. A friend of Niu's came up to slap his neck, something he'd gotten used to by then. But eight-year-old Liu went up and kicked the man in the shin.

"Fuck off."

Outraged, the man gave Liu a backhanded slap, making the boy cry and drawing the attention of shoppers.

"He was just goofing off," Niu complained to his nephew.

Once they were outside, Niu rubbed the boy's head.

"Rely on blood brothers when fighting a tiger and your own army in battles," he said.

That drew uncle and nephew close. By the time Ren Baoliang went to prison in Luoshui, Liu Yuejin was already married. Ren was a long-distance trucker, hauling coal, foodstuffs, fertilizer, and cotton; depending on the season, he transported anything that brought in money. One day, he drove a truckload of live crabs from Gaoyou in Jiangsu to Tongguan in Shaanxi, where he was stopped at a checkpoint by the Luoshui police. The overloaded truck was too high, so Ren quietly stuffed a couple of hundred yuan into the policeman's pocket. The policeman said nothing, so Ren started the engine, but before he could get back on the road, another policeman came out of the kiosk to check his papers, telling him he was missing something and that he'd have to confiscate his truck. Unwilling to pay off another cop, he checked on the bug-eyed crabs, which were foaming at the mouth, a sign that they needed to get moving. It was bad enough that the second cop was giving him a hard time, but the one who'd taken his money, instead of helping him, turned and walked off. Incensed, Ren ran after him, demanding his money back. The affronted cop insisted he hadn't taken any money from Ren and clubbed him three times before Ren snatched the club and hit back. Ren had been struck three times, on the shoulder, the hip, and the back, while he only hit the cop once, but on the head, sending him thudding to the ground. Hitting an ordinary person was no big deal, but hitting a cop on the head meant big trouble. It was a minor wound with a little blood, but the doctor at the hospital turned it into something much worse—a concussion. That, along with interfering with police work, earned Ren two years and eight months in prison.

One day, when Liu Yuejin was in town to buy piglets, a classmate from middle school, Li Ailian, asked him to take a roast chicken to prison for her cousin, Feng Aiguo, who had stolen a neighbor's cow and her two calves, for which he'd landed an eight-month sentence.

Li, an orphan raised by the cousin's mother, was grateful for the care she'd received. She was permitted one monthly visit, but this was not visiting day, and she knew that Liu's uncle was a cook at the prison, so she asked him to go in her place. After buying the piglets, Liu went to the prison and handed the roast chicken to Uncle Niu, who summoned Feng from his cell to the kitchen. Niu gave the man the chicken and told him to take it over to the corner. But when Feng had finished about half of it, another man shouted from his cell:

"He's not Feng Aiguo. I am."

The man squatting in the corner was Ren Baoliang. Earlier, Feng had been on the toilet with a case of diarrhea when his name was called, giving Ren the opportunity to come up and enjoy the chicken. Niu slapped Ren.

"Isn't there any roast chicken in fucking Hebei?" Niu followed that up with a kick.

"You think you can get away with that because I'm blind, is that it? I don't complain when they cheat me out there, but how dare you try to cheat me in here!"

Then he picked up a rolling pin and began hitting Ren, who froze, protecting his head with his hands, but was still quietly chewing on the chicken. Liu felt so sorry for him he went up to stop his uncle.

"That's enough, Uncle. It's just a roast chicken. You can beat him all you want, but you're not going to get the chicken back."

"It wasn't for the chicken," Ren began to cry. "It's that no one has visited me in all this time, not once."

After Ren served his term, the first thing he did was go to Liu Family Village to see Liu Yuejin, taking along ten ready-to-cook chickens. Five years later, Ren was the foreman at a construction site in Beijing. He and Liu had not seen each other during all those years, though they had written. Another five years passed, and Liu, now divorced, did not know what to do. So he left Luoshui and came to see Ren in Beijing. Before he hired on as a cook at the construction site, they were close friends, but that changed once Liu got the job. Or put another way, it was all right for Ren to tell people that Liu was his friend, but Liu had to treat Ren differently. Or, they were friends in private, but with people around, Ren was the boss. Liu understood the need for hierarchy, so he always called Ren "Baoliang" when they were alone and switched to "Foreman Ren" when someone else showed up.

In addition to the fact that Ren liked Liu's proper manners, he also owed the younger man on account of the roast chicken years before, so he turned a blind eye to Liu's shenanigans in the kitchen. But then one day, Liu went out drinking with some of the migrant workers, who began criticizing Ren. Liu was a different person when he was drinking, giving no thought to what came out of his mouth and forgetting who he was. With nothing much to say about Ren's present state, he brought up the prison term and told how Ren had been beaten in the kitchen on account of a roast chicken. Eventually Ren got wind of what Liu had said. Never shy about his past, Ren was in fact quite proud of it.

"So I've been in a fucking prison," he said. "What makes you think I'm afraid of you punks?"

He could talk about that experience, but no one else could. Or someone else could say it, but not Liu Yuejin, and that is when their friendship soured. Ren wanted to send Liu packing, but was concerned that such a move would make him look petty. So without letting on that he knew, he let Liu stay on; he just took away his shopping privileges, hoping that Liu would leave on his own once his skimming days were over.

It so happened that Ren had a niece who had come to Beijing from Cangzhou to look for work after failing to get into college. Ren arranged for her to be in charge of shopping for the kitchen. Aware that his drunken utterance had gotten him into trouble, Liu thought he might as well leave, since staying would make it awkward for both men. But the one thing China has a surplus of is people, and it would not be easy to find another job on short notice. He could get a job digging ditches and climbing scaffolds, but not work in a kitchen, so he forced himself to stay and wait for something better to come up.

Ren Baoliang's niece, Ye Jingying, was a nineteen-year-old, flat-chested girl who weighed over two hundred pounds. She started work with great enthusiasm, riding a tricycle to the market each morning and recording every item in exercise books, noting even the cost of a bunch of green onions or a head of garlic. When her first month was over, she had filled two books with her accounts, and yet, thanks to her inexperience regarding the ins-and-outs of market purchasing, she spent two thousand yuan more than the previous month, while the dining hall food got worse. At the end of the month, when they went over the accounts together, she handed Ren her books, which he ripped apart and tossed to the floor.

"You're quite the honest one, I must say." He added with a sigh, "I guess it's better to hire a thief than an honest person."

So Ren removed Ye from the job and sent her into the kitchen to steam buns and rice, handing the shopping duties back to Liu Yuejin.

"Foreman Ren," he said, sucking on his teeth, "I'm getting old and am no match for those vendors." He even spoke up for Ye: "You really can't blame your niece, you know."

"You fucked me over before, Liu Yuejin." Ren said impatiently, "And I've fucked you over. So let's drop the act. If you continue to put on airs, I'll fire you for real."

That put a grin on Liu's face as he got on the tricycle and headed for the market.

3

Han Shengli

Liu Yuejin owed Han Shengli thirty-six hundred yuan, stemming from something else he'd done while drinking. He'd gotten into the habit of talking to himself after he turned forty. He'd blurt out something while he was chopping vegetables in the kitchen, walking down the street, or undressing for bed after a long day's work. Later, when he thought this over, he realized he was recalling terrible things from his past and what he muttered was regret for them; he never talked to himself about good things. In recent months, he'd begun saying to himself:

"I have to stop drinking."

Three months earlier, Lao Huang, who sold pigs' necks in the market, held a wedding for his daughter. Unlike other vendors, who sold mainly the meaty parts, with the rest on the side, Huang dealt exclusively with necks and entrails, which made his products cheaper; Liu Yuejin was a regular customer. As time passed, they became such good friends that if, after buying necks, Liu took some pork intestines without paying and put them on his three-wheeler, Lao Huang would let it pass. Sometimes, after all that, Liu would stay behind to chat with Lao Huang. So when Lao Huang's daughter got married, Liu took a wedding gift of money and attended the banquet, where he drank more than he ate and was soon drunk. The woman sitting beside him was the wife of Wu Laosan, who also dealt in chicken necks and other byproducts. Liu sometimes bantered with Wu's wife when he was shopping. For instance, Wu and his wife were both from the northeast, where women are particularly buxom. Liu would say:

"Look, your breasts are filling up. It's nursing time."

"Call me mama, and I'll nurse you," Wu's wife might reply.

Her husband would smile silently while smoothing out his chicken necks.

So when Liu sat down next to Wu's wife at the banquet, they ate and drank and began their usual bantering. Liu started out with jokes, but as soon as he had a little too much to drink, he lost his common sense and control of his hands, which took their lead from his mouth and grabbed her breasts. She didn't mind, even giggled, but her husband, who was sitting across from them, would have none of it. He might not have cared if he too hadn't drunk too much, but he had and he was livid. He picked up a plate and flung it across the table at Liu. Had Liu not been so drunk, he'd have known he was in the wrong and wouldn't have fought back. Completely forgetting who and where he was, he wiped the food off his face and splashed a bowl of chicken-neck soup all over Wu, so enraging him that he picked up Huang's butcher knife and climbed over the table to use it on Liu, who sobered up fast. Others tried to stop Wu, but that only further enraged him.

"Keep your hands to yourselves. I'll use this on anyone who tries to stop me. This has been going on too long and I'm not going to take it any more."

The disturbance ended only when Lao Huang stepped in to mediate and the two sides struck a deal. Liu would give Wu thirty-six hundred yuan for the damage caused by his roaming hands. Since he had only three hundred yuan on him, he hit up a man from his hometown, Han Shengli, for the remainder. They went to the bank, where Han withdrew thirty-three hundred, and lent it to Liu at three percent interest. Liu then handed the full thirty-six hundred to Wu, putting an end to the altercation. Still feeling the effects of the alcohol, Liu didn't feel too bad about the money, especially because he'd managed to cop a feel, but by midnight he'd sobered up enough to be besieged by remorse and fury with Wu.

"It only costs eighty yuan to sleep with a hooker. I didn't even touch the important parts and I had to shell out thirty-six hundred. It shouldn't cost that much to screw your wife *and* your sister!"

Then he turned his anger to Lao Huang, who had negotiated the amount.

"You took advantage of me when I was drunk. What kind of man are you?"

From then on, he bought his pig and chicken necks from different vendors, ending his dealings with both Wu and Huang. But his troubles with Han were just beginning. They had agreed on a three percent interest rate, and Liu was to pay him back within three days. Three months had passed, and Liu had yet to pay back a single yuan, which could mean one of two things. Either he didn't have the money, which was Liu's excuse, or he had it but refused to pay his debt, which was Han's belief. They had several arguments over this.

"No good deed goes unpunished," Han said with a shake of his head. "Once you do something good, your friend becomes your enemy."

Now that they were enemies, Han disregarded the niceties of friendship and came for his money, once a week at first, then every night. Liu changed his tune, refusing to say whether he had the money or not. Instead he said:

"There's money, but it's with Ren Baoliang. He's slow in paying me. Do you expect me to drag it out of him?"

Or: "Go see Ren Baoliang and get him to pay me, then I'll pay you back."

Han did not know what to do with him.

"You've got it all turned around. You owe me, so why should I go see Ren Baoliang?"

Han came one day, not in the evening, but at noon. He was partial to Western suits, which he bought from a vendor at the night market near the construction site; they cost him twenty or thirty yuan, all second-hand goods of dubious origin. But on this day, he was wearing a bloody white T-shirt. His pants were also stained with blood and his head was bandaged. Liu was selling food at the dining hall, where several hundred migrant workers were in line with their lunch boxes. Acting like a different man, Han pushed through the crowd of hungry workers and reached the window.

"If you don't give me my money today, Liu Yuejin, I'm going to kill you."

Liu panicked when he saw the blood.

"What are you doing? Trying to scare me with makeup?"

Liu handed the ladle to Ye Jingying, who was doling out rice, and walked out of the kitchen. It took all the nice things he could say to finally drag Han to the back of the dining hall, where he had him sit on a pile of steel rods before sitting himself.

"How could you come yelling like that in front of everyone for that little bit of money? Aren't you ashamed of yourself? I am, for your sake."

"I was beaten." Han shook his bloody shirt. "Because of you."

"Who did it?"

"You don't need to know. I owe people money, too." He glared at Liu. "People I ought to learn from. They don't just want my money—they'll take my life if it comes to that. All I ask from you is my money."

Liu knew that Han stole from people in the area. He must have been caught and gotten a serious beating.

"Eight stitches." Han pointed to the bandage. "Cost me a hundred and seventy, and that's on you too."

Liu lit a cigarette and steered the conversation in a different direction:

"No matter what we do, Shengli, we can't be cold-hearted. Do you remember back home eight years ago, when your stepmother kicked you out, how it was snowing and the wind was like a knife? Who took you in and gave you a bowl of hot noodle soup?"

"I guess I should call you uncle for what you did for me that day. But you've brought that up a thousand times, and it's old hat. Let's not get sidetracked, dear uncle. They want their money back fast, so I need it now."

"I really don't have it. Honest. Give me a few days."

Han looked around before jabbing at the rods he was sitting on.

"Look at all these. Get some out at night and we'll call it even."

Liu wasn't quite sure how Han got all bloodied, but the suggestion of thievery had him leap to his feet.

"I don't care what you do all day, Shengli, but I don't plan to become a thief."

Han was upset. So was Liu. "Don't get me mad, or thefts will be the least of your worries. It might involve something like a clean knife in and a bloody knife out."

"I want my money back, but you say you don't have it," Han shouted. "And you won't steal for me. What do you expect?"

A group of workers who had finished their lunch appeared around the corner, so Liu grabbed Han's hands and lowered his voice:

"Three days. Give me three more days."

4

Liu Pengju

Besides talking to himself, Liu Yuejin learned an important lesson upon turning forty, and that was, people can be divided into two types, one that's qualified to talk and the other that ought to keep their mouths shut. Those in the latter group always get themselves into trouble by saying things they shouldn't say; you can die for saying the wrong thing. For Liu Yuejin, there were things he was qualified to talk about, such as what they'd be having for lunch that day. He could offer turnip stew with cabbage, or cabbage stew with turnips, with or without pigs' necks, and how much; he ran the show, just like his uncle at Luoshui Prison years before, a man who decided what the inmates would have for lunch. But like his uncle when he was away from prison, Liu had no authority once he left the construction site; he could say what he wanted, but it would have no effect. If he laid it on thick, he had to deal with the consequences, which could be considerable. Everything was fine if he was able to deal with those consequences, but he could really be in hot water if he couldn't. Yet he loved to lay it on thick—it excited him.

Liu's son, Pengju, was a high school student back home. Liu had laid it on thick in regard to the son, which made him feel terrific when he did, but it wound up becoming a crushing burden for six years. If not for this son, Liu wouldn't have been so shameless as to keep from paying Han back, even though he had the money. He'd been on the up and up before turning forty, but now he was a different man.

"How did I get to be like this?" he often muttered.

Six years earlier, his wife, Huang Xiaoqing, divorced him. Before the divorce, he was working as a cook in a restaurant called Xiang's Diner in a county town in Henan. He did everything, from preparing the food to making the noodles and buns. A year into the job, he found an opportunity to talk the owner into hiring his wife to serve and clear tables. He made seven hundred yuan a month; she made three hundred.

A man named Li Gengsheng, one of Liu Yuejin's elementary school classmates, ran the Luoshui distillery. When any of the students in the class lost a fight, they took their anger out on Li, the class sissy. Like everyone else, Liu had vented his frustrations on Li, a big kid who earned the nickname, "Big and Dumb." No one could have predicted that thirty years later Big and Dumb would be the general manager of Pacific Distillery, which, though small, produced "Little Leaping Chick," which sold for two-fifty a bottle, and Maotai, which went for thirty-eight. The big and dumb sissy of thirty years before had grown into a man with backbone. One day, Li came to Xiang's Diner with some friends and, when he heard that the waitress was Liu's wife, he went into the kitchen to bring Liu out to drink with them. One of Li's friends asked Liu how much his wife earned at the diner. When Li heard three hundred, he immediately offered her six hundred to work in his distillery bottling Maotai. Both Liu and his wife were elated by this unexpected good fortune.

"I'm doing this for no other reason," Li said, pointing to Liu Yuejin, "than the kicks you gave me when we were kids."

Everyone laughed.

Huang Xiaoqing left the diner the next day to work at the distillery and by the following spring was transferred from bottling to sales, a promotion that often took her out of town with Li to sell their products all over China. She received a percentage of the profits, as much as fifteen hundred a month, much more than Liu made as a cook. Believing that his old classmate was helping them out, Liu would take Li's hands when they met and say:

"You've been very good to us, and I, your elder, will never forget it."

In the meantime, rumors about Li and Huang were flying around town; everyone knew about the affair, everyone but Liu Yuejin, until one winter night, that is.

Pacific Distillery had a security guard named Zhang Xiaomin, the son of Li Gengsheng's cousin, which was how Zhang got the job. On the night of the winter solstice, Li drove back to the factory after a night of drinking; Lao Zhang, who'd also had a lot to drink at a class reunion, was dozing off in the guardhouse. Li called out at the entrance, but no one responded. Then it began to snow and the drunken Li shivered in the cold wind; he called again and still got no response. So he opened the gate, stormed into the yard, and kicked open the guardhouse door. Once inside, he picked up a club like a police baton, which Zhang carried on his belt on his rounds. Emboldened by the alcohol, Li gave Zhang a savage beating, something he'd gotten used to doing in recent days. At one point, the club smashed a mirror hanging above the bed, sending glass shards raining down; one made a gash on Zhang's face, but the blood did not stop Li.

"You fucking idiot." Li spat into Zhang's bloody face. "I'd be better off keeping a dog around than keeping you."

He tossed away the club and left. Lao Zhang took the beating and cursing without complaint, but was left with a scar on the left side of his face once the wound healed. His girlfriend broke up with him because of it. Upset, he went to Xiang's Diner one day when Liu was making lunch and whispered something to him. Liu put down his spatula and ran to Pacific Distillery, where he kicked open Li Gengsheng's office door and found him and Liu's wife, both stark naked. Liu went up and began hitting Li, who did not fight back, until he couldn't take it any longer. Zhang Xiaomin ran off when he saw them fighting, while Liu's wife got dressed and left without trying to stop them. In the end, Liu lost the fight; no longer big and dumb, Li, the victor, crouched on a chair, still naked, and lit up a cigarette.

"It is what it is, so sue me."

Soon Liu's sad tale of being beaten by his wife's lover when he caught them in the act spread around town, giving Liu the reputation of being gutless, sort of like Li back when they had been in elementary school, except that it was all right for a kid, whereas, for Liu the cuckold, it was a tremendous loss of face. Early the next morning, Liu went back to the distillery with a bunch of relatives, but Li had already left with Lao Huang to sell their liquor in Hainan. Unable to vent his anger on Li, Liu stormed the workshop with his helpers and smashed bottles, sending Maotai flowing like a river. But that didn't ease his frustration; instead, he felt his mind was a total blank. As he lay in bed that night, he was puzzled, not over why he hadn't known about his wife's infidelity for a whole year, but over why the two of them had got together in the first place. Liu could understand why his wife had fallen for Li, probably for his money, but he wondered what Li had seen in Huang Xiaoqing, who wasn't pretty, with tiny, slitty eyes, a thin face, and a nose covered in freckles. She was past thirty, and Liu saw nothing attractive about her. Why would Li pick up with her, since he could probably have any woman he wanted? Was it simply because Liu had kicked him back then? But Liu wasn't the only one. All the others who had abused Li were now married, so was Li going to get involved with every one of their wives? That wouldn't be possible, would it? For Liu, it was exasperating to be cuckolded and truly unbearable to be puzzled like that. Still confused, he went to ask a friend he could trust, Lao Qi, a flatbread vendor with a stall by Xiang's Diner.

"I'm puzzled, too." Lao Qi was turning the cakes as he scratched his head with a greasy hand.

Liu went to ask other people he trusted, but instead of giving him a satisfactory explanation, they thought something was wrong with him, that he was on the verge of losing his mind. Liu was the only one who knew he was more normal than usual. In the end, he gave up and called Li Gengsheng, who was in Xi'an at the moment. Li didn't pick up at first, and when he finally did, he was caught off guard by what Liu wanted to know.

"I just like her waist," Li said. "So tiny I can put my hands around it."

That made Liu's head buzz. During the thirteen years of their marriage, he hadn't noticed any difference between her waist and those of others; now he felt worse than when he'd learned of the affair. Li had seen something special in her waist, which justified the affair and turned Liu into the guilty party. Putting down the phone, he felt that all the days of the past forty-two years had changed color, but that was not something he could share with his friends. If he did, it would be turned into another joke.

That was when he began to drink, and when he was drunk he was a different man. The upside of being drunk was the ability to forget things; the downside came the day after, when he sobered up and was so sad he could cry. Yet when no tears came he simply sat, lost in thought, eventually turning suicidal, not over the affair or the reason behind it, but because everything was all twisted and he couldn't wrap his head around it. In the past, when he heard about a suicide, it brought fear to his mind, but now it felt like a liberation. There were many ways to kill yourself—drinking pesticide, slitting your wrists, jumping into a river, or electrocution—but all he could think of was hanging. His neck started to itch at the thought of it; he could even feel the sweet sensation of a rope around his neck. At times he shouted in his sleep:

"Someone bring me a rope."

Committing suicide sounded grand, but in the end he did not go through with it, because of his son, who had been dragged into Huang's affair. He was twelve. Based on what she'd done, people began to speculate on her past, saying it was hard to tell whether he was indeed Liu's son. So Liu took his son to the county hospital for a DNA test, whose result showed that they were indeed father and son. Three months after the test, Liu and his wife were divorced. Huang wanted the son with her, but Liu said he'd club the boy to death before he'd give him up. Being the guilty party, Huang knew she had no right to insist, so she said:

"You can have him, and I'll give you a monthly allowance."

Still upset with her, Liu blurted out:

"I don't want your slutty money. I wouldn't take anything from you even if he and I had to beg on the street."

Those words made him feel wonderful, even winning a thumbs up from the man in charge of the divorce decree work. The bravado felt fantastic, but six years later, Liu realized how foolish he'd been, for his words had gotten him into a load of trouble and backbreaking hardship. In the meantime, he was also aware of his own inconsistency: he'd said he didn't want her slutty money and yet he'd asked Li for a compensation of sixty thousand yuan during the settlement. Money was money, nothing slutty about it, but Liu had spoken too fast.

5

Yan Ge

Yan Ge, the CEO of the Greater East Asia Real Estate Development Company, was originally from Hunan. He'd always been on the slender side, even when all his friends put on weight after turning thirty and walked around with drooping paunches. With peasants as parents, he lived in poverty until he was thirty-two; as a college student in Beijing, he had to save half of his lunch for dinner, which he managed by adding more rice. Ten years after graduating from college, he still had little to show for himself after switching jobs seventeen times. Everything changed in his thirty-second year, when he met a special person. When you are down and out, the dark nights seem never ending, but once your luck changes you can become rich and famous overnight. It had been less than two decades since meeting his "patron saint," and he had already been transformed from a penniless man to a billionaire, no small feat for someone whose major in college was ethics, not real estate, architecture, economics, or finance. Courses in ethics had taught him nothing; he became a member of the upper class by building houses. Now photos of him appeared on billboards along Fourth Ring Road, from which he looked out at his real estate empire.

Troubles cropped up once he became rich, not because of his wealth, but because of the people around him. After turning forty, he detected two major changes in China: one, people were getting fatter, and two, they had become more petty. Traditional Chinese beliefs have it that people get more broad-minded as their bodies fill out. But not the people around Yan Ge—the larger they got, the pettier they became. As if that weren't enough, they were also stubborn hair-splitters with whom he had to deal constantly. He didn't mind if other people, even his friends, were stubborn, but his own wife was getting fatter and pettier by the day, and that was a major headache. Qu Li had been a quiet, slender girl, but after the age of thirty she began squabbling over every little thing. There she was, the wife of a businessman worth billions, bickering with the people at the neighborhood beauty salon over something as simple as a hairdo.

Before his rise, Yan Ge never brought up his past, and now, whenever he mentioned eating leftovers in college, people laughed and complimented him on his sense of humor. But he sighed over his conviction that Chinese people had no understanding of humor. He had always thought that humor was linked to language, but now he realized that it was tied to race, that those with a sense of humor were a different animal altogether. The twist was, people with no sense of humor could do lots of comical things. Take a look outside and you'll see how the world has changed: bath houses are now called cleansing plazas, a diner has become gourmet city, a barber shop is a beauty center, nightclub girls are ladies, later changed to princesses. He felt he was in the minority whenever he went out, and he had to learn to be humorous.

"This is Mr. Yan, CEO of the Greater East Asia Real Estate Development Company." He played down such introductions:

"No need for that. I just build houses."

When people commented on his fitness, he'd say:

"You have to eat to get fat."

When people said his business was so big that his company had built half the houses in Beijing, he'd shake his head:

"I'm just a laborer, moving bricks and cement. Please don't laugh at me."

Once people started saying he was funny, he stopped joking with them, not because he disliked being funny, but because he'd suffered as a result. He was surrounded by fat, petty people, who were ruthless in life and in business. Water boils at a hundred degrees centigrade—for them it was fifty; water freezes at zero—for them it was fifty. Their boiling and freezing points were exactly the same.

In his view, the biggest change after the age of forty was that he stopped being funny and turned into a stern person; as time went by, he grew to dislike jokes. If one of his subordinates joked with him, he would reply with a frown:

"Can't you be serious for a change?"

Instead of responding to a friend's joke, he would simply repeat what had been said verbatim, without so much as a smile. Looked at differently, Yan was more or less the same as the people around him, except, of course, he was not fat.

More than a dozen Greater East Asia ventures were in progress, each headed by a foreman, of which Ren Baoliang was one. Yan Ge often went to the sites, where men from all over China—Hebei, Shanxi, Shaanxi, Anhui, and Henan—labored. He enjoyed listening to the migrant workers, who were extraordinarily witty, even though they survived on turnip stew with cabbage or cabbage stew with turnips. They revived Yan's residual sense of humor. His foremen thought he came to inspect their work; he did that, but mainly he wanted to listen to the migrant workers talk, for a breath of fresh air. As the sages said, ancient traditions often reside in crude places and wisdom emerges from the common man. Fat, petty people had gobbled up all amusing things and words along with their abalone and shark's fins, while what remained managed to survive among unpolished people who lived on turnips and cabbage. The slaves write history, Chairman Mao said. He was right.

Among his dozen or so foremen, Ren Baoliang was Yan Ge's favorite, because he was funny sometimes and obtuse at other times. The workers thought Ren was a shrewd man, but to Yan, Ren was simply foolish, crude maybe, or just obtuse, though with a sound logic. That is, Ren spoke the truth, which sounded ridiculous at first, but its veracity came through clearly if you paid attention. There's nothing funnier than the truth.

One evening, Yan went to Ren's site, where construction was underway on the CBD building, which was already fifty-some stories high. Yan and Ren rode the elevator to the top, where they could see all of Beijing in the sunset.

"What a view!" Yan said with an admiring sigh.

"The girls ought to be on the prowl again," Ren said, pointing to the street below, where the people moved like ants. He spat. "They're whores," he said angrily, "but now everybody calls them ladies.

"Let's forget about building houses, Mr. Yan," Ren continued. "Let's open a whorehouse. It's a much easier way to make money."

It was a non sequitur that sounded stupid at first, but was actually quite funny. Yan had been bothered by something when he arrived; now doubling over from laughter, he forgot his problems and stayed an hour longer than planned, even though he had a dinner engagement that evening. All lit up, Tiananmen Square had never seemed so beautiful. So Yan started coming to Ren's site once a week, mainly to listen to the workers and Ren talk; he ate in the dining hall if he came at mealtime. The workers had eaten so much of Liu Yuejin's turnip stew with cabbage that their stomachs churned when they picked up their rice bowls; but not Yan, who thought the food was delicious. He could easily down two bowls, eating so heartily that sweat bathed his forehead.

"Time for another revolution," Ren would say when he saw Yan enjoying the food. "You'll have food like this every day when the revolution comes."

That made Yan laugh.

One day Yan came to the site at lunchtime. Tired of the food in the dining hall, Ren bought a boxed lunch to eat on the steps in his little yard. It wasn't much of a yard, just a small enclosure some three meters from the work tent, beneath a date tree, with a table he fashioned out of discarded planks. Ren was having roast chicken with chestnuts when he spotted Yan. Thinking Yan was there for lunch, he said as he chewed:

"Wait here. I'll send someone to get you some."

But Yan was not there to eat or to listen to them talk that day. He was looking for someone, not anyone in particular, just someone who could pretend to be someone else. After Yan's involved, prolonged explanation, Ren was still confused.

"Are you putting on a play, Mr. Yan?"

"Acting out in real life, not in a play."

"Why do you need to act something out in real life?" Ren laughed after a momentary pause. "You can see real life going on all over the place."

"If you don't do something right, you'll have to act it out again, won't you?"

Yan followed up with a detailed description of what he meant by something not done right. It turned out that he had been carrying on with a pop singer who specialized in songs praising the nation and motherhood; she'd done that so long she'd become anorexic. In fact, she was faking anorexia; it was just that the songs were so nauseatingly saccharine that her fans were disgusted by the nation, by motherhood, and by her. She used her lost appetite as a ruse to divert people's attention and change her style in the process, for she was also sickened by the nation and motherhood. Put differently, it was a ploy.

One day Yan went to see her, not for the nation or motherhood, but for their own sake. When they finished what he'd come to do, she put on a pair of dark glasses and walked him down the stairs, which was next to a small lane bustling with all sorts of business that made life possible—a shoemaker, a mutton barbecue vendor, a bike repairman, a popcorn maker, a boiled corn vendor, and a baked sweet potato vendor.

Before they parted, the pop star went up to buy a baked yam, at the very moment a tabloid reporter was eating soup across the lane. Surprised to see her there, he snapped a picture. No problem if it had been anyone else, but he was a journalist, so naturally it appeared in the next day's paper, filling half a page. There were two pictures, actually: one, a street scene with bustling crowds and the various businesses, the other, a close-up in the upper right corner.

The pop singer was standing in front of the stall, about to stuff a yam into her mouth. Beneath the photo was a caption: ANOREXIA, ANOTHER PUBLICITY STUNT? Being in the paper didn't hurt her, nor did claims of a publicity stunt; she needed to stay in the public eye, and however that was accomplished didn't matter. The problem was, Yan Ge's head was peeking out from behind the singer's right shoulder; he looked like he was the anorexic.

He didn't mind being in the paper, since his picture was on a billboard on Fourth Ring Road, but in this particular photo he was not alone. To be sure, not many people would recognize him either from the billboard or the paper; but his wife would, especially because she'd long suspected him of having an affair, a suspicion that became fact thanks to the picture in the paper.

His wife, Qu Li, was in Shanghai visiting her parents, and when she returned that afternoon, she'd see the photo as soon as she stepped off the plane. If she could quarrel with a beautician because she was unhappy with her hairdo, just imagine what she'd do when she saw Yan Ge with another woman in the paper. Burying a knife in him was not out of the question.

Before she lashed out at anyone, Qu Li was in the habit of conducting an investigation, which was always more unpleasant than the actual fight. Based on this logic, it was safe to assume that, after reading the paper, she would check out the "scene of the crime." To deceive his wife, Yan thought he could re-enact the previous day's events, so that when Qu came to ask around, people would say he hadn't arrived there in the company of the pop star. If Yan "happened" to be at the wrong place at the wrong time, he could claim he did not know the singer, and there was a chance that Qu Li would believe him enough to spare him.

Yan had dealt with every vendor in the lane, all but the one from Anhui who sold boiled corn. An easily frightened man, he trembled when he talked and posed a threat to Yan's scheme, which was why he needed to find a replacement, someone who looked like the corn vendor. Since there were plenty of men who looked like him at the work site, Yan came to see Ren Baoliang for help. The explanation wore him out, but Ren at least understood what Yan wanted, though he was not completely convinced.

"Won't it be a waste of effort if she doesn't read the paper?"

"Someone will tell her if she doesn't see it herself. She's surrounded by fat, petty people."

Ren knew all about Yan's theory of fat, petty people.

"Why go to all that trouble?" he asked with a sigh. "If it was me, I'd have divorced her long ago and put an end to it."

"It's not as simple as you think." Yan glared at Ren. "If a divorce were possible, don't you think I'd have done that long ago?" He added, "Haven't you seen how it's done on TV? They set up a fake scene when an official goes to inspect a place, just like I plan to do with my wife. That fits a range of problems."

Now Ren was resigned to the fact that they would have to put on a show. Still, he scratched his head and said:

"But you've come to the wrong place for play-acting. I've got hundreds of workers here, but they have trouble taking care of real life. They don't have time for acting."

Yan's cell rang. He looked at the screen and decided not to get it. Instead, he studied Ren's face.

"I think you'll do."

Ren jumped, as if he'd been insulted.

"How did I give you that impression? You could skin me and I'd still be the most honest, trustworthy person in the world." He changed the subject. "Let's talk about serious matters, Mr. Yan. We're six months behind in payment, and you really need to take care of that. I could postpone payment for the material, but the workers haven't been paid for six months, and they're beginning to cause trouble." He gestured to stress how serious it had gotten: "My car tires have been slashed five times this month."

Ren drove a secondhand VW Santana.

"I am talking about serious matters." Yan stopped Ren from going off track. "How will you get your money if my wife kills me?"

That got Ren's attention; he was about to respond when the gate to his yard was flung open with a clatter and in walked Liu Yuejin. Neither greeting nor looking at them, he walked straight to the date tree, took out a rope, and tossed one end over a branch. Ren and Yan were shocked.

"What are you doing, Liu Yuejin?" Ren shouted.

"I've been working here for six months and haven't been paid yet." Liu put his head through the noose. "My wife and child are gone, so there's no reason to go on living."

Liu had just seen Han Shengli off with two hundred yuan, grocery money for the dining hall, which, as he told Han, he'd have to make up when he went to the market later. In fact, Liu had already skimmed enough to get the two hundred yuan, but he made up the story because he didn't want to pay Han back.

Han had acted differently that day; before leaving, he told Liu he'd give him two days to come up with the remaining thirty-four hundred. If he failed, Han would have to get rough with him. He didn't appear to be joking.

Liu had more than three thousand yuan, but that was his emergency fund, which he wouldn't touch unless absolutely necessary. He needed at least five thousand to feel comfortable.

After Han left, Liu could not stop worrying. His son, Liu Pengju, had just called from Henan, reminding Liu of his tuition, 2,760 yuan and fifty-three fen, which also had to be paid in two days, or his son would be kicked out of school. Liu owed Han money, his son needed money, and Ren Baoliang owed him wages; the logical step, of course, was to ask Ren for his pay, with the call from his son serving as the perfect excuse. On the other hand, he knew that Ren had no money, which was why he had to resort to an unusual measure to squeeze it out of him.

Lucky for him there was a precedent: just the month before, Lao Zhang had resigned to go back to Anhui for some family matters. When Ren refused to pay him, he climbed onto a tower crane and threatened to jump, drawing the attention of several hundred onlookers, as well as firefighters and the police.

"Come down from there, Lao Zhang," Ren shouted. "I know what you want."

Zhang came down and Ren paid his wages, so now Liu Yuejin wanted to copy Zhang's ruse to get his. A decade-long friendship with Ren caused him to hesitate at first, but he was forced to go through with the ruse, partly because of his urgent need for money and partly because of their falling-out over shopping for the dining hall. But he did himself no favor by this tactic, since Ren knew exactly what he was up to.

"What do you think you're doing, Yuejin?" Ren shouted angrily. "What's your family got to do with me? It's been six years since your wife ran off with another man." Ren pointed at Yan. "Know who this is? It's Mr. Yan, our CEO. He built half the houses in Beijing. You work for me and I work for him."

"Did you see that, Mr. Yan?" Ren said with a flick of his hand. "You have to take care of the workers' pay. This goes on every day."

Yan, who had remained quiet the whole time, clapped his hands softly when he saw the two men arguing.

"What a great show!" He turned to Ren. "Did you set this up? You could be a director, and you're telling me you can't act?"

Ren was so outraged he flung his boxed lunch to the ground, sending chestnuts and chicken pieces all over the place. "You keep saying that, Mr. Yan, and I'll go hang myself, too."

Then, pointing at the high-rise that was by then nearly sixty stories high, he went up and gave Liu a kick.

"You want to die? Then go jump off that building."

Yan stepped in and stopped Ren.

"No need to look for anyone else." He pointed to Liu. "He's the one."

6

Qu Li

On this afternoon, Liu Yuejin, dressed in someone else's clothes, squatted at an intersection to boil corn, pretending to be someone he'd never met. Yan Ge had told him that the man from Anhui was about the same height, weight, and appearance, though it didn't really matter if there were differences. This was all created to deceive one woman with a photo, and no one could tell the difference between the two corn vendors; the other man was about the size of a pea in the photo, so all they needed was overall similarity. They were the ones Yan Ge's wife would likely question. Besides, the focus of the photo was not the corn vendor, but the yam vendor and the mutton vendor next to him. Having a fake corn vendor, like drawing a tiger based on a cat, was for reassurance.

This was Liu's first time playing someone else, for which Yan paid him five hundred. Pocketing the money, Liu was immediately in character.

"Didn't you say the man's from Anhui?" he asked Yan. "I'm from Henan. What if she hears the difference when I talk?"

Yan was caught off guard. Liu was right about the accent. Why hadn't he thought of that? But then he realized Liu's mistake; the man didn't talk in the photo. Yan was the only one who knew he was from Anhui; Qu Li wouldn't know. Relieved, he said to Liu:

"Just speak in your Henan dialect. Don't worry about it. The key is not to get nervous." He added, "You're not the protagonist, but still you need to be careful. My wife is like a weasel that can smell a rat. That's why I need you."

Liu nodded. Putting the Anhui accent aside, he asked another question: "What did the photo-taker want, money?" He pointed at the photo and then jabbed the other side of the paper with his finger. "He's putting you through a lot of trouble."

Yan sighed.

"Money and something else, resentment. Resenting someone who has a better life."

Liu nodded.

A newly constructed shopping center lay in the background of the photo. Yan Ge pointed to the top of the building and said, "If we'd put a sniper there, *bang*, he'd be dead by now."

Liu had another question, same as Ren's: why couldn't Yan, a CEO, no less, simply come clean with his wife? He liked someone else. What was wrong with that? If his wife knew, she knew, and he could get a divorce and marry the singer. There'd be no need to sneak around. Why go through all that trouble to re-enact a scene in order to deceive her? In this regard, Yan Ge was no match for Li Gengsheng, the phony liquor maker at Pacific Distillery, who wasn't at all shy about stealing Liu's wife. Liu didn't bring up the last point, figuring that everyone has his own issues. In fact, he even felt sorry for Yan, who had wife trouble even though he was a wealthy CEO. They were in the same boat—maybe not the same boat, but neither wanted the truth to come out.

Yan told Liu not to be nervous; what Liu felt was discomfort, not anxiety. When he put on the Anhui man's clothes, he could tell they were secondhand, bought at the night market, because of the smell. Who knew how many times they'd changed hands, given the musty underarm odor? But though the clothes smelled bad, the Anhui man was good at his job of boiling corn in the large stainless steel pot sitting atop a coal brazier. Customers showed up the moment Liu set up shop, and many were obviously return customers; selling corn can amount to something, Liu said to himself with admiration for the

Anhui man. Yan Ge had told him that the man trembled whenever he had to say something, but in Liu's view, he had a good work ethic, and that gave Liu the idea to take up corn selling if he ever had a falling-out with Ren Baoliang.

"Just follow the Anhui man's example and do what he does," Yan reminded him when he took over the stall. "Don't change a thing."

But Liu made a change right off—the price. The Anhui man had charged one yuan per ear of sweet corn, and now Liu wanted 1.1 yuan, fully implementing his grocery shopping policy. With one additional *mao* for each ear of corn, he would have ten extra yuan after a hundred ears. Liu had no intention of working for free.

"Isn't it one yuan?" a customer asked. "How come it's more today?"

"Huairou had a hailstorm yesterday that destroyed a field of corn, so the price has to rise."

"Hey, you're not the same guy."

"The other guy had too much to drink last night. I'm his cousin."

After three hours, Yan Ge's wife had yet to show up to conduct her investigation. It was getting late and she likely wouldn't come that day, which didn't matter to Liu, since he'd already been paid five hundred yuan for his performance and five or six extra yuan from selling half the corn in the pot. If he had to play the Anhui guy the next day, he'd be paid again and earn some extra from the corn. If he kept that up, he'd be rich.

But Liu's bubble burst, because as he was dreaming about the money, a Mercedes glided up and stopped. A fat woman emerged from one side of the car, followed by Yan Ge from the other side, a sign that the play was about to begin, even without the customary gongs and drums to signal the raising of the curtain. Yan's wife looked heavy, but Liu could tell she'd been slender when she was younger and wasn't bad looking. She had a dog on a leash in her left hand and was holding a newspaper in the right, the page with the photo of Yan Ge and the pop singer visible. Liu readied himself for action.

Qu Li had landed in Beijing at four that afternoon, two hours later than scheduled owing to a thunderstorm in Shanghai, where she'd gone to visit her family, with whom she hadn't always had a good relationship. As a girl, she'd been close to her father, but not her ill-tempered mother, who beat her daughter whenever she was in a foul mood. Qu had a younger sister, whom the mother scolded but never hit. Obviously, her bad temper was not directed at everyone indiscriminately, and she had the upper hand in a family that was divided into two camps—father and mother.

People from Shanghai are known for their attachment to their hometown, but Qu Li had decided to go to college in Beijing precisely to break free of her mother's control. When her father died a year after she got married, she no longer felt the need return to Shanghai and did not visit her mother when she happened to be in the city. But over the past year she'd begun going back, sometimes once a month, a development Yan found puzzling. Who had changed, Qu Li or her mother? It didn't really matter to him. In fact, he liked it, because that freed him to see any woman he wanted in Beijing when she was away.

What he didn't know was that she went to Shanghai not to visit her mother, but to see a psychiatrist, for she was convinced she was suffering from severe depression, something she chose not to tell her husband of twelve years.

During the first five impoverished years of their marriage, they'd fought a lot. Back then she'd been gentle and quiet, and their fights had been of the cold-war variety. After five years, their fortunes turned, she put on weight, and they no longer fought quietly. That was followed by another cold-war period, though with a difference.

Suddenly she thought she was ill—psychologically, not physically, always worried about something. She worried about Yan's fidelity, so she checked his underpants each night. Then she worried about her own sanity. Yet it wasn't just the two of them that occupied her thoughts; she was also stressed out about the world in general. Whenever something changed around her, be it a new shoe repairman or a new leader for the nation, she felt that the world was out of whack and that everything was wrong, even if it had nothing to do with her. That was no doubt a sign of depression. Other people who suffered the same illness had trouble sleeping and looked sallow from weight loss. In her case, she could never get enough sleep or food. Hamburgers were her choice of comfort food. When something bothered her, she would not stop eating until she was about to burst; she then would go straight to bed.

So she decided to see a psychiatrist, but not in Beijing. She believed that Shanghai psychiatrists must be better, since more people suffered from depression in her hometown. She wondered if her problem was rooted in her childhood and her mother. Going to Shanghai meant being closer to where it all began, so she flew once a month to see a doctor, but with scant results. She found that, unlike people who were lucky enough to have their issues resolved, her problem seemed to get worse.

Her psychiatrist was a man in his thirties from Chiang Kai-shek's hometown. His hairstyle and the movements of his hands led her to believe that he was gay, but that didn't matter, because he was so adept at psychoanalysis. He explained things clearly and convincingly, proceeding from the surface to the center, from the simple to the complicated, and seeing through symptoms to get at the core issues.

Of course, he did not hit on the core issue immediately; it took half a year before he nursed it out of her that she had had three miscarriages in twelve years. That revelation cleared up everything. Nodding slightly with his fingers daintily steepled, the psychiatrist said in accented Mandarin, "That's it." Her miscarriages were the root cause of her problems, which had nothing to do with her childhood or her mother; all along she'd been thinking about the babies, not worrying about Yan Ge, herself, or the world.

She checked Yan's underpants because she did not want him to have a baby with someone else, while the cold war with him and the quarrels with the beauty salons were all transferences of responsibility. Her eating problem, well, that was a sign of capitulation.

If they were to take it a step further, then the core issue was not the baby, but the fear of childlessness and the lack of an heir for the family inheritance. In other words, money.

Everything clicked for the doctor now that they'd found the cause of her depression, but not for Qu Li, who actually felt worse for not being able to solve the root problem. Her worries about the world worsened, but they focused on Yan Ge after hearing the doctor's analysis. She began paying closer attention to his behavior and speech. She was fully aware that her actions might produce an unwanted result, but maybe that was what she needed. With the unintended effect would come a full-blown argument, perhaps even the worse possible outcome—homicide—but that would prove it was all someone else's fault.

In the past she'd been concerned that Yan was having an affair, but now it was more worrisome if he was not. She might wish for him to have as many women as possible so she could see her hopes fulfilled. Her most recent trip to Shanghai was simply one of habit, not really to see the doctor.

A close friend had called the day before from Beijing to tell her about the photo with Yan and the pop singer. This friend, also the wife of a wealthy man, and fat to boot, expressed her emotional reaction to the photo with a hint of excitement, which led Qu Li to see through the so-called altruism. The woman had been eagerly waiting for someone she knew to run into trouble, a sign that she too was psychologically ill.

Unbeknownst to this friend, Qu Li was not upset by the news. She was, rather, enlivened, like a warhorse detecting the smell of the battlefield and blood. She could sense the blood boil and course through her body, though she pretended to be upset on the phone to fool the friend. Biding her time, she wanted to savor the bitterness and pain; the longer a volcano remains dormant, the more splendid the eventual eruption.

Yan Ge, newspaper in hand, picked her up at the airport, which she knew was a ploy that would let him strike first and give him an edge. After she got in the car and took her dog in her arms, Yan opened the paper to show her the picture.

"Can you believe this? I didn't realize who she was when I was buying a yam."

His intention was so obvious it outraged her. Despite her decision not to give her friend the satisfaction of having a fight with Yan, despite her plan to wait and be ready, she could not hold back.

"What are you so nervous about? I'll know what's what when I go there and ask around."

"Who could still remember what happened yesterday?" Yan said.

Ignoring him, Qu Li told the driver to take them to the street in the picture, exactly as Yan had hoped. He was playing cat and mouse. In the past he'd been apprehensive whenever she went to visit "the scene of a crime." But this time was different; he did not want the performance to be wasted. Moreover, the playacting was not meant to deny his involvement with the pop singer; he intended it to deny his wife a victory. So he feigned reluctance.

"Go ahead and check it out if you want to."

They arrived at the scene of the occurrence.

Liu Yuejin had thought he'd be the picture of calmness, but he tensed up at the sight of Qu Li and Yan emerging from the car. The show was about to begin. Lacking any acting experience, this was going to be a challenge. Liu spent his days with construction workers, all working class types, with whom he shared a lingo and work. With Yan Ge and Qu Li, rich people he'd never before encountered, he had no idea what they did or what they'd say or how he should respond.

She did not rush into her investigation; instead, leash in hand, she let her dog take the lead in walking around the various stalls.

"Go ask the yam vendor if you don't believe me," Yan said impatiently.

Ignoring his suggestion, she continued to roam the area—once again, just what he wanted her to do. She was coming back to Liu Yuejin's stall, and, just like the Anhui man, Liu began to tremble. Noticing him, Qu Li stopped, opened the newspaper, and asked:

"Did you see this singer yesterday?"

By then Liu could not utter a sound, so he nodded.

"Did she come alone?" Qu Li asked casually.

"No," Liu was stuttering. "There—were—two of them."

Color drained from the face of Yan, who stood behind his wife.

"Who was the other person?"

"Her mother."

"How do you know it was her mother?" Qu Li asked, after a pause.

"I heard her say, 'Ma, here's the corn. I'll go buy yams.'"

Qu Li breathed a sigh of relief. So did Yan, who slipped Liu a thumbs up. Though only a migrant worker, he was a good actor. Qu Li did not ask anyone else after that, but, even if she had, Yan was not concerned, not with that good beginning. So, dog leash in hand, she went back to their car, followed by Yan, who climbed into the car before her and, as if suffering a great injustice, slammed his door.

"Just a moment," Qu Li said to the driver. "I want an ear of corn."

She came back to Liu Yuejin with her dog.

"How much is an ear of corn?"

No longer tense, Liu was upset that he'd been nervous earlier, realizing that acting was easy. He loosened up and turned into a genuine corn vendor.

"One yuan ten."

She picked over the corn in the pot and asked casually. "What time did the singer show up, was it in the morning or the afternoon?"

Liu was caught unprepared and, with no script to follow, made up an answer on the spot.

"In the morning. I'd just opened."

She nodded and smiled. Liu smiled too, figuring he'd gotten it right. Qu Li picked out an ear of corn and handed Liu two yuan. "Keep the change."

Then she returned to the car with her dog. Liu thought the play-acting had been a great success, as did Yan. The driver started the engine and the Mercedes tore down the street while Qu Li gnawed on the ear of corn.

Convinced that he'd won, Yan pressed on with his complaint: "The paper dealt with whether she was eating or not, and you thought it was about sex. You must have a one-track mind. I won't let you off the hook so easily the next time you get so paranoid."

He was stunned when she snapped her head up and flung the corn into his face, sending his glasses flying and frightening the dog, which looked up and started barking.

"What do you think you're doing? What's that all about?"

Pointing at the paper, she said with tears in her eyes:

"You should be more careful when you lie like that, Yan Ge. The corn vendor said it was in the morning but, here, look at the clock behind you."

Retrieving his glasses from the floor of the car, he put them on to read the paper. A digital clock had been installed in the corner of a distant shopping center. The read-out was blurred, but clear enough for him to see 17:03:56. He was struck dumb.

7

Ma Manli and Yang Yuhuan

Ma Manli was the owner of Manli Hair Salon, which was located on a corner one lane over from Liu Yuejin's construction site, the entrance illuminated by a revolving light. The salon's hundred and sixty square feet were divided into two rooms, one in front and one in the back. Manli was in charge of haircutting and was helped by a young Shanxi girl named Yang Yuhuan, who washed clients' hair and performed odd tasks, like giving massages in the back room. A small, simply outfitted, inexpensive place, Manli Hair Salon drew its clients from the construction site and the nearby market. At other salons, a haircut cost twenty yuan plus ten for a shampoo, while Ma charged five yuan for both a haircut and a shampoo. A massage cost twenty-eight, and even with some additional service during the massage, the bill would not exceed a hundred.

Ma herself never offered additional service, and took thirty percent of whatever Yang earned in the back room. As a result, Yang usually made more than Ma, which gave her bragging rights that she was the salon's backbone. In both behavior and conversation, it was clear she did not think much of Ma, and she acted as if she were the boss and Ma her employee.

Some days at noon, Yang would be idly nibbling on watermelon seeds instead of getting lunch ready, so Ma had to cook for her after she finished cutting hair. That caused arguments, but nothing came of them, except to add some life to the place.

Ma, who was thirty-two years old and hailed from Liaoning, lacked the full breasts typical of women from northeast China. It was a secret known only to a few, for she wore a padded bra to cover up. One of those who did know was her former husband, Zhao Xiaojun, who said to her during the divorce proceedings:

"Are you really a woman? You look like a man in drag."

The other person was her six-year-old daughter, whom Ma left in the care of her mother back home before coming to Beijing. As a baby, her daughter cried a great deal because her mother did not produce enough milk to nurse her.

There was yet another person who knew; that was Liu Yuejin. One night near closing time, Ma was alone after Yang left on the back of her boyfriend's motorcycle. Ma was having her period and, when she went inside to change the pad, she also changed into her PJs; since she was alone and was about to close shop, she skipped her bra. But when she walked back into the front room, she was shocked when Liu rushed in; he was surprised by the difference in her.

"What's your problem?" she screamed angrily.

Liu was a frequent visitor to Manli Hair Salon, no more than a ten-minute walk down a small lane. He came not for a haircut or a massage, but to kill time, watch people, and listen to women's voices, a rarity at the site, where several hundred men worked. Ren Baoliang's niece was female, but, at two hundred plus pounds, she was more a sight to behold than a voice to appreciate.

To be sure, Liu could have gone to other places to hear women's voices—on the street, in shopping malls, or at subway stations. And before he met Ma, he'd enjoyed sitting by subway exits, where it was cool in the summer and warm in the winter, so he could watch people and, more importantly, listen to their voices. After a hard day's work, women's voices calmed and reassured him.

Small-breasted Ma Manli had a different voice, however—slightly hoarse, sounding like a man when you first heard it, and yet the pleasing, mellow huskiness was more tantalizing than the average female voice. He loved hearing her talk, and there was yet another reason why he visited so often. When he learned that Li Gengsheng liked his wife, Huang Xiaoqing, because of her tiny waist, Liu became infatuated with small waists, which Ma Manli happened to have.

He could not help but marvel over how things had worked out. It was, as people say, true that the lost horse is the biggest and that a deceased wife is the most virtuous. He hadn't noticed his wife's waist during their thirteen years of marriage, and now he missed that waist fully six years after she left him. The two women shared another feature: slender eyes, though Ma was fair skinned while his wife had a sallow face. Huang was not the talkative type, while sharp-tongued Manli was merciless in an argument. Gradually, he felt a sense of loss if he was away from her for three days.

"Tell me," he once said to Manli, "can we call this being in love?"

She glared at him. "You miss your mama sometimes. Would you say you're in love with her?"

"I've been alone for six years now." He sighed, feeling sorry for himself. "And I don't even have a lover."

"Over there." She pointed to a corner. "Go take care of yourself there."

He smiled and let her comment pass, but he was telling the truth about not having been with a woman for six years. Sometimes he felt like going to a prostitute, but simply could not bear the thought of spending money that way. So, as Manli suggested, he took care of it himself. But that just increased his infatuation with women's voices. On days when he bought pork for the dining hall, he made a point of bringing her some pigs' necks in a plastic bag. At other times it might be a bag of chicken necks. When she was busy and he sat there crossing and swinging his legs, she would order him to do something:

"Don't just sit there. Look around and get busy."

He'd get off the stool, pick up a broom and dustpan, and sweep up the hair on the floor. Ma did not mind that he was there so often, but Yang did, since his presence had a negative effect on her massage business. A man in the mood for a massage would stick his head in and, if he saw another man sitting there, would turn and leave. Liu knew he was in the way, but he couldn't help it. So if a man stuck his head in, he'd say:

"It's all right. Come on in. I'm just a neighbor."

That may have been all right with him, but not with the potential client, who would turn and leave anyway. So whenever Yang saw Liu Yuejin walk through the door, she made noise and pulled a long face.

Originally named Yang Ganni, she had changed her name several times after coming to Beijing, from Yang Bingbing to Yang Jingwen to Yang Yuchun, none of which was grand enough for her. Eventually she settled on Yang Yuhuan, the name of a famous Tang dynasty consort.

A scrawny little thing when she first arrived, Yang ballooned into a ball of flesh in a year. Though not as big as Ren Baoliang's niece, she looked chunky because she was so petite. Now she wanted to lose weight, but that was not as easy as putting it on, and everyone said she was overweight. That, however, was precisely what attracted her massage clients. Aware of her desire to slim down, each time Liu Yuejin saw her he said, "You've lost some more weight, Yuhuan."

If not for that comment, she would never have let him into the Manli Hair Salon.

Liu knew that Manli had been divorced three years before, but had no idea what her former husband did for a living. He'd asked, but she wouldn't tell him. Liu had seen Zhao a few times at the salon and each time Zhao was bathed in sweat. Dressed in a Western suit, he looked like a traveling salesman, and he came for one thing only: money. As Liu listened to them argue, he learned of their dispute over thirty thousand yuan. It was Manli's brother, not her, who owed Zhao the money. But since Zhao could not find her brother, he came to her. She denied responsibility, and that inevitably led to an argument.

Zhao showed up once when Liu was at the salon, and this time the former couple got into a real fight, during which the mirror behind the barber chair was smashed. Manli was hit in the nose, smearing her face with blood. When Liu went up to stop the fight, Zhao turned on him.

"You're here with the salt and here with the vinegar? Are you going to give me my money?"

"Stop fighting," Liu urged. "She's bleeding. Can't you talk this over?"

"I'm through talking. I want satisfaction today or a clean knife will go in and come out red." Zhao was about to hit Manli again, when, spurred by the sight of her bloodied face, Liu took out a thousand yuan and handed it to Zhao, who took the money but muttered angrily all the way out the door.

"What kind of man comes to collect for a debt after a divorce?" Liu said.

But regret settled in the next day. Not over trying to stop the fight, but because he had managed to do so with his own money. There with the salt and there with the vinegar, he was essentially meddling in people's domestic affairs even though they were no longer married. What was he thinking? The money would have been well spent if he and Manli had something going, but there was nothing, not even a stolen kiss. Why be so chivalrous? He had to be the biggest fool around. When he returned to the salon that night, he tossed out hints about getting his money back.

"You're the one with all the money, and you were happy to give him some." Manli would have none of it. "Go see him if you want your money back. Don't come to me."

Now he felt like an even bigger fool, after helping to pay off a debt for someone who did not appreciate the gesture. Fortunately, it wasn't much, though his heart ached each time he thought about it. It did, however, make him feel like he could stroll proudly into the salon any time he wanted.

The day after playing the man from Anhui, Liu Yuejin came to the salon, not in his usual clothes but in a dark green suit he'd bought at the night market. He even wore a tie, though he still wore a fanny pack; a Western suit was his preferred attire whenever he had something to celebrate. He was on his way to the post office to send his son some money, and Manli Hair Salon was on the way; since he had plenty of time, he walked in to chat. The idea of sending his son money would be the excuse to remind her of what he'd spent on her.

Yang Yuhuan was leaning against the door applying lipstick and watching people walk by. She pretended not to see him when he arrived, and did not even move her feet to make room. Liu was about to say she'd lost weight again, but, annoyed by her lack of manners, he walked right past her.

Manli had just finished washing the hair of a client whose head was dripping wet and was dragging him over to the mirror for a blow-dry. Seeing she was busy, he looked around and spotted a large peach; he picked it up and ate it. After finishing the peach, he thought his nose hairs were getting long, so he picked up a pair of scissors to trim them at the mirror. When the client left, Liu said:

"I'm here to say good-bye."

"Are you leaving Beijing?" Manli was surprised.

"No, not Beijing—this world," Liu said, shocking her even more. "My son gave me an ultimatum yesterday." He continued, "If I don't send him the money for tuition, he'll leave and move in with his mother. Do you know how much trouble I had to go through six years ago to gain sole custody? Now he's threatening to leave. Does he know how much I've struggled over the past six years? Moving in with his mother? Wouldn't that be the same as moving in with his mother's new man? I wouldn't care for myself, but what would people say? So you see, I'm backed into a corner and have decided not to live anymore."

It was not the first time he'd told her about his sad past, so at first she was not entirely convinced. Convinced or not, he continued the act by talking to himself in the mirror as if it were his son.

"You little bastard. Do you not have a sense of right and wrong? Do you know what kind of woman your mother is? She's a loose woman, a worn-out shoe. And who did she marry? A man who sells fake liquor and should have been in jail long ago." He began to feel sorry for himself. "Is there no place for an honest man these days? The bold man dies from overeating, the timid man starves to death. They'd better not force my hand. If they do, I won't kill myself. I'll go see that mutt and his bitch with a knife and it'll come out stained in blood."

After having put on a show the day before, he had gained a feeling for the stage. Today he was in character, getting angrier and angrier until his face turned red and his neck thickened.

"I came by to tell you on my way to the train station."

Tricked into believing him, Manli became part of the performance. "It's not such a big deal, so why all this talk about a knife?"

"The tuition is more than three thousand!" he said, raising his voice. "And I can't pay it in full. So what should I do?"

Finally she caught on, realizing that he was playacting, a new strategy to get his money back. "I have to give it to you for putting on such a production for that little money."

She took a handful of small bills out of a drawer and tossed them at him, either because she was tired of arguing, or because the money had been owed too long, or because she knew he was not a generous person.

"Don't come in here anymore."

He picked the money up from the floor and counted it. 210 yuan.

"Now who's putting on a big production?" he said earnestly. "Everything I said was true."

8

Yang Zhi

Liu Yuejin felt that his fortunes had changed for the better over the past couple of days. He'd acted in a street-corner drama and been paid five hundred yuan. The money was less important than the opportunity to meet Yan Ge, Ren Baoliang's boss. From now on, Ren would have to change his tone of voice when he spoke to Liu. Then he'd had another performance at the Manli Hair Salon, and had gotten 210 yuan out of Ma, which, similarly, was less important than the fact that she'd begun paying him back. The first payment was an admission that she owed him money. Added to the money he'd saved, he now had a total of forty-one hundred, a grand sum that allowed him to walk proudly to the post office. The street was fouled with exhaust fumes, but he felt refreshed and energized.

On the phone his son had said he needed 2,760 yuan and fifty-three fen for his tuition, but Liu had no intention of sending the full amount. He'd send fifteen hundred, not to save the rest for an emergency, but because he did not trust his son to tell the truth. The little bastard had always been a handful, so Liu had to be careful and watch his step.

A newsstall next to the post office sold ninety different newspapers and magazines. The previous day's tabloid with the pop singer and Yan Ge was still displayed prominently, and many people bought it instead of the latest issue. When Liu walked by, he saw a crowd looking at the paper and smiled knowingly at the thought that the readers only knew half the truth. They believed what the paper said, which he'd helped change into something false; it had just been a show and he'd made it seem real. The sight of people reading the paper gave him a superior feeling, like the proverbial sage who was the only sober person in a world of drunks.

A familiar sound in the air made him pause on his way up the post office steps. A man in his fifties was playing the two-stringed *erhu* in front of a post box on the corner, with a porcelain bowl on the ground containing a few coins. Seeing someone playing for spare change on a Beijing street was nothing special, but this man was different; he was singing a popular song in a Henan accent. The *erhu* was out of tune, so was the man, producing the squeals of a pig being butchered, and it grated on Liu's ears. Normally he wouldn't have paid the man any attention, but after two great performances he felt good enough to do something. Sticking your nose into other people's business is related to status; don't try if it's someone more powerful than you, but go ahead and jump in when it's someone inferior. A mere cook at a construction site, Liu nevertheless felt superior to a street musician, essentially a beggar. Besides, the man was also from Henan, a familiarity that further bolstered Liu's confidence. Turning around, he walked down the steps and went up to the post box, where the man continued singing with his eyes closed.

"Stop!" Liu yelled. "Stop! I'm talking to you."

The old man, who had been under the spell of his own voice, was startled by Liu, whom he mistook as an official from Urban Management. He stopped playing and snapped his eyes open, only to discover that Liu was not in uniform.

"What?"

"What were you singing?" Liu asked.

The man stared blankly before replying: "It's 'Love and Dedication,' of course!"

"You're from Henan, aren't you?"

"So what? You unhappy with that?" The man stiffened his neck.

"Unhappy with that? Have you ever listened to yourself? Who cares if you lose face, but you're bringing great shame to all the people from Henan."

"Who do you think you are?" The man bristled at Liu's criticism. "What business is it of yours?"

"See that over there?" Liu pointed to the construction site. "I built that."

He was bragging, of course, but vaguely enough for it to be acceptable. There were several CBD buildings in the area, all under construction, one of which was Liu's—not his alone, but his, as in his crew. His declaration could lead a person to think that he was either the boss or a construction worker, but he was neither; yet it was acceptable because he was the cook at the site. In any case, the man was bluffed by Liu's posturing, especially because Liu was dressed in a suit and tie, giving the impression of a construction foreman, his better, which led him to say dispiritedly:

"I was a folk singer back home in Henan."

"Then you should keep singing folksongs."

"I did." The man sounded unhappy. "But no one wants to hear them."

"I do." Liu took out a coin and tossed it into the bowl.

The man looked at the coin, rolling around in his bowl, and then at Liu, before tuning his instrument and playing the Henan folksong, "Second Sister Pines for Her Husband." He'd been out of tune with the pop song, but now he hit every note and sounded every word correctly, which, to his surprise, drew a crowd, something he'd been unable to do when he was butchering "Love and Dedication." They gathered not to hear him sing, but to watch two men from Henan engaged in a debate. And yet the singer, thinking they liked what they were hearing, really got into it. Eyes closed, head raised, he bellowed out Second Sister's feelings until the veins in his neck bulged.

As for Liu Yuejin, he felt quite good about correcting one of the world's mistakes, so he looked around to size up the crowd, spotting a man by the newsstall who'd been there awhile, flipping through the paper. The noise drew him to look in Liu's direction. When their eyes met, he smiled, obviously amused by the scene with the folk singer. Liu returned a knowing smile. Tossing the paper aside, the man came over and stood behind Liu to listen to the Henan tune. No one really knew what the singer was singing, because it was in the Henan dialect, but Liu Yuejin had heard the tune before in his hometown. As the only one who truly enjoyed the song, he closed his eyes and swayed with the music, when he felt a nudge at his waist. He ignored it at first but then, sensing something was wrong, he opened his eyes and reached for his belt. The man behind him had cut the strap on his fanny pack and taken off with it. Liu looked around for the man, but he had snaked his way through the crowd and run off. It happened so fast all Liu could manage to yell was "Thief!"

Then it occurred to him that he had feet and that he ought to give chase. The thief was obviously a pro, for instead of running along the main street, he sprinted to the back of the post office and ducked into a clothing market specializing in wholesale imported garments. Although located in a back alley, the market dealt exclusively with famous brands, which, of course, were fake, but in high demand owing to the low prices. There were crowds of people with bags of various sizes, including a substantial number of Russians. By the time Liu had run into the market, the thief had disappeared amid the crowds of shoppers among the seemingly endless clothing stalls.

Liu did not even have time to get a clear view of the thief's face; the only thing he could recall was a large dark green mole shaped like an apricot flower on the left side of his face.

9

Lao Lin and Chief Jia

Yan Ge, thin to begin with and a vegetarian to boot, was skinnier than his peers. Born into an impoverished peasant family in Henan, as a child he'd sometimes subsisted on rice and fried chili peppers for three days because his family could not afford to buy anything else. The spicy taste made the bland rice go down easier, and when they couldn't afford chili peppers, they made do with lumpy pickled vegetables.

After college, but before his marriage, he moved from job to job; life was hard because much of the little money he earned he sent home to help his family out. During this period, he ate mostly turnips and cabbage with rice, so later on, after he made his fortune, he ate lots of meat, then seafood. For a while he was addicted to an extravagant dish called saucy rice with shark's fins, which he'd have for lunch and dinner, with guests or when he was alone. He finally reached his saturation point after three years, when he realized that most of the shark's fins he'd consumed were fake, for there couldn't possibly be that many sharks in the ocean. He came full circle back to turnips and cabbage, and lost the weight he'd gained during his feasting days. As we've seen, he was a fan of Liu Yuejin's turnips and stewed cabbage, which differed not just from the turnips and cabbage he'd had to eat as a child, but from what his personal chef cooked as well. During the lean days, he'd eaten them every day; they were tasteless. Now his chef made the dish into a delicacy, slowly stewing the ingredients in a pot suspended over a fire, like decorative art. Only Liu's dish at the dining hall was to Yan's liking; it was prepared in a huge, communal pot into which mounds of turnips and cabbage were thrown to stew until piping hot and mushy, producing a taste that conjured up the act of mingling and eating with the masses. All he needed to comfort his stomach and soothe the beast were two steamed buns or a bowl of soupy rice.

Lao Lin in Chief Jia's office, on the other hand, had been a carnivore all his life, with an appetite only for such delicacies as crab, lobster, sea urchin, abalone, and, of course, saucy rice with shark's fins. He never touched turnips stewed with cabbage. Whenever Yan Ge invited him out, they went to restaurants that offered plenty of meat or seafood. Obviously, Lao Lin had yet to move to the next level in dietary evolution. On this day, instead of a seafood café—Lin had eaten seafood for lunch—they went to a hotpot restaurant, where, once the water was bubbling hot, they each dipped in his favorite, meat for Lin and vegetables for Yan.

The two men had known each other for six years. Thirty-eight-year-old Lin had started out as Chief Jia's secretary and was later promoted to office director. Originally from Shandong, where men tend to be big and tall, Lin was an exception; he was short and small-boned, the sign of a dirt-poor childhood, like Yan Ge. He had once been scrawny, but you would not know it by looking at his current roly-poly figure. His face, though, remained thin, as if chiseled by a knife, and that, along with his small bones, gave the illusion that he was slim.

Another trait that marked him from other Shandong men was his soft voice, so soft you might miss something if you didn't listen carefully. At least he spoke slowly, pausing after every phrase to give you enough time to figure out what he was saying. With a pair of white-framed glasses for extreme myopia, he reminded Yan of an old party member from his childhood, Zhang Chunqiao, one of the Gang of Four. Yan had known Jia first, so Lin treated him politely, though Yan was fully aware of Lin's temper.

Once, when they were sharing a meal of saucy rice with shark's fins (or maybe Lin was eating shark's fins while Yan had vegetables), Lin received a call from one of Chief Jia's bureau chiefs. At one point the conversation took a wrong turn. Lin changed his tone and began to speak rapidly, like a machine gun, to the point of rattling the glass in the window. How the man on the other end reacted, Yan did not know, but he got a fright, and began to see Lin in a new light.

Yan had met Chief Jia fifteen years earlier, when Jia was a section chief and Yan was a branch manager for a private company. They met at a dinner hosted by a mutual friend with more than a dozen people in attendance, which meant that no serious business could be discussed. After a few rounds of drinks, they began telling dirty jokes, bursting into laughter after each one. Everyone was having a great time, all but Jia, who quietly kept his head down the whole time. When someone asked him why, he sighed and said:

"You're all managers at private companies and I envy you. I work in a government office, with a salary that's barely enough to get by on."

No one thought much about his complaint, which to them was common knowledge, not some elevated truth, so they ignored him and continued to eat and drink. Yan Ge was the only one who sensed something beneath the man's complaint and, as they happened to be sitting next to each other, Yan got Jia to talk. It turned out that Jia's mother, who had been diagnosed with liver cancer, needed an operation, but he was eighty thousand yuan short, with nowhere to get the money. Jia was worried sick and in no mood for merriment; he'd come that night only because he'd hoped to touch up some of his wealthy friends for a loan. Now that everyone was having so much fun, he couldn't broach the subject and could only sigh.

The response made Yan rue his curiosity, as he did not know what to say. Jia didn't ask him for a loan, but his intention was clear after telling him the whole story. At the time, a mere employee at a private company with a fixed salary, Yan did not have that kind of money, and besides, they had just met. He let the subject drop, though he felt awkward.

Yan forgot all about Jia's situation after the dinner ended. The next day, when he was sorting business cards he'd collected the night before, he was surprised to learn that Jia, though only a section chief, worked in a department that was at the heart of China's economy. That triggered something in Yan's mind and, as if seized by a premonition, he put away the cards and drove to Tong County, then east to Hebei, where a college friend, Dai Yingjun, lived. They had shared a dorm room, and in their sophomore year Dai had attempted suicide over a failed romance, after which his father came to take him home. Who could have predicted that a possibly tragic event would turn into a blessing? Dai and his father opened a paper mill producing sanitary napkins and were rich within a few years. Yan saw him several times after college; good food had ballooned Dai to the point that his eyes were as tiny as mung beans. He had also developed a dirty mouth, no longer the genteel young man who had tried to kill himself over love.

Dai was happy to see Yan that day—at first—but pulled a long face as soon as Yan mentioned a loan.

"Why the fuck are so many people coming to me for money? It doesn't blow in on the wind, you know. It's not easy selling sanitary pads one at a time for women to stain with their blood."

"I'd never ask your help for just anything, but my pa is in the hospital."

Feeling cornered by the mention of a sick father, Dai continued to grumble while calling over his bookkeeper to get eighty thousand yuan for Yan. With the money in hand, Yan returned to Beijing and went straight to the government office, where he called for Jia at the gate, telling him he happened to be in the neighborhood and decided to stop by to say hello. Jia came out of the office building and invited Yan in, but Yan said he had another engagement. He handed him the money wrapped in newspaper.

Jia was momentarily speechless. "I was just venting yesterday, but you took it seriously."

"I'm glad the money will be put to good use." Yan added, "You can put off other matters, but not when your mother is ill."

Deeply moved, Jia said with moist eyes:

"I'll accept your help then." He held Yan's shoulder tightly. "I'll never forget it."

Jia's mother had the operation but did not live long after that; about six months later the cancer spread and she did not recover. But Jia never forgot Yan's kindness. When the two men first met, Jia was forty-six, seemingly too old for any kind of career advancement, but for some reason his luck changed and he was promoted to deputy bureau chief the following year; two years later he was bureau chief. After that, he became the deputy director, a ministerial rank, and eventually the director. When they first met, they were friends who shared difficult times. Then, along with Jia's promotion, their friendship entered an elevated state. When making friends, it is always better to start with a humble background together, for no one in a high position will be in need of friends. Once, during a meal after Jia's latest promotion, he pointed at Yan with his chopsticks.

"You're someone with a long view." He added, obviously having had too much to drink, "Other people mean nothing, but you are a lifelong friend, all because of that eighty thousand yuan."

"That was nothing, Director Jia." Yan waved him off. "I've forgotten all about it, so please don't bring it up now."

Jia's office was in charge of construction permits for commercial and residential real estate. After Jia's promotion, Yan Ge quit his job at the computer company and started his own real estate development company, which made him a billionaire in a mere twelve years. Jia, in other words, was the special person in Yan's life, his angel, his patron saint. A patron saint is never someone who walks up to you with a smile to lend a helping hand; no, he exists for people with a long view who know to make advanced preparations.

Yan detected subtle changes in their relationship during that period, not caused by him, however. Jia was the one who initiated the changes, to which Yan had to passively react; he had no choice. They were friends, but the difference in status meant that Yan was a friend to Jia but that Jia could not really be a friend to Yan. Put differently, before Jia's promotion, they had been friends, but no longer. Or put yet another way, they could treat each other as friends in private, but in public the distinction in status must be maintained. As someone who was well versed in social etiquette, Yan showed Jia the requisite respect in public, but was mindful of propriety in private. To be sure, Jia got wealthy right along with Yan. Yan would never have gotten rich if not for Jia, which was why Yan was so generous with his money where Jia was concerned. He gave it to him on several occasions, with a fixed set of rules: cash only, no bank transfers or deposits to credit cards, and always face to face, leaving no trace. Naturally, pleasures of the flesh were generously funded. Over a period of twelve years, Yan believed he had gained insights into a man's insignificance in the face of money and power. Take sex for example. Some people do not need to go looking for it; it comes looking for them, pants off.

Jia became an even gentler person after his promotion, always eager to extend a soft hand with a moist palm for anyone to shake. When he smiled, his round face took on the shape of a watermelon. In the past, he had been straightforward, saying what was on his mind. But no longer. He developed a fondness for metaphors and bullet points, even for jokes. For instance, when talking about the type of woman he preferred, he would say she must be doe-like: one, a small head; two, a long neck; three, a big chest; and four, slender legs. His audience had no trouble conjuring up an image. Then he'd add:

"All society's warlords chase after the doe."

He sounded contemptuous and sinister, as well as confusing, and it was hard to tell whether he was talking about women or something more important. That was when Yan realized that Jia was not the same man.

One weekend, Yan drove Jia and his family to Beidaihe for the ocean air. The two men were walking along the beach at night, the wind playing with Jia's hair, when Jia blurted out under his breath:

"You can't know how humble an official is until you're one yourself."

Unsure what Jia was referring to, Yan held his tongue. And Jia was not done:

"You think you're with the powerful, the wolves and jackals, but in fact you're down there with the worms and maggots."

Now Yan understood that Jia was talking about the difficulty of being an official.

"It'd be a lot better if some of them died," Jia concluded.

Yan shivered, as he wondered who Jia was referring to. Why did these people need to die and how would that improve things? Yan again held his tongue. Just as years ago, when he intuited that Jia would be important to him one day, Yan now sensed that sooner or later Jia would abandon him. They could not be friends for life, not in a relationship grounded in money and sex. One day, Jia would turn on him, and when that happened, Yan would have to let it happen, lacking the power to counteract it.

The day finally came, in the wake of a problem-filled year. In late April of the previous year, Jia had attended a meeting in Zhongnanhai and invited Yan out for dinner afterward. He asked Yan how much disposable cash he had.

"A billion or more, I guess," Yan said after some mental calculations, making sure it was a conservative figure.

Jia told him there would very likely be some adjustments in the national finance policy after the first of May, and suggested that Yan ought to invest his money in the market, either commodity futures or stocks.

"How much can you make building houses?" Jia said, swirling the wine in his glass. "Don't take the long way around. You have to let your money make more money for you."

To be sure, Yan wanted to make more money, but not too much. How much was enough? He felt secure profiting from each construction project. Besides, he knew nothing about financial markets and could not say if he was capable of letting his money make money. When he told Jia his concern, Jia said:

"You can always learn. You weren't born knowing how to build houses, were you?"

Yan had to agree; but even if he disagreed, he had to listen. Owing to the difference in their status, they understood the world differently. Jia had just attended a meeting at Zhongnanhai, the seat of government, after all. So Yan invested the money earned through real estate into commodity futures and stocks, and did very well at first, as predicted. But he began to lose money after six months, not owing to his lack of knowledge about financial markets or his inability to find new ways, but because the government instituted another adjustment in finance policies after the first of October.

Yan was screwed, screwed by the country, for who was better at taking the long way around issues than the government? He tried to tough it out, but a year later he not only lost the one point four billion he'd invested, but he owed banks more than four hundred million. And his failure in the financial markets also affected his real estate business. He'd been making money from real estate, but now he had owed money for materials and wages for workers at over a dozen construction sites for six months. In a little over a year, Yan Ge was transformed from a billionaire to someone in serious debt. He could, of course, refocus on real estate, but he needed money for that. With four hundred million owed, plus six months' interest, he'd be lucky if the banks didn't take legal action. They would never give him another loan. His only hope was Jia, who he hoped would speak to the banks on his behalf.

Jia turned on him. At first he gave Yan various excuses, saying he wasn't in charge of the banks, though he had been able to get them to help Yan in the past. Now that Yan was in serious trouble, why couldn't Jia do something? They'd shared difficult times together before, but this problem seemed to be Yan's alone. Wasn't it Jia who had told him to invest? If only he'd just kept building his houses. It had been two months since Jia last agreed to see him; in the past all Yan had to do was place a call and Jia would be there. Now either Jia would not pick up or the call would go to his secretary. Sometimes,

Yan tried Jia's office director, Lao Lin, who remained cordial and friendly, and who said he would let Director Jia know. But Yan never heard back.

Finally, he realized that Jia had jettisoned him. He'd have had no complaint if it had happened at some other time, but now he was in dire straits and found Jia lacking in moral decency. Putting aside the financial mess Jia caused him, and Yan's help when Jia's mother was ill fifteen years before, Jia had reaped tremendous profits by giving Yan building permits over the past twelve years. A rough count of the money going to Jia, a government official, would be enough for him to lose his head several times over. But Yan did not want to sour their relationship, for that would do him no good.

The day after the photo with Yan and the singer appeared in the paper, Lin called Yan and asked to see him. They agreed to meet at a hotpot restaurant.

Although Lin and Yan treated each other with courtesy, deep down Yan did not like the man. Stern and secretive, Lin was inflexible once he made up his mind on something. Money, for instance. Yan had never used Lin as a middleman when delivering money to Jia, since that was their business alone; though Lin feigned ignorance of the arrangement, he went to Yan for loans. While Yan and Jia were old friends, Lin merely worked for Jia. But since he was at Jia's side all day long, a word from him could work for or against Yan, which was why he always tiptoed around the man.

After lending money to Lin three times, Yan began to give it to him without being asked. He gave Jia much more, but he did that willingly, while he offered Lin less but was forced to. It felt different. It was as if Jia were the Buddha, waiting for believers to come and light incense, while Lin was a dog or a wolf, who would take a bite out of you whenever he felt like it.

Jia thanked him and said, "just this once" when Yan handed over money, whereas Lin didn't even bother with the nicety, acting as if he was entitled to the money, and one bite was never enough. It was understandable that Jia, a sixty-year-old man nearing retirement, wanted money, even if it was tainted. Lin, on the other hand, was not yet forty, with a long way to go in his career, and if he began seeking bribes at such an early age, when would he stop? Yan wondered what Chinese society would be like when someone from Lin's generation took over from Jia.

And then there was the way Lin treated women. Yan usually procured women for Jia, some Russian and some Korean, but Lin always wanted to get his hands on them first at the hotel. He would heave a contented sigh afterward, which told Yan that Lin's submissive attitude toward Jia was fake. Yet Lin was, after all, working for Jia and was someone to reckon with. Yan Ge did not think it would work to his advantage to expose Lin's scheming to Jia. On his part, Lin was as respectful as ever with Jia, which only intensified Yan's fears.

Besieged by worries from all sides and a failing business, Yan had yet to find a way to set things right when the photo appeared in the paper, creating another mess. After re-enacting the day in question, he'd thought he had his wife deceived, but he'd overlooked the clock and the time of the encounter, which had made a bad mess worse. Qu Li had had a fit in the car and, after they were back home, had demanded a divorce, which was to be expected.

But then she simply vanished. It was a ruthless tactic, no matter how you looked at it. Although she never let on, everyone knew she suffered from an illness of some sort, and her disappearance would have everyone believing it was Yan's fault. When a sick woman disappears, she must be found, so Yan put aside a company in disarray and went looking for her. With her cell phone turned off, it was impossible to know where she might be, Beijing or Shanghai, or somewhere else. He contacted everyone he could think of, but still there was no sign of her.

At this juncture, he received the call from Lao Lin, who asked to meet. Since it could be related to his business, he had to forget about looking for his wife and go meet Lin. During lunch, Lin kept his head down as he dipped pieces of meat into the pot and kept Yan in the dark about the purpose of the meeting. Yan knew he had to wait until Lin finished two plates of meat, when, with sweat bathing his forehead, Lin put down his chopsticks and lit up to take a break.

"Busy lately?" Yan probed.

Ignoring his inquiry, Lin took a sheet of newspaper from his bag and spread it out on the table. It was the one with the photo of Yan and the singer. Lin belched when he poked the photo with his chopsticks.

"You're really something. I hear you had a real-life re-enactment yesterday."

The reference had Yan breathe a sigh of relief. He shook his head.

"It didn't work," he said. "It only brought me more trouble."

He recounted his wife's disappearance. Lin listened with a smile, but then abruptly turned stern:

"The re-enactment was meant to deceive your wife, but what was going on with the real thing? How much did you pay the photographer? Director Jia was very upset when he saw this."

The comment told Yan that Lin knew everything. He had failed on two accounts. He had staged the re-enactment to mislead, but also to avoid setting off the stick of dynamite that was his wife. As for the photo, it had not been the work of a passing paparazzo; Yan had arranged for it to be taken for one person, Director Jia. Yan's business was at a crossroads, and yet Jia had refused to help him, so Yan grew resentful. He held out hope that Jia would change his mind when he saw this as a warning.

The pop singer had been with Yan for three years, and it was his money that had made her famous and given her the opportunity to sing the praises of the nation and motherhood. In the spring of the previous year, he had taken her to dinner with Jia. During the conversation, Jia used metaphors and similes, mixed in with his customary bullet points of one, two, three, etc. He was more penetrating and profound than usual, eliciting nods from the singer and indicating to Yan that Jia was interested in the woman. Sex is nothing compared to money and power. Yan secretly pushed the singer toward Jia, and eventually they became involved, though not for long. Jia was first to back out, for, as a seasoned official, he knew that kind of dalliance should not be overdone. On the other hand, he'd had a relationship, no matter how long it lasted.

After failing to see Jia for two months, Yan tricked her out of her apartment to have her picture taken by a man he'd hired. He'd planned to send the photo to Jia as a reminder, only to be betrayed by the photo-taker, who'd sold the picture to a tabloid instead. The photo-taker had nothing against Yan, since he had no idea who his object was until he was on site, when he realized it was the singer, an anorexic eating roasted yams, and saw his chance to make even more money. When the photo appeared in the paper, Yan was caught off guard and, before long, his wife left home. But disaster turned into opportunity for Yan now that Director Jia, having seen the photo also, told Lin to meet with Yan. Hearing that Jia was upset, Yan was not alarmed; in fact, he was happy that the picture had had an effect. You don't need to pound a drum to get sound out of it. Now that Lin had shown his hand, Yan knew he had to come clean.

"I really didn't mean for the photo to appear in the paper," he said, explaining that the photo-taker had betrayed him. "It's really very simple," he added. "I could save the day if Director Jia could put in a word for me with the banks and get me a loan of two billion."

"Are you serious?" Lin laughed coldly. "Do you honestly think a couple of billion is going to make this mess of yours right?"

Lin took off his glasses, wiping the steam off the lenses, and sighed.

"Director Jia did not mean to abandon you. It's just that he's had three tough months. Someone has been secretly working against him."

Yan was surprised, though unsure if he should believe the story; then his better judgment of Lin and Jia told him it was simply an excuse.

"The boat is leaking and you can't toss me over the side," Yan said anxiously. "I know where to go if the banks sue me." He circled his neck with one hand, and continued. "I might not be able to keep this either. If you decide not to help me," he pointed at the paper, "I'm not going to hold back. If I could get an anorexic to go out and eat yams, I could get her to talk about her relationship with the director."

"You're not scaring anyone." Lin was nonplussed. "She can talk all she wants. At worst, it'll be just another sex scandal."

Seeing Lin's nonreaction, Yan looked angry, though he was faking it to make the next step easier. Snatching up the paper, he tore it into pieces.

"That was just a warning. If you ignore it, don't blame me if I cut off all means of escape." Then he took out a USB drive and laid it on the table. "I've sorted the contents into categories."

That got Lin's attention. "What's on it?"

"Several conversations. You know what we've talked about over these years. Oh, there are a few video recordings, clearly dated to show when I made my offerings to you and Director Jia. There are also clips of the director with Russian girls and Korean girls. By the way, the time stamps show that you did it all with these girls before the director had his share."

Lin was so stunned his face and neck were perspiring profusely.

"You're really something." He stared at Yan. "I didn't expect you to do this."

"I didn't do it." Yan lit a cigarette. "It was one of my assistants. He was killed in a car accident two months ago, and when I checked his computer I found this. He'd planned to use it to blackmail me, but in the end it will serve me well."

It was Lin's turn to wonder whether to believe his story, as Yan continued to marvel over the situation.

"It really is a case of knowing the depth of a chasm but not the scope of the human heart. I was so good to him when he was alive; I told him everything and entrusted him with the most important tasks. Who'd have thought that the one you trust the most often turns out to be a ticking time tomb beside you?" He wasn't done yet. "But, as they say, everything has its purpose, and we can say the man did not die in vain."

Lao Lin picked up the USB drive and turned it over in his hand.

"That's for you," Yan said. "You can share it with the director. I have another copy with me."

That was more or less the knife that went in clean and came out red. It was not like Yan Ge, who had no respect for people who did that. Only the fat, petty people pull the clean knife/red knife stratagem. He couldn't believe he'd actually become just like them. Then he was astounded to see Lin toss the drive into the hotpot, where, wrapped in thinly sliced meat, it bobbed in the boiling broth.

10

Han Shengli

After losing his fanny pack, Liu Yuejin was on the verge of killing himself, for real this time, because his life had depended on the forty-one hundred yuan it held. But that was not the only reason for suicidal thoughts. In the pack were his ID card, his phone contacts, and a double-sided account book for the dining hall, one side detailing the amounts spent, the other side recording the difference between actual costs and his bargain price. Losing these items would not have been the end of the world. The problem was, his divorce decree was also in the pack. It had been six years since the divorce, but he'd kept the paper until its original yellow color turned light brown. Since he carried the pack wherever he went, it got greasy from the extended period of time he spent in a smoky kitchen, and the paper began to turn oily black and got much heavier. Since the divorce was finalized, there was no point in carrying the paper around, especially since it presented an annoying sight, but it was precisely because it annoyed him that he kept it. Sometimes he woke up in the middle of the night, took it out to have a look, and muttered:

"It worked. It really worked." Or:

"I'm going to have my revenge one of these days."

It was sort of like the old land reform days, when an aging land-lord had a restoration account unearthed in his house, though Liu would not have wanted to kill himself if he'd lost one of those. He knew that revenge was only a pipe dream. The key was the IOU tucked inside the paper, showing the amount owed, sixty thousand yuan. When Huang Xiaoqing, his wife at the time, asked for a divorce six years earlier, Liu had asked Li Gengsheng for that amount as compensation for pain and suffering. Li was agreeable:

"No problem, as long as you agree to sign the paper."

Liu knew that Li was agreeable not because of Liu but because of Huang, or Huang's waist. Li added that he had to wait for six years for the money, so long as Liu left the couple alone during that period. If he caused them any trouble, the agreement would be annulled and Liu would have no money.

"If it works, it works. If not, well, you're a dickhead," Li added.

Liu had to do what they asked, on account of sixty thousand yuan, for which Li wrote an IOU, detailing the condition. It wasn't until later that Liu realized the mistake he'd made regarding the amount. During the custody fight, he'd fought hard to keep their son but had let his emotions get the better of him and turned her down when she offered to send four hundred each month for their son's support. Li Gengsheng and his son were two separate matters. He accepted the IOU, and it would take him years to realize that money is money no matter where it comes from.

Then there was the difference between an IOU and ready cash; four hundred a month would be just under thirty thousand after six years, which was why the sixty thousand had increasing importance to Liu.

Now it was a month before the six years were up, and he stood there listening to a Henan tune, not bothering anyone, when his pack was snipped off. No pack, no divorce decree; no divorce decree, no IOU. Would the fake-liquor maker give him the money without the IOU? Back when Liu caught Li and his wife in the act, Li was in the wrong and yet he beat Liu up and squatted on a chair, buck naked, smoking a cigarette. Now without the IOU, Liu could easily imagine Li's reaction:

"You lost what? I've never owed you any money." Or: "Has poverty made you lose your head? Are you trying to cheat me?"

Huang Xiaoqing knew about the IOU, so she could serve as his witness. The problem was, she was no longer his wife and he no longer meant anything to her, so why would she take his side? Over the past six years, Liu had seen her only once. In the previous summer, He had traveled to Henan for the wheat harvest. On his way back to Beijing, he stopped at the Luoyang Train Station, where, after buying his ticket, he squatted in the square to wait for his train. It was hot and he was thirsty, but he couldn't spare the money for a bottle of water. Instead, he walked up to a nearby hotel, where there was a carwash; he drank his fill at the faucet. An Audi drove up and stopped next to him. Out stepped two people, Li Gengsheng and Huang Xiaoqing, who were likely taking the train somewhere to sell fake liquor. Li didn't see him. Huang was telling the driver to remember to feed the dog when she turned and spotted Liu with a hose in his hand. Their eyes met. Liu stood up despite himself. Without a word to him, she followed Li into the station.

They had become strangers. Why would she help him now? The money was as good as gone. The amount would mean little to Li, but to Liu it meant his survival. He could never tell anyone where the money came from, but the note gave him a sense of security and hope. When the six-year period came to an end, he would have the money, which could be turned into a weapon. When his son asked him:

"Why haven't you sent me the money? Don't you have any at all?"

He could then justly respond:

"Money? I don't have much, but I do have sixty thousand."

"Then what are you waiting for?" his son would say. "Send me some."

"It's in the bank, a CD account," he'd reply.

Sixty thousand yuan had bolstered his courage and given him something to rely on. Now that it had vanished, what he missed was no longer just money but also the assurance, as if the floorboards had been pulled out from under him.

After a fruitless search for the thief, Liu emerged from the garment market and squatted by the side of the street, his mind a blank. He felt utterly hopeless, just as he had six years before when he'd caught his wife in bed with another man. He returned to the construction site, oblivious as to how he got back, and told no one about the theft, since it served no purpose.

How in the world would he explain to people the cash, the divorce decree, and the IOU? Particularly the IOU, which he'd gotten because he'd been cuckolded. Now that the note was gone, he might as well have been cuckolded for nothing. It was bad enough being robbed; he'd be a laughingstock if he mentioned the IOU, so he had to keep it to himself. In the end, he could only blame himself. He'd been on his way to the post office. Why did he have to be such a busybody and go over to correct the itinerant singer? Nothing would have happened if he'd simply sent the money. Yes, he'd gotten the man to change his tune, but at what cost? He'd lost his pack because the thief's hands could not resist the temptation, but mainly because Liu wanted to show how keen his ears were. He had it coming.

All these thoughts ran through his head until nightfall, when thoughts of suicide resurfaced and his neck tasted the sweet sensation of a noose. With all the steel girders at the construction site, hanging himself there presented no challenge. Or, if he preferred, there was the dining hall, whose rafters were surely strong enough to bear his weight.

But he didn't kill himself after all, not because he couldn't bring himself to do it, but because he suddenly recalled how the thief, after snatching his pack and running off, had turned to look at Liu and smiled before taking off running again. For that smile alone, Liu would have to find the thief and hang him first, after which Liu would have plenty of time to hang himself. Or, if he retrieved his pack, he wouldn't have to.

It would be like searching for a needle in a haystack. How would Liu Yuejin ever be able to find the thief by himself? It was then that it occurred to him to report the theft to the police.

The fat duty policeman's head was bathed in sweat even though it wasn't all that hot. He wrote down everything Liu said about the pack, which contained little. At some point, Liu lost the thread of his narrative, causing confusion on the part of the policeman, who stopped writing as Liu rambled on. He didn't seem to believe Liu, especially the part about the divorce decree and the IOU. He yawned grandly. Liu was anxious to give more details, but the policeman closed his mouth and stopped him.

"I've got it all. Go home and wait for news."

The policeman might have been able to wait, but not Liu.

"I can't wait. I'll be as good as dead if he throws that note away."

His anxious look seemed to have convinced the policeman, but he said:

"We've got three murders to solve, so tell me, which is more urgent?"

Liu opened his mouth but no sound came out. As he left the police station, he knew he could not count on the police. Then he happened to think of Han Shengli, a petty thief who must know other thieves. If he could find Han, maybe the thief and his pack could be retrieved quickly, a shortcut compared to seeking help from the police.

When Han saw him, he thought his earlier threat was working and that Liu was there to pay him back, so he was disappointed to hear about Liu's lost pack and his request for help. When Liu mentioned the cash it held, Han was especially upset.

"Liu Yuejin, you have a flawed character. You'd rather let someone steal your money than pay me back so I won't have to hide like a thief from people I owe money to."

Liu brought up the divorce decree and the IOU, afraid that Han might laugh at him. He didn't, though no sympathy was forthcoming either.

"Who are you, anyway, Liu Yuejin?" Han stomped his foot and stared at him wide-eyed. "You're too calculating to be a cook." He wasn't done yet. "I knew I could never outwit you. You're so devious."

Han was obviously focusing on a different matter, so Liu had to bring him back to his lost pack.

"Shengli, I haven't always done right by you, and we can talk about that later. Now can we work on finding the pack?"

The urgency did not affect Han; in fact, it gave him the opportunity to posture.

"Sure, I can help you find your pack, but what's in it for me?"

"I'll pay you back as soon as we find it."

"So it's come to that, but is it really about paying me back?" Han glared at him.

Seeing that Han was taking advantage of the situation, Liu was getting upset, but he needed Han's help, so he had to swallow his anger. As the saying goes, keep your head down when standing under someone's eaves.

"I'll give you five percent of the amount on the IOU."

Han held up his thumb and index finger to show the figure "8," a sight that nearly made Liu erupt. He had no choice but to give in to the greedy Han.

"Six percent, if you do a good job."

"Let's put it in writing," Han said.

Liu wrote out an IOU to state that Han would get six percent of the amount of cash in the pack if it was found, and so on and so forth. Six percent of sixty thousand came to thirty-six hundred, an amount that made Liu's heart ache.

"Where did you lose it?" Han asked as he took the note.

"Ciyun Temple, by the post office."

"Ai-ya! That's the worst place to lose anything."

"How come?"

"It's not my territory. A couple of days ago I worked in someone else's territory and got a good beating for it, plus a twenty-thousand-yuan fine. The rules among us are stricter than the law."

"So what do we do?" It was like seeing a cooked duck take wing.

"What else?" Han glared at him again. "All I can do is put you in touch with someone."

11

Cao Wushang and Baldy Cui

Cao Wushang, originally from Tangshan, Hebei, was a forty-two-year-old man with a long face. Since his arrival in Beijing five years earlier, he'd been a duck butcher at a peddler's market in the Beijing outskirts, where he had a good-sized pen, more than four hundred square feet, a former car wash with a ready source of water. Though he advertised only local ducks, in fact he slaughtered ducks from all over. Cao was afflicted with several eye ailments—trachoma, glaucoma, and cataracts—making it hard to see clearly beyond ten paces, much the same problem as Liu Yuejin's uncle, the prison cook Niu Decao. Liu took an immediate liking to the man.

Of course, Cao would have been just another transplant if he'd been known only for duck slaughtering, but over the years he'd become the ringleader of a den of thieves in the Beijing outskirts, elevating his status to that of "Brother Cao," a moniker that was better known than his real name. Brother Cao had never stolen a thing, as a boy or a man, and now it was too late to take up the profession, since his blurry vision would not let him see where people or things were. And yet, even with his bad eyesight, he controlled a group of men with sharp eyes, quick hands, and fast feet.

While his shed served as a thieves' training ground and base camp, he spent his uneventful days supervising duck slaughtering; directing the activities of thieves was like a sideline occupation. But not at first. Tangshan was famous for its thieves, some of whom eventually showed up at the duck shed. They often argued over hauls and territory, and Brother Cao mediated a few times, smoothing over potential blood-shedding incidents, which earned him the respect of the thieves, who then came to him whenever there was a dispute.

At some point he became their leader, with expanding territory as thieves from other cities and provinces waged territorial battles with those from Tangshan. These other thieves worked alone or in small groups, shooting in the dark, as it were, without a Brother Cao and his strategic leadership.

So after a few battles, the Tangshan group's territory grew as other thieves either dispersed or came to join Cao, increasing the size of his gang.

It was at this juncture that Cao revealed his true identity; he was a college graduate who had not started out slaughtering ducks in Tangshan. He'd taught at a suburban high school until his eye ailments made it hard to see the board and his students and he was forced to quit. First he sold fish at a peddler's market—grass carp, silver carp, and crucian carp, in addition to fathead fish.

Back then he had a mynah bird that had learned to say, with a Tangshan accent, words such as "You're here," "Have you eaten yet?" and the Chinese New Year's greeting, "Happy New Year." When he started to take the bird along to the market, it picked up curses like "Fuck you," "Need a fuck?" and "Drop dead." The bird was attached to Cao, who never shut it up in a cage, but let it fly around the stall, for he knew it would stay close by.

One day when Cao went out of town to buy fish, his wife and the bird stayed at the market. The woman who ran a stir-fry stall with her husband, Lao Zhang, came to buy fish and got into an argument with Cao's wife over the scale.

"Fuck you!" The bird began to curse when it saw someone arguing with Cao's wife.

"Need a fuck?"

"Drop dead."

Zhang's wife leaped up to hit the bird, but it flew away as she slipped and fell into a muddy puddle by the fish enclosure. Now enraged, she got up, grabbed a chopping board and smashed the enclosure, sending the fish flopping around on the ground. Cao's wife was incensed. She ran up and pushed Zhang's wife into the muddy water, then sat astride her and began slapping savagely. Zhang ran over, took Cao's wife by her hair, and returned the slaps. He also caught the bird with a fish net and snapped off its head. By then Cao had returned with his fish purchase. He was not upset that someone had smashed his fish enclosure or hit his wife, but the death of his bird really set him off. Picking up a liquor bottle, he flung it at Zhang, not to kill him but to vent his anger.

But, even with his poor eyesight, he was not wide of the mark. No, he hit Zhang in the head and sent him to the ground with blood pouring from the wound. Convinced he had killed the man, he fled the market with his family during the commotion and, after making it to Beijing overnight, opened a duck butcher stall in the peddler's market.

A month later, when he heard that Zhang had not died, even though he'd lost a lot of blood, his family begged him to return to Tangshan. But having spent a month in Beijing, he liked it better than Tangshan. So he sent them back home while he remained in Beijing. And though it was purely accidental that he became the leader of a gang of thieves, ultimately it gave him a sense of accomplishment that was missing from butchering ducks alone.

Before his sight turned bad, Cao had been a voracious reader and a good student, slowly developing a motivation for something better. When reading *Records of the Grand Historian*, he felt a kindred spirit with Zhang Liang, and when reading *Annals of the Three Kingdoms*, he found similarities with Kong Ming, and in *The Water Margins* with Wu Yong, also a rural teacher. He would close his book and sigh deeply, ruing the day of his belated birth that made him miss out on such great opportunities.

His pupils were imps who sometimes seemed to understand him and sometimes not. Later, when he became a fishmonger, he finally found "someone" to talk to when he bought a mynah bird. In the end, it was the fight with Lao Zhang that necessitated his move to Beijing, where he became the leader of thieves, finally putting his talents to good use.

Only people born in tumultuous times have the potential to accomplish something spectacular. Cao had to settle for presiding over petty thieves to strive for a different kind of accomplishment. The thieves stole money, but money was not what drew Cao to be their leader.

Liu Yuejin took a liking to Cao Wushang when they first met, for Liu's uncle also had eye problems, the only difference being that acquaintances of his uncle's never thought twice about coming up to bitch-slap him. In contrast, Cao always had people serving as his eyes when he walked down the street. After the duck stall closed for the day, he played mahjong with the thieves. It took him forever to read each tile up close, a habit that would have displeased players at other boards. With him, however, the mahjong partners actually fought to show who could be more patient or obliging.

"No hurry, Brother Cao," they'd say.

When all is said and done, it was because of a mynah bird that Cao got to where he was now. So after everything settled, he bought another bird, but this time, to prevent the bird from learning curse words, he sealed its ears with wax after teaching it a few phrases. And the bird never left the cage. Not being able to hear what people said, it repeated the only three phrases it knew: "Let's talk it out," "Peace is priceless," and "It's not too easy."

In his early days, Cao had learned calligraphy and was quite good at it. So he wrote a couplet that he put up on either side of the shed entrance.

A *single lamp can extinguish a thousand years of darkness.*
A *wise person can expel ten thousand years of foolishness.*

Unable to comprehend the profundity of the couplets, none of the thieves made a comment, good or bad, and the couplet stayed.

Han Shengli, with Liu Yuejin in tow, wove his way through the market and arrived at the shed, where Cao, who was reclining on an old-fashioned armchair, was reading a paper with a magnifier, stopping to wipe away tears with a tissue every few lines. In the corner a chubby young fellow was slaughtering a duck, his every move showing that he was new at the job. Turning his face away, he laid the knife against the duck's neck and, as the bird struggled, sent blood spurting all over the place, except into the intended plastic basin. The duck flapped around, spraying its blood onto the wall, so flustering the fellow that he reached out to push the duck's head down, only to see the blood spurt in a new direction, onto Cao's newspaper and hand. A bald fellow at the rear of the shed, watching a TV show with long-legged models, quit the show, walked up, and gave the chubby youngster a kick.

"Now you see, you little prick? If you can't even kill a duck, how are you going to work on the street?"

Cao calmly laid down his paper and wiped the blood off his hands with the tissue.

"It's not such a bad thing that he wants to go out," Cao said to Baldy before turning to chubby:

"What's out on the street, Hong Liang?" he asked amicably.

It took Hong Liang some time to come up with an answer. "People."

"That's what your mama told you." Cao sighed. "Let me tell you, there's nothing on the street but wolves."

"They'll eat you up the moment you're out," Baldy said.

Effectively silenced, Hong went to select his next victim in the cage, so scaring the ducks they began quacking all at the same time.

"Brother Cao." Not daring to barge in, Han Shengli called out, "Is this a good time?" keeping his hands on the doorframe.

Cao could not see all the way to the door and didn't recognize Han's voice. He turned to the door.

"Who is it?"

"It's Shengli, from Henan."

"Ah, it's you, Shengli." Cao seemed to recall who he was.

"I came to tell you something, Brother Cao. One of my relatives had his bag taken near Ciyun Temple, and I know those are your people."

Not liking what he heard, Brother Cao frowned.

"They're not really my people. Same hometown. I know some of them, that's all."

He picked up another newspaper and, ignoring his visitors, recommenced reading with his magnifying glass, leaving Han Sheng-li and Liu Yuejin standing there, feeling awkward. The slaughtered duck was still flapping on the ground when Baldy tossed it into a feather-shedding roller that was filled with steaming hot water. He pulled back the electric brake and the roller began to move.

Baldy clapped his hands and walked up to the door.

"How much was in the bag?"

"Forty-one hundred."

"It's not the money," Liu shouted from behind Han. "There's an important document in it." He added, "The thief had a dark mole on his face."

"You'll have to pay a thousand earnest money," Baldy said, ignoring the additional information.

Han looked at Liu, who was tongue-tied, as he hadn't expected to pay in order to get his bag back. Knowing it must be how they did things, he didn't dare ask questions as he began pulling money out of his pocket. Nothing but fives and tens that totaled slightly over a hundred.

"Do you really want to find your bag?" Baldy frowned.

"It's all I have, Brother Cui. I'll borrow some money and bring it over."

At that moment, Cao looked toward the door, but before he could say a word, the mynah bird that had been asleep in the cage woke up and said:

"It's not too easy."

"You've got it." Cao looked at the bird and nodded.

Baldy Cui put the money away and turned back to watch TV, while Liu spoke into the shed to the bird and Cao:

"Thank you. Thank you very much."

12

Qu Li

Yan Ge found Qu Li.

She had been in Beijing all along, and Yan knew that. If he'd wanted to find her, he could have done it any time after she left, but he pretended he could not so he could put on an act of continuing the search. He knew her whereabouts because his driver had her driver in his pocket, or put more accurately, under his control. Qu Li's driver was Yan's mole.

Her driver, Lao Wen, had taught Little Bai, Yan's driver. Back when Wen was driving a truck for the Beijing Automated Lathe Factory, Bai had been his assistant and later landed the job of Yan's chauffeur, thanks to Wen's recommendation. Yan Ge had a stud farm in a southern suburb where Bai had been sent to tend horses when he first arrived. By then the lathe factory had closed. Bai liked the job because he made more feeding Yan's horses than working.

Among the horses Yan kept was a Dutch mare called Stephanie, a gentle and highly intelligent animal that was his favorite. If he said fast, she galloped; if he said slow, she loped. He spoke and she reacted. The understanding between man and horse reminded Yan of times in bed with certain women. Horses and women of that caliber were rare, in his view.

He had been drinking before coming out with friends to ride around the farm on the day of the Dragon Boat Festival three years earlier. Some fighter planes from a nearby airbase were circling the air above them, and no one paid them any attention, until one went into a steep dive and buzzed the farm, trailing red smoke and flattening the grass. The riders were shocked, but Stephanie was the only horse that was spooked, and by the smoke, not by the airplane itself.

It was partially Yan's fault for not putting on blinders like all the others; he'd thought the mare was so gentle there was no need for it. She charged Yan's friends and their mounts. Some riders were too dazed to act; others jumped out of their saddles and fled to the stable. Even the trainers froze, having no experience dealing with a spooked horse. All but Little Bai, who was chopping grass in the stable. He ran out and grabbed Stephanie's reins. She dragged him along the ground but he refused to let go. The horse kept running and dragging him, until with a "bam" he slammed into a tree and the horse stopped. Bai suffered four broken ribs and spent three months in the hospital. When he was discharged, he no longer tended horses. He was now Yan's driver.

Forty-eight-year-old, Hubei-born Wen stayed in Beijing after being discharged from the army. A generous man who was always ready to lend a helping hand, he was not obsessed with money; he did, however, have a huge appetite for sex, had since he was young. At the lathe factory, he'd gotten involved with the bookkeeper and received a split lip from the woman's husband.

Soon after starting out driving for the Yan family, he began a secret dalliance with one of their maids, a young woman from Anhui who had stolen some of Qu Li's jewelry the previous spring over the period of a month. No common jewelry, the rings, necklaces, and earrings were all studded with gemstones—a sapphire in a ring, an emerald in a necklace, diamonds in earrings, altogether worth tens of thousands.

Since the maid lived in the house, she had no place to hide the stolen goods; she asked Wen to take them, but he was opposed to the thefts, for fear of being found out. Ignoring his advice, the maid told him that Qu Li had so much jewelry she'd never miss these few pieces.

Unable to talk her around, Wen took the jewelry home and hid it behind the heating grate. A month later, when Qu Li could not find some of her jewelry, she suspected the maids, but wasn't sure which of the three had stolen it. Nothing was found when their rooms were searched, and the matter was dropped.

The day before National Day, Wen's wife found the jewelry while cleaning house. Knowing nothing about jewelry, she thought they were fakes from night market stalls. In fact, she didn't care whether they were real or not. All she knew was that they were women's jewelry, which meant that her husband was having another affair and had bought the jewelry for his new woman. She was right, but not completely, and screamed at him when he got home that night. He had no way of coming clean, which angered her even more. She smashed the pieces along with their TV set.

Little Bai had the habit of paying his teacher, Lao Wen, a visit every year on the eve of National Day, a ritual he'd developed back when they worked at the factory. He arrived with a case of soft drinks and a fruit basket, only to be greeted by a domestic fight. The shattered jewelry on the floor told him everything he needed to know, but he feigned ignorance and went home after trying to smooth over the situation.

The next day he told Yan everything in the car. It wasn't his intention to betray his teacher, but he was savvy enough to know who, between Yan and his teacher, would be more useful to him. Besides, Bai was worried that Wen's wife might raise a stink, and once Yan Ge and Qu Li got wind of it, they'd figure he was in on it too. Wen had gotten him the job, so it was to Bai's advantage to bring it up with Yan first, thinking his boss would be upset and fire Wen.

That did not happen; instead, Yan told him not to mention it to anyone and to pretend that nothing had happened, leading Bai to assume that Yan was being charitable to a man who had worked for him for so long. Bai thought Yan wanted to give Wen a chance to make amends; he could not have been more wrong. Yan simply wanted to use this opportunity for Bai to have Wen in his pocket, to control him, as it were.

To be more precise, Wen was Qu Li's driver, and could serve as Yan Ge's eyes and ears where his wife was concerned. He would be informed of her movements through Wen and then Bai. Originally he'd only wanted to know where she was at all times so he could carry on with his other women. What a pleasant surprise to find other uses as well.

"The ancients were right when they said that helping others is helping yourself," he announced emotionally. "That's why the great retainer of old, Meng Changjun, made friends with small-time crooks."

Bai thought he understood, but wasn't sure, but that didn't matter. As long as his boss was happy, he'd keep his job.

Qu Li had thought no one but her driver knew where she'd been the past three days, since she'd told Wen not to tell anyone. He disobeyed her by calling Bai, who relayed the information to Yan Ge. Yan, on his part, pretended he didn't know, and continued the search, with two purposes in mind: one, he wanted to know exactly what she had in mind while buying himself time; and two, he needed that time to deal with Director Jia and Lin. Based on reports he received, Qu Li had gone to eight places in three days, including hotels, friends' houses, the suburbs, and some spas, sometimes during the day and other times at night.

"Who did she see?" Yan asked.

"She always told Wen to wait outside, so he doesn't know."

Yan grew suspicious at the reports, not about her going to see people, but about the purpose of these visits, which seemed to have nothing do with the pop singer. Qu Li had left home because of that photo, but she might be plotting something unrelated now. Not being able to figure out what she had in mind unnerved him.

The Qu Li surveillance came up empty, and the matter with Jia and Lin hung in the air. Yan hadn't heard from Director Jia after showing his hand to Lin over the USB drive, even though, as he knew, Lin would tell Jia all about their meeting in the hotpot restaurant. Lin had conveyed an attitude of indifference when he tossed the USB drive into the pot of boiling water, but Yan was sure he was just acting tough. Director Jia had wasted no time in sending Lin to meet with Yan after seeing the photo, and would be utterly shocked once he learned about the USB drive.

Yet Jia had remained silent after the existence of the drive was revealed. Yan was aware that the revelation of the USB drive carried different consequences than the exposure of the pop singer. The latter would hurt Jia's reputation—a mere sex scandal at most, no permanent injuries. But the USB drive could inflict mortal damage. Jia would not sit idly by and let things spiral out of control.

Before their relationship soured, Yan had often invited Jia out for a round of golf. During one game, Jia needed a bathroom break, so Yan offered to drive him over in a golf cart.

"No need to trouble you," Jia said.

Instead, he walked off a few steps, turned his back, opened his fly, and began pissing on the grass. Forced to do the same, Yan became Jia's urinating companion, and was treated to an impressive sight. After holding it in for some time, Jia released a strong, muddy, smelly stream that was characteristic of an older man, yet different from other older men in that it was powerful and bold, signaling to Yan that beneath Jia's mild appearance was a ferocious quality. This experience made Yan aware that he was too inexperienced to be a worthy opponent to Jia.

In a way, the ball was now in Director Jia's court, and all Yan could do was wait for him to hit back. It had never been his intention to cause mutual destruction, and the only reason he brought up the singer and the USB drive was to repair their relationship. Spinach was Yan's food of choice whenever he was on edge, like hamburgers were for Qu Li; he gobbled the stuff up till his belly bulged, releasing the tension and letting him breathe again. Hamburgers, of course, were fattening; spinach was not.

On this day, Yan was eating spinach and, before the relief came, he received a call from Little Bai, telling him that Qu Li's driver had just told him that she was at the bank.

Yan jumped up from the sofa at the news. Banks were tied to money, and her trip to the bank meant something different than her visits to friends. Finally understanding what she had been planning, Yan knew he could no longer pretend to search for her. He told Bai to get the car ready and take him to the bank, where he intercepted her. It had only been three days since he'd last seen her, but she'd changed. She had been the impulsive type, someone who could get into a fight with a beautician.

Now, however, faced with her husband's lies and infidelity, she was able to keep her cool. Instead of blowing up, she was gentle, more civilized. She appeared to have lost weight also, a change that puzzled him more than her new attitude, though she did not seem surprised or cross to see him.

"We need to talk," Yan said.

Wordlessly, she pointed to a coffee shop nearby, so they went in and sat down. Yan knew he could not rely on his usual vague insincerity. So, rubbing his hands, he told her everything about the pop singer and ended with:

"I don't have feelings for women like that." Then he added:

"It was all an act, and I left when it was over. We weren't an item and I never spent a night at her place."

He'd thought she would erupt in anger again, which was what he had hoped for, because then they'd be able to focus on the pop singer and talk it out, even if she was irate, until they patched things up. But she didn't fall for it; she did not seem irked, and in fact appeared not to care at all, as if she'd been listening to someone else's sex-capade. Obviously, her mind was elsewhere, which, to him, was a ray of hope in turning things around. Imagine his surprise when she came straight to the point. Stirring her coffee with a silver spoon, she said with her head down:

"Stop talking about your women, Yan Ge. Our problems are worse than that."

Tears welled up in her eyes, and she seemed able to breathe more easily once she'd gotten that out. Like smashing an object or splashing water on the ground, nothing was salvageable now that the truth was out. She had laid her cards on the table, and Yan knew he had to follow suit and change tactics.

"You're preparing a way out, aren't you?" Yan pointed to the bank.

"Like they say, husband and wife are birds in the same forest, but when disaster strikes they fly off in different directions for safety."

Astounded, Yan began to suspect that she had been faking her depression all these years.

13

Liu Yuejin

Liu Yuejin suffered a cracked head during a fight. Wrapped in a bandage, it presented a sight similar to Han Shengli of a few days ago, under a baseball cap with a fake logo. If it had been anyone else at any other time, he would not have let the man off so easily, but it had been someone from Brother Cao's duck shed, and in the end it didn't matter, as he had to find his pack as soon as possible; he could not afford to argue with the one who hit him.

As he was leaving the shed with Han that day, after asking Brother Cao for help in finding Liu's pack, they had agreed that they would return the following evening to see if there was any news. But by the following afternoon, Liu had hatched a scheme to get rid of Han, so he went to the shed by himself. Cao's style and authority had convinced him that, once Cao said yes, he would have no trouble recovering his pack.

As a middleman between Cao and himself, Han was no longer needed now that Liu had made the connection. Besides, with his cataracts and blurred vision, Brother Cao reminded him of his uncle. And Han had displeased Cao, who struck him as a decent man for interceding when Baldy Cui insisted that Liu pay him the full finder's fee, even knowing that Liu did not have that much money.

If Han was present when he retrieved his pack, Liu would have to follow through on their agreement and pay him the money he owed, plus a percentage of the sixty thousand yuan. But Liu had other plans for the money—his son had called again to say he had been kicked out of school for not paying his tuition after the three-day deadline. Liu had doubts that he was telling the truth, but the boy did sound earnest, so this time he mustn't delay.

When the pack was missing, paying Han seemed reasonable, but once it was within reach again, Han would not deserve the money, in his view. He'd pay Han back sooner or later, just not right away. So instead of waiting till evening, he showed up at the shed in the afternoon.

This time no duck was meeting its death. There was a whole gang of people there, playing mahjong with Brother Cao while Hong Liang, the fat boy who was killing ducks the day before, was serving tea. A meticulous person in everything he did, Cao was a serious player; so were the others. He held each tile up close to study and took his time to make a move, slowing the game down. That was one sign of his earnest approach. Another was, no idle talk around the table, which was littered with bills of various denominations. Liu waited at the door. When a round ended and he heard sounds of tile shuffling, he called out:

"Brother Cao."

Cao looked up but could not see Liu's face clearly. It was also a new voice.

"Who's that?"

"The one who lost his pack. I came with Han Shengli yesterday."

When Liu stepped inside, Cao recalled who he was.

"Oh, you. Sorry, we couldn't find the thief."

Having come filled with hope, Liu would have fallen to the floor from the news if not for the doorframe he held onto. A lost pack meant nothing to Cao and his people, but for Liu the news was devastating. Dazed, he tried to think and, as he was lost in his own thoughts, he said what was on his mind, instead of what he should have said:

"He's one of yours, how could you not find him?"

Just as the day before, when Han had said that every thief on the street worked for Cao, the man was not pleased, but he merely frowned and said nothing. Noticing Cao's expression, Baldy Cui yelled at Liu:

"Have you got your head screwed on straight? The man's got feet, so how are we supposed to find him so fast?"

Still thinking his own thoughts, Liu said:

"I handed over the earnest money for nothing, then, didn't I?"

Then a thought struck him.

"Could it be that you've found him and you're hiding the pack from me?"

And then:

"I don't care if the money's gone, but you have to give me the other stuff."

Liu's lack of tact made Cao sigh. Still not responding to Liu, he said to the people around the table:

"I made another mistake."

Bewildered by his comment, they looked at him nervously.

"Confucius said, petty men and women are hard to deal with."

The others were still confused.

"I'm not going to help anyone from now on. Every time I do I make people unhappy."

Now they got it, though it really didn't matter if they had or not. The most important matter for them was the realization that Brother Cao was upset, self-reflection being a peculiar habit of his whenever he was angry. Baldy Cui leaped up from the table, ran to the door, and kicked Liu.

"What kind of fucking talk is that?"

The attack caught Liu in his stomach, catching him off guard and sending him to the floor. He landed on his back, overturning a basket full of duck feathers, which flew into the air and quickly blanketed the shed. On any other day, he would not have fought back after such a kick, but judgment failed him now that he had no hope of getting his pack, his money, and the IOU back. With a sudden infusion of courage, he got up from the pile of feathers and, ignoring Baldy Cui, picked up a knife, jumped forward and waved it at the people around the table.

"I've lost everything. Do you know what that means?"

They froze, surprised by Liu's reaction and attitude, not out of fear of the knife, since they were used to those, both to slaughter ducks and to fight other gangs. Brother Cao frowned as he pushed the tiles away and walked out of the shed. Unhappy that Liu had ruined not only a game of mahjong but Brother Cao's mood, Baldy was about to kick Liu again when another player, a fat fellow, beat him to it and first kicked the knife out of Liu's hand before landing a flying kick in the abdomen. Despite his bulk, the man was light on his feet; with two swift kicks, Liu flew into the air before landing by the table where ducks were slaughtered. He banged his head on a corner of the table; the sight of his own blood sobered him up; he quietly curled up on the floor, buried his face in his hands, and began to cry over the injustice.

Liu returned to the dining hall and bandaged his head, a minor injury that stopped bleeding once his head was wrapped up. He could not sleep that night. It was bad enough that his pack was stolen, but now he had to avenge a beating he'd received because of it. But finding the pack was still the first order of business, for it would be harder to locate as time went by. He had to put aside the thought of revenge and focus on the pack, but he had no idea how. The police were no help, neither was Brother Cao; it was also pointless to enlist the help of Han Shengli and people like him. Liu had reached a dead end, for there was no other solution. By the time dawn broke, he had reached a decision: he had no one but himself to rely on, so it was up to him to find the thief.

The following morning he asked Ren Baoliang for three days off without telling him why; he did not want Ren to laugh at him and, besides, it was too long a story to condense into a few words. He just told Ren he'd been beaten up and needed to go to the hospital. Convinced by the bloodstained bandage, Ren chose to say nothing. Liu rode out onto the street, his first stop the post office where his pack had been stolen. The man from Henan, still there playing his *erhu*, had reverted back to the popular song, no longer singing the Henan tune. This time, of course, Liu was in no mood to argue over that; his mind was on something else. Ever since the day the pack was stolen, he had hoped the thief would return to the spot, which was why he gave the Henan man two yuan each day to keep watch. Now, after the beating the day before, he was in a bad mood and flew into a rage at the sight of the man belting out "Love and Dedication" with his eyes shut, as if he were a casual bystander.

"Stop, stop!"

The man opened his eyes and stopped singing when he saw Liu.

"I haven't seen him again."

"You have your eyes shut, so how are you supposed to see him? What did I give you money for?"

"I'm supposed to do your bidding for two yuan?" he grumbled. "I'll give you back your money. I think there's something wrong with you. He's not that stupid. Why would he come back after making off with your pack?"

Liu had to admit that the man was right, so he rode off, knowing full well that it was pointless to argue.

He spent the whole day out on the street. It had seemed like a good idea, but where to begin? He knew that thieves are territorial, so the thief would likely stay close to the post office, if not to the same exact spot, just about every day. So he made a round of the markets, the bus stops, and the subway entrances, all places with crowds, the best areas for thieves to ply their trade. But when the day was over, he had laid his eyes on just about everyone but the thief. Several people had looked familiar from behind, but his joy had turned to disappointment each time he moved in front of them. There were also a few who had resembled the thief, but no dark green mole on the right cheek.

By the time the streets were lit up, it dawned on him that he had forgotten to eat, though he wasn't hungry. He was about to call it a day and return the following morning when it occurred to him that thieves also work at night. After buying a flatbread at a stall, he squatted at the roadside to eat and study the people emerging from the subway; the thief was not among them. He got back on his bike and rode along, so intent on watching pedestrians he failed to see a car slowly pull up to the curb, where the driver opened his door. Too focused on the people around him, Liu slammed into the door and hit the asphalt; his bicycle's front wheel, twisted out of shape, continued to spin. The owner of the car, a Lingzhi, was a heavyset middle-aged man who was alarmed at first. But once he knew what had happened, he ignored Liu and went to check on his car. There was a dent on the front door and a long scratch on the back door from the bike pedal.

Incensed, he ran up to Liu.

"Do you have a death wish?"

Liu appeared to have escaped with no broken bones, but his back had hit the curb and the pain was so intense he nearly fainted. He tried to stand up but couldn't, so he struggled to sit up, when another piercing pain led him to pull up his pants leg. There was a big bruise on his leg.

"Do you know how much this car cost?" the man shouted, ignoring Liu's injuries.

Liu could not but wonder why he was having such lousy luck. His pack had been stolen and not recovered, and now he'd banged into a man's car. One problem had yet to be solved and another had come on its heels.

"I don't have any money," was all he could think of to say.

The man could tell, from Liu's accent and clothes, that he was a migrant worker, but he clenched his fists and shouted anyway:

"You're going to pay for the damage even if you have to sell your house."

"My house is in Henan," Liu rubbed his leg, "and no one will buy it."

Before the man could say any more, a traffic cop on a motorcycle, light flashing, rode up and stopped. Some long-haul, privately owned, unlicensed gypsy cabs were using loud speakers to hustle for fares to Tangshan and Chengde, but drove off when they saw the cop. Ignoring them, he turned off the motorcycle and flashing light to study the scene, as calls came through the walkie-talkie on his shoulder.

"Make him pay for the damage," the car owner yelled, " to teach him a lesson."

The cop looked to be new on the job, a square-faced young man in his twenties. The day before he had responded to a traffic accident on Fourth Ring Road and, due to his lack of experience, had been tricked by both sides. He'd made a mess of the investigation, placing the blame for the accident on the wrong driver, first one then the other, upsetting them both. They had filed a complaint at traffic court earlier that morning. He'd just emerged from a tongue lashing by his squad leader, and was in a bad mood to begin with. If the driver of the car had been calm and reasonable, he'd have examined the scene of the accident more carefully, but the man sounded as if he was issuing him an order. He frowned.

If that weren't enough, the man pressed his face so close the cop could detect a sour smell from the man's dinner. Rich people all have sour breath. They sit in their air-conditioned cars all day long, safe from the elements, while he was exposed to the elements, inhaling dust and car exhaust. The man's tone tried his patience. Pushing him away with his helmet, he skipped the scene survey and said in measured tones:

"Teach who a lesson? How come I think it was probably your fault."

Surprised, the man began to argue:

"Look closely. My car wasn't moving. He was the one who hit me."

"This is a sidewalk," the cop stared at him, "not a parking spot."

Finally realizing he had parked in the wrong place, he was deflated.

"I just stopped to buy a pack of cigarettes," he muttered. Then he blurted out, "I know your squad leader."

Everything would have been fine if he hadn't brought up the squad leader. But when he heard that, the cop walked over to check on Liu Yuejin, who was sitting slumped on the curb, foaming at the mouth, by all appearances nearly unconscious. The bandage on his head made the injury look serious, so the cop said to the driver:

"Drive him to the hospital, right now."

Wondering if Liu might be seriously wounded, the driver panicked. He tried to slink away.

"Where do you think you're going?" the cop shouted.

That stopped the man in his tracks. Seeing he was not in the wrong, Liu struggled to his feet. He had faked the foaming.

"I'm not going to the hospital," he said to the cop. "Tell him to pay for my bicycle."

The cop looked over at the man, who looked at Liu, then at the cop, and then at his watch. He took out two hundred yuan and flung the money to the ground.

"What the—"

He glared at the cop before getting into his car and driving off.

"It's not that I don't want to go to the hospital," Liu said to the cop. "I just can't, because I need to take care of something else."

"You're not innocent either." The cop wasn't happy. "What were you thinking, not watching where you were going?"

Liu Yuejin had a good feeling about the cop, who had, after all, helped him. It had been days since he'd had anyone to talk to, and he felt sorry for himself because of the accident, so he opened up to the cop, as if he were family. He told him everything, the stolen pack, its contents, his visit to the precinct station, his search on the street, and so on. He was revealing to a complete stranger all the things he'd kept from Ren Baoliang, but he wound up confusing the cop, who doubted the existence of sixty thousand yuan. He took a close look at Liu and said:

"You're from Henan, aren't you? You people are born liars."

Then he got on his motorcycle and rode off with the light flashing, leaving Liu behind, half dazed.

14

Yang Zhi

Yang Zhi was feeling seriously out of sorts.

Four days earlier, he'd stolen a fanny pack near the Ciyun Temple post office, though it had been his day off and he hadn't planned on working. Normally he worked five days a week and took two days off, unlike other thieves, but much like office workers, the only difference being the days he took off—Wednesdays and Thursdays. Stealing the pack that day was like working overtime. The Temple area was not his territory, so this had been a violation of professional ethics, a risk he usually shunned; money was always good, but you had to know when to stop, like anyone engaged in business dealings.

The mark that day was the reason why Yang worked overtime—the man was asking for it. Dressed in a Western suit and sporting a fanny pack, he was chastising a street artist. Yang hated the idea of the strong bullying the weak, and if that weren't enough, the man was gesturing wildly, pointing to the distant CBD structure and claiming he'd built it. He didn't look like a developer, at most a foreman at a construction site, and the bulging pack was a sign of hefty contents. Yang simply could not abide the man harassing the street singer and showing off his wealth, which was why he made a snap decision to work that day.

After snatching the pack and shaking off the man chasing him, Yang went into a public toilet and opened the pack, only to be disappointed by the contents, which he had thought could be tens of thousands. There were a few thousand, nothing to scoff at, but disappointing. The rest was junk Yang did not deign to examine. He'd been tricked by the man's appearance and ruined his day off, but he put it out of his mind after leaving the toilet.

Unexpectedly, he'd owned the pack for less than four hours. After leaving the toilet, he'd gone to a public bath and then strolled over to Lao Gan's Xinzhou Restaurant, where he'd run into Zhang Duanduan, the girl from Gansu. If she'd looked like an ordinary hooker, nothing would have happened; it was precisely because she didn't that he'd been attracted and gone with her. It had been a trap.

If it had been only the money and the pack, Yang would have eaten the loss and swallowed the humiliation; but it was like a flood inundating the Temple of the Dragon King, the deity in charge of rain—people in the same trade not recognizing each other.

The problem was, he was doing the you-know-what with Duanduan when the three men stormed in and surprised him. By itself, that was no big deal; it was just that his you-know-what was shocked into inaction. In the heat of the moment, he'd been in a hurry to grab his clothes to cover himself and paid it little attention when his clothes were snatched away.

So when they took off with everything after kicking him around a bit, he slinked back home and realized that something was amiss down below. He broke out in a cold sweat; this was serious. The loss of the money and the pack now paled in comparison. Unwilling to accept the prospect, he lay down in bed to play with it, but the more he did the worse it got, until finally he panicked. Grabbing some money, he went out and found a streetwalker; still no good.

So he went to another one, this time a big-breasted prostitute, with no better result, maybe even worse than with the first one. The next one was neither too skinny nor too plump. She initiated a stirring down below as they walked back to his place. But when they got into bed, it turned into a limp noodle; he refused to give up. He worked really hard at it, his head bathed in sweat; the woman didn't object for a while, but after half an hour, she impatiently tried to squirm out from under him.

"Aren't you done yet?" She added, "Don't blame me if you can't get it up."

That earned her a slap that shut her up; she lay back down and remained motionless as Yang continued his hopeless rally. Finally, he knew it was wasted effort. He'd only stolen the man's pack, while the three men and a woman had robbed him of his manhood, yet his anger was focused on the woman only. How could she trick and frighten him like that?

All he could think of the following day was finding the offending team. He went back to Lao Gan's diner, then to the little house, as well as to streets and areas frequented by prostitutes, but he never saw them again, which intensified his anxiety. For three days, Yang Zhi searched for them, with no interest in thievery; he would not do anything else until he found them, or more precisely, her, Zhang Duanduan, the cause of all his trouble. He'd kill her to vent his anger and expel the fear inside, which, hopefully, would help restore everything down below. Before long he was blaming it on the pack; it had created so many problems it led to his murderous thoughts of revenge. In the process, he'd forgotten that he'd stolen the pack in the first place, from a man called Liu Yuejin, a cook, not a boss, at a construction site, who was looking everywhere for him. The pack would rob Yang of his manhood and Liu of his life.

A lane dotted with food stalls lined one side of the Tonghui River, a stinky ditch that had seen better days, with clear water and boats, during the Republican era. On the left side of the river were rows of CBD buildings and to the right were the food stalls; the area was quiet in the day, a filthy mess that was obscured by bright lights at night. The turbid, foul-smelling water reflected the high rises along its bank, giving off the illusion of a bustling city as the water traveled east. The row of stalls sold just about everything edible: barbecue, entrails soup, stew and wheat cakes, spicy hotpot, spicy prawns, Korean cold noodles, Turkish barbecue, and so on. Smoke permeated the air above the crowds of diners, so tightly packed they could barely move. Standing along the railings were working girls looking for business.

After three days of a fruitless search, Yang recalled that Duanduan was from Gansu and that the three men also spoke with a northwestern accent; after asking around, he learned that there was indeed a Gansu gang working the Tonghui River bank, an area with no clear territorial demarcation that drew petty thieves for minor work. Now Yang changed his tactic from searching to waiting. On the third night, going stall by stall to ask for answers, he got one at the spicy hotpot stall, where he was told that three men from Gansu often came for midnight snacks with a woman. That had to be them, Yang said to himself. He sat by the stall and waited for them from six o'clock till two in the morning, with no sign of them. The stall owner, also from Shaanxi, thought Yang was waiting for friends.

"They come just about every day," he said. "I wonder why they aren't here tonight."

Yang was in no hurry. He came the following night, but instead of the Gansu gang, Liu Yuejin showed up. Liu had learned about Yang waiting at the stall from Hong Liang, the inept duck slaughterer. Liu had been out all day searching unsuccessfully for Yang, planning to wait all night if necessary. But a downpour drenched him and gave him a minor fever, so he went back early to the dining hall, where a small makeshift room of broken bricks against one wall served as his living quarters and a guard house for the dining hall. With the light from the site, he bent down to open the door as someone patted him on the shoulder from behind. Startled, he turned and saw it was Hong Liang, the fat youngster from Cao's shed, a sight that set him off right away.

"What do you want?" he asked gruffly.

"I didn't help beat you up," he said, then came straight to the point: "I want to make a deal with you."

"I'm busy," Liu grumbled.

"I'll tell you where the thief is for a thousand yuan."

Liu paused, his elation quickly replaced by disbelief. If even Brother Cao couldn't find the thief, how would this fat little guy, who had trouble killing a duck, know where he was?

"You still have my earnest money," Liu said, convinced that he was being conned. "Don't get on my nerves, or I won't let you off easily."

Undaunted, Hong Liang held out his hand. Liu thought he looked like he meant business, and though he wasn't entirely convinced, in the end, his desire to find the thief won out and he decided to trust him for now. He could always square things later if he was lying. He took out a hundred yuan, one of the two hundred he'd gotten from the accident.

"This is all I've got. Blood money."

Hong Liang took the money and stuck his hand out again. Liu was beginning to believe him, but did not want to give in.

"Search me if you don't believe me." Liu raised his arms. "I'm running a fever and I'm not even willing to buy a bottle of water."

"It's not for this piddling amount." Hong Liang flicked his finger at the bill. "I'm doing it because the thief hit me once." He added, "I should have told Brother Cao, but Baldy Cui and the others have beaten me too, so I didn't want to share anything with those bastards." He wasn't done yet:

"I sneaked out early this evening to try my luck at the snack stalls by the Tonghui River. I didn't steal anything but I saw the man you're looking for. He was having something from the spicy hotpot stall."

Leaving Hong Liang behind, Liu got on his bicycle, with its second-hand wheel, which had cost him thirty yuan, and sped over to the Tonghui River. It was not quite ten at night, the busiest time for the area. After locking his bike, he began inching his way through the crowd, his eyes on the spicy hotpot stalls. After checking out several he spotted Yang Zhi at a stall by the bridge. The sight of his old nemesis brought back all his anger; he was surprised to find him here, since he'd been to this spot before, but maybe he hadn't looked carefully enough. Who could have predicted that he'd find the thief with the help of a hapless duck slaughterer, after spending so much time searching fruitlessly on his own?

His fever vanished at the sight of the thief, and he was energized; locating him was like finding his pack, and finding his pack was getting his money back. But all that paled in significance compared to the IOU it held. He was overjoyed, as if he hadn't been looking for his pack, but for the world at large. When a lost object is found, it seems to double in value.

Liu took a deep breath to calm himself, wondering if he should just pounce on the man, but a glance around the area changed his mind. The place was packed nearly to capacity with diners, and the thief might escape again if they got into a fight. Taking another look, Liu realized that the man wasn't eating, but, like him, was checking his surroundings, as if searching for someone.

Cautiously pulling down the bill of his cap, Liu strode to the next stall and ordered a bowl of wontons. He took his time eating while watching the thief, biding his time; he'd make his move once the crowd thinned out.

Now that he'd found the thief, he had to make sure he didn't get away again. The thought occurred to him that if he made his move out in the open, the thief could get away during a struggle. A better course of action was to watch him and follow him back to his place. When the thief went to bed he'd return to the construction site to get some help and corner him in his own house, like catching a tortoise in a water vat. That would be the only guarantee that he'd catch the thief. Finally hitting on the right solution, he stopped worrying; the idea of following the thief, not fighting him, erased his fears.

Now with his mind at ease, he realized that he hadn't had a thing to eat all day, so he settled down to enjoy the wontons. But then, worried that the bandage might draw unwanted attention, he took off his cap and unwound it before putting the cap back on. It had been two days since his unfortunate visit to the shed, and a scab had formed over the wound; it had stopped hurting, and the cap felt looser.

When Liu finished his wontons, Yang the thief was still sitting at the hotpot stall, showing no sign of leaving. By eleven o'clock, Yang was still there, so was Liu, neither in any hurry to leave. The owner of the hotpot stall was upset that by sitting there all night, Yang was interfering with his business.

"It's getting late," he said to Yang coldly. "No need to wait any more. If they're not here by now, they're not coming."

Yang stood up and looked around before heading toward the Tonghui River bridge, followed by Liu, who had quickly paid and retrieved his bike. After crossing the bridge and heading down a lane, Yang walked out onto the street and boarded a bus. Liu quickly gave chase. At every stop, people got off and people got on. Luckily for Liu, it was nighttime, and there weren't so many people; he'd have lost Yang if it had been daytime.

After five stops, Yang got off and took another bus to the suburbs, alighting after six stops. He entered a small lane, the sight of which had Liu breathing a sigh of relief. Finally they were at the thief's place. He secured his bike to a locust tree before following Yang into the lane, a filthy place with three public toilets from which dirty water flowed into the street. The streetlight was broken, so he had to watch his step.

When they reached the end, Yang turned and walked into another lane, all the way to the end, where there was a house whose door faced the lane. Liu noticed that the wall was haphazardly whitewashed, a clear sign that the door, a sheet of particleboard in a frame of three wooden slats nailed to the wall, had been newly opened on the wall. It was padlocked. Liu knew it was the right place—it had the look of a thief's den.

What he hadn't expected was to see the thief, instead of bending down to unlock the door, press his face against the window to look inside. Maybe this wasn't his place after all. Then the thief tried the lock, and when it didn't budge, he aimed a frantic kick at the door, which wobbled a bit. It broke after the second kick and fell open with the third. Feat accomplished, he spat and stopped. From his hiding place, Liu was confused. After kicking in the door, the thief walked off with his head down, and Liu had no choice but to keep following him now that he knew this was not where the thief lived.

He relaxed his personal state of alert at the thief's dejected appearance and wondered if he should just pounce on him and settle things once and for all. How long would he have to follow him otherwise? What if he wandered the streets all night long? He'd have no trouble fleeing the next morning, surrounded once again by crowds. As the thief turned into another lane, Liu sped up to get closer to him, but two men suddenly emerged and blocked the thief's way. Stunned, Liu ducked into the toilet closest to the lane entrance and peeked out at this new development.

One of the men blocking the thief was Baldy Cui, and the other, unknown to Liu, looked like a student in a restaurant uniform. Cao's people had also been looking for Yang for a few days, but to settle a score, not to help Liu find his pack. They were searching for the same person and, though for different reasons, their efforts overlapped and could have been combined, if not for the furor Liu had raised at the shed.

Yang Zhi was from Shanxi, while Brother Cao and his gang of thieves were from Tangshan; different places of origin meant different territories. One must always think twice before provoking people from Tangshan, a fact known to every thief in Beijing. If you did, you were either obliterated or decamped over to their side. It was simple: do not venture into Tangshan territory and everyone can practice their craft in peace, like well water not mixing with river water.

When Yang came to Beijing some six months earlier, neither the area nor the rule was familiar to him. His expertise was picking locks. After someone was caught trying to break in, Yang could go to the same house the following day and emerge loaded with loot. Emboldened by his superb talent and gutsy attitude in lock picking, he gave little thought to the Tangshan gang and operated in their territory four times in a month. Nothing happened at first, but after the fourth time, he was caught by Cao's people, who took all his loot before hanging him up to whip him with a belt.

"Brother," Cao sighed, "I let you go three times." He continued, "You're a smart man, so how could you not know that three times is the limit?"

That taught Yang that Cao was not someone to mess with, and he knew he had two options: one, stay away from Tangshan territory, like other thieves, or two, join them and share in the profits. The territory under their control was residential housing for the rich and some high-end business districts, also frequented by the rich, both of which offered great potential. What could he expect to get if he went to places for the poor? But he'd have to follow their rules once he joined them, which would mean unwanted restrictions. He could not make up his mind.

After getting to know Cao's gang from the run-in, Yang became a frequent visitor to the shed—on his days off, of course. They played mahjong, which, unlike picking locks, was not Yang's forte, and within weeks he had racked up a debt of forty thousand yuan. He tried to win it back, and the more he played the more he lost, until the debt was over two hundred thousand by the end of the month.

It finally dawned on him that it might have all been a setup, but it was too late for him and he couldn't say anything. From then on, he began to steal for Brother Cao, whom he paid back whenever he got something. Stealing for the Tangshan gang but not in their territory meant he had to limit himself to the areas of the poor for petty cash. How would he ever be debt-free that way?

A loathing for the Tangshan gang's sinister scheme began to rise inside him. Who qualified as a real thief? Not someone who stole from ordinary people. No, a real thief was someone who stole from other thieves. Ordinary victims could go to the police, but someone in his shoes had to swallow the losses. Only by robbing a bank could he ever hope to pay off his debt. So to avoid his debtors, Yang stayed away from the shed, which led Cao's people to come after him. That was why he had been preoccupied.

Yang thought that Cao's people were after him for the money he owed, but it was actually about something else, and they were in a hurry to find him, for something had come up and the pressure to find him had intensified. Ordinarily, they might give up after failing to find him after a few days. This was something Brother Cao knew but Yang did not. There was no need to search for Yang during the first half of the month, but now something was up. Hong Liang, the duck butcher, had sneaked out that night, which was a violation of the rules. Baldy Cui caught him when he returned and slapped him around, and Hong Liang, given his guilty conscience, mistakenly took that as a sign that Cui knew everything.

"Who did you go see?" Cui wanted to know.

It was a casual question, but Hong confessed, revealing Yang's whereabouts, but omitting the deal he'd made with Liu, for fear that Cui would confiscate the hundred yuan. So when Yang Zhi left the snack stall, he was unaware that he was being followed by Liu Yuejin, who did not know that Yang had grown two additional tails. The only difference was that Liu was on a bicycle while Cui and his lackey were in a used VW. With one on the pedestrian walkway and the other in the fast lane, they were oblivious of each other's presence. Yang was not alone in being startled when Baldy Cui blocked his way at the lane entrance. Liu was equally surprised. The appearance of Brother Cao's people told Yang that he had been found out, so he tried to talk his way out of it.

"Can we talk later, Baldy? I'm looking for someone. It's urgent."

He took out a penknife from the small of his back. It reflected a cold glint under the streetlight but had no effect on Cui, who took the knife from him and ran his finger along the edge of the blade. Liu Yuejin was the one who was frightened; he was lucky Baldy and his lackey had shown up first, for who knew what might have happened if he'd gone up against the knife-carrying thief?

"Who are you looking for?" Cui asked, still fingering the blade.

Yang had wanted to tell them about the stolen pack and the scare he'd endured, but he stopped at the last minute. For one thing, it wasn't something he was proud to bring up, and besides, talking would solve nothing. Most of all, his problem down below could easily be turned into a joke.

"None of your business. Just someone who'll be in big trouble when I find him."

"Let's forget your business for now." Cui stopped him. "What about our business? You owe us money and it's long past due."

Now somewhat fearful, Yang continued to explain:

"If you kill someone you pay with your life; if you owe money you pay your debt. I understand the rules, Baldy. I'm not trying to get out of anything."

"As Brother Cao said, money is a small matter; being upright is more important."

"It's an important principle I uphold."

Baldy was about to say something, when the young fellow in the restaurant uniform stopped him.

"Since Lao Yang here knows the principle, let's not belabor the point, Baldy Cui. We should get to the more important matter." He took out a piece of paper.

"We need you to do something for us tonight, Lao Yang."

He spread the paper out to show him a sketch.

"This here is Beethoven Villa." He pointed to a spot. "The people in this house play mahjong and order in food every night."

"Brother Cao's idea is for you to make up for your mistake with this." Cui jabbed at the paper. "An indoor job, your kind of work."

Cui took out a cigarette and said, "You're one of us. This is Brother Cao's territory." He added, "It's for your sake, too. A rich family and an easy job. After that, we'll forget the money you owe us."

Yang was speechless. Liu, on his part, was too far away to hear what they were saying; all he could see was three men jabbing at a piece of paper, a disquieting sight.

15

Yang Zhi

Yang Zhi changed into a restaurant uniform and got on a delivery bicycle, followed by Liu, who had a different purpose for tailing Yang now. Earlier, when finding his pack was the sole aim, he'd hoped to catch Yang at a quiet moment and place. Now the plot had thickened and the thief was on the move, engaged in something else, which Liu needed to keep track of before he could recover his pack. He had lacked the nerve to intervene and Baldy had returned the knife to Yang, who had then put it back in his pocket; now Liu had to follow Yang to keep from losing him after going through all the trouble to find him. So all he could do was watch the man until he finished whatever he needed to do, when he'd be easier to deal with—either that or wait to catch him where he lived.

Yang turned into a different person in his uniform. Puzzled, Liu wondered where he was going and what he planned to do there. In the meantime, Liu was sure that the thief was onto something big, for he wouldn't need to change clothes for a small job.

With Yang going at a measured pace, Liu had no trouble keeping up on his bike; it was so much easier than trying to follow a bus. When they reached Honglingjin East Bridge, Yang looked at his watch and got off, parked the delivery bike, and sat down on the curb to smoke. Liu had to get off on the other side of the bridge to wait. Yang smoked and gazed vacantly at the passing pedestrians and vehicles. It was getting late and the traffic was thinning out.

Staring at the increasingly deserted street, he sighed and mumbled something to himself before lowering his head to continue smoking. All that was familiar to Liu, who was also given to gazing into the distance, sighing and mumbling to himself whenever something bothered him. Surprised to find similarities between them, Liu sighed.

But the man was a thief, no matter what, and Liu was determined to catch him and get his pack back. Yang finished his smoke and got back on the bicycle; Liu followed suit. They rode down the main street through seven intersections before turning left, and after three more intersections they turned into an alley that led to another lane.

An open vista greeted them once they emerged from the lane. It was a gated community fronted by a fountain, where a pair of stone lions spewed water even late at night. Colorful lights swirled on the gate, and the wall below was inscribed, Beethoven Villa. Two security guards in berets and puppet army uniforms stood at the gate.

Yang had appeared listless on the way, but the bright lights seemed to animate him, energizing Liu at the same time. At a leisurely pace, Yang rode up to the gate, while Liu got off his bike and hid in the lane to watch the man's movements. Pointing to a piece of paper he took out of his pocket, Yang said something to the guards, one of whom spoke into his walkie-talkie, after which he waved Yang inside. The thief pushed the bicycle through the gate and got back on to ride into the villa.

Liu was able to see him at first, but he soon disappeared from sight, which caused Liu considerable anxiety. After following him for half the night, he'd hate to lose him now, but he had no reason to enter the villa to keep track of him. Even if he could make up an excuse, he might do such a terrible job telling his lie that the guards would make him out to be a thief. Besides, Yang was bound to finish whatever he went in to do, and once he was done, he'd have to come out through the gate. So Liu parked his bike and crouched down to smoke as he waited patiently. At some point, he sighed and, like Yang before him, muttered to himself:

"What the hell is going on here?"

Unaware of his tail, Yang rode up to the villa feeling uneasy, but not because he was about to do a job. It was because of what had happened in recent days. He still hadn't found the gang that stole his pack after searching for four days. As he stewed in anger, his problem down below was getting worse; at first it was all right when he was alone and only stopped working when he was with a woman. But since the day before, it even refused to respond while he was alone. It was clear that he was spiraling down an abyss, and he was worried that if he couldn't locate Zhang Duanduan soon, he'd be beyond salvation by the time he found and killed her.

As if that weren't enough, now there was a new problem: Brother Cao's people had tracked him down and sent him to burgle a house in Beethoven Villa. He'd considered killing himself, and was in no mood to burgle, yet he had no choice, because Brother Cao's people would never take no for an answer.

Luckily, he was a professional, able to forget his troubles and worries and focus once he was on a job. The impressive villa enlivened him and helped him concentrate, like a ball player walking onto a brightly lit ball field. That was the difference between a pro and an amateur. Concentrating on the job forced all worries to the back of his mind, which in turn helped him relax. So he felt he had the job to thank for forgetting his problems. Why had he become a burglar? To forget his troubles.

Now energized, he wanted to do an especially good job this time, so he paid close attention to the buildings as he rode along. After seven or eight turns, he reached the clubhouse, which, at this hour, was shrouded in darkness. He rode past and got off his bike to look at a number on one of the buildings. After checking it against his paper, he went up and rang the doorbell twice before the door opened. He could hear the sounds of mahjong tiles and of men and women talking and laughing. In the open door a longhaired man in his PJs raised his head and yawned grandly for a minute or longer, until he was all snot and tears. Finally finished with his yawn, he began exercising his neck, making loud cracking noises. Obviously, they had been playing for quite some time. With all that done, the man finally looked at Yang, who knew he had to be in character immediately, quickly becoming a deliveryman.

"Same as yesterday, Boss," he said guilelessly. "Eight orders of fried rice and five fried noodles."

Yang opened the warming case on the back seat and took out thirteen boxes. The man took the boxes while Yang put the order form on a pad, took a pen from his pocket, and uncapped it with his teeth before handing it over for the man to sign. The man sized him up while taking the pen.

"You're new." The man looked suspicious.

"The regular guy isn't feeling well, so the boss sent me." Yang was unfazed.

Clearly satisfied with the answer, the man signed the form, raised his head to yawn again, and went back inside with the food, trailed by the sound of the door slamming shut.

Yang turned the order form over and looked at the paper pasted on the back; it was a sketch of the compound, with an arrow pointing from this villa to another. Hopping onto his bike, he followed the arrow to the back of the compound on small, winding, uneven paths past lawns with chirping insects. Going deep into the compound, he passed a manmade lake alive with the intermittent calls of cranes and circled round it to reach a house in the corner. After dismounting to check the number, he looked around to make sure he was alone before hiding the bike in the grass. Then he took a sack from the warming case and went around to the back of the house, where he drew a steel wire from his belt to pry open the window and crawl inside.

It was a large house, likely over five thousand square feet, with high arched ceilings. Aided by the streetlights, he could roughly make out the furnishings in the dark—there was a pool table in the middle of the living room. He picked up a ball and sent it rolling across the felt. No dogs barked, no people moved about, and Yang was reassured that the house was empty and that Cao's people were telling the truth. For him, there were two kinds of jobs: the ones with certainty and the ones without, depending on whether the house was occupied or not. Moreover, he always felt better about stealing from the rich. Even so, he knew he had to be in and out as quickly as possible or he'd have trouble explaining the delay to the guards.

After determining the lay of the land, he got down to work, starting with the living room, then to the study, the sitting room, the bedrooms, the bathrooms, and the storage space; proceeding from the first floor to the second and then to the third, he worked methodically, with practice and experience, an old hand at tidying up people's houses. Ignoring visible drawers, he went for areas that might offer surprising results, such as the inside of a bookcase, kitchen drawers, or under a sofa. In the storage space on the second floor a safe was hidden behind the mops and brooms, but it was attached to the wall, so he passed it up.

Twenty minutes later, he had collected all the valuables—except those in the safe—including money, fine jewelry, gems, watches, cameras, video cameras, and two brand new cell phones. A rough calculation told him that the jewelry and gems alone should be enough to pay back the people at the duck pen. It had been a productive trip; the rich truly were a thief's best friends. After he cleaned out the place, it looked neat and tidy as usual, with no sign of a break-in, which distinguished Yang from amateur burglars.

During his search, he had unearthed a number of intriguing objects; for instance, in the bookcase in the first floor study, he found a stack of American dollars and two boxes of virility pills, which led him to wonder if the man of the house had a problem similar to his. He decided to take them. Between the mattresses in a third floor bedroom he came across two bankcards and a colorful box that held a dildo. Looking at it, he was confused at first, but it made sense when he recalled the virility pills he'd taken from the first floor. The dildo would do him no good, so he put it back. In the heater cover he rooted out some jewelry and a box of business cards. He could understand the need to hide the jewelry, but what was the point of keeping business cards out of sight? He took one out; there were words on it, but it was too dark to read them. The shape, triangular as opposed to the usual rectangular shape for cards, intrigued him enough to pocket one.

"An upright person has nothing to hide," he said to himself. "I'll count this as a souvenir."

After a complete round, he tied up the sack, slung it over his shoulder, and got ready to go downstairs, when he heard the crunch of car tires on the road outside. The car stopped and someone unlocked the door, letting in the voices of both men and women. Yang was startled. Cao's people had said the house would be empty, so where did these people come from?

"Damn. Tricked me again."

He opened the window to jump out, but the three-story house, with its vaulted ceilings, was as high as a five-story building. He'd break a leg in the fall, and even if he lucked out, he'd make a noise when he landed. So he rushed back to the bedroom, where he planned to hide and sneak out later after the people left. To his dismay, someone was coming up the stairs, all the way to the third floor, heading in his direction. Alarmed, he hid his sack in the entertainment cabinet and, finding no better place to hide, went to stand behind the curtain.

The bedroom door opened and the light snapped on. From behind the curtain he saw it was a woman in her thirties, heavyset but quite good-looking. She entered the room, kicked off her heels, and tossed her purse and cell phone onto the bed, before beginning to undress. Her blouse came off first, then the skirt, bra, and panties. In an instant she was stark naked, a somewhat chunky figure, but with fair skin and full, rounded buttocks. She walked into the bathroom, closed the glass door and started her shower. Through the frosted glass, he could make out her naked body, a sight that enthralled him, and before he knew it, something began to stir between his legs. He didn't sense it at first, but was elated when he noticed. He'd thought the scare from Zhang Duanduan had completely deflated him, and he'd vowed to kill her to restore his manhood. To his surprise, that restoration came at the sight of a stranger whose house he had just burgled. It was truly a productive trip; not only was the loot enough to pay off his debt, but he was himself again. You can never predict how things might work out. Just when everything seems hopeless, there's a turn of events.

As Yang was waxing the moon, the cell phone on the bed began to ring, shocking him out of his reverie and sending his hand down to cover his crotch. The door to the bathroom opened and the woman, wrapped in a towel, came out to answer the phone. As the curtain fluttered from a cross current between the window and the bathroom door, she spotted a pair of feet under the curtain and, after a momentary pause screamed, effectively shrinking the growth between his legs. But that was the least of his concerns, for two men yelled out from the first floor:

"What's wrong?"

Then came the hasty footsteps of people running up the stairs. Knowing he mustn't be caught, he pulled the curtain aside, looked down, and, of course, it was still a three-story jump. With no other way out, he put his leg over the ledge and was about jump when he thought about the sack of loot; he couldn't go back for it now, but, refusing to leave empty-handed, he picked up the woman's purse before taking the plunge.

The house was certainly high. He emerged unscathed, except for a sprained ankle, which he ignored as he took off running along the lake all the way up to the compound wall, which he climbed and then continued to run. A watchman at the lake spotted him and, as Yang made the climb, the gate guards sounded the alarm. The two men came running out, one heading into the compound and the other staying outside, shouting to each other through walkie-talkies the whole time.

Instead of fleeing from the area, Yang crouched down behind a tree and waited until the guard ran past before hightailing it into a lane across the way. Then he ran as if his life depended on it, straight into Liu Yuejin, who had been lying in wait for over an hour. Liu had his eyes trained on the compound gate, and a long time had passed with no sight of Yang. He wasn't sure if the man would come out that night or if he'd left through another gate. After following him all night, he'd lost him. What a lousy break. If he'd known this would happen, he'd have pounced on him earlier around the snack stalls. Yang had a knife, but Liu thought he might get some help from the crowd if they got into a fight. Following him had been a safe plan, but it would be a failed trip if he lost him. Besides, hiding out in the lane had drawn suspicious attention to him.

Earlier, an old man walking by thought Liu was a thief lying in wait in the lane. He was about to ask what he was doing there when Liu stood up and beat him to the punch by asking for a light, then telling the man he was waiting for a friend who had delivered food to the villa compound. Liu was more or less telling the truth and the old man did light his cigarette for him, but he gave Liu another suspicious glance before walking off. Just when Liu felt it was a hopeless wait, the alarm went off inside and he saw the guards running around. A shocking development. Then he saw Yang coming toward him, a pleasant surprise. Liu had no inkling what Yang had done inside to alert the guards and set off the alarm, but he couldn't let the opportunity pass. He had to catch him now.

"Thief!" Liu shouted.

He held back for fear of the knife. Yang Zhi froze at the sight of Liu, unnerved by his unannounced appearance, when he suddenly recalled how he had stolen the man's pack. But this was not the time to mull that over. Seeing Liu block his way, he drew his knife. Not really interested in fighting, he waved it as he ran past Liu, who naturally gave chase. With his sprained ankle, Yang knew that Liu was catching up so he flung the purse at Liu's face. Liu tried to dodge the object, slipped and fell. He got to his feet and resumed the chase, but Yang had already turned into another lane and was out of sight.

Liu was upset at how close he'd come to nabbing Yang, though he had managed to avoid his clutches. Reminded of something by the noise at the gate, Liu returned to the lane and picked up the object, the purse Yang had used to fend him off. He then sneaked off into one of the lanes.

16

Yan Ge

Yan Ge met with Lao Lin again, but not for seafood or hotpot this time. They went to Hometown Congee, where Yan had a bowl of cold congee with lotus seeds and silver fungus and Lin had hot congee with shark's fins. After they finished, Lin looked calm and unruffled, not affected at all by the mouth-burning, nonvegetarian congee, while Yan was sweating from his cold congee, for he kept wondering if this meeting would end well.

The last time they met, Yan had delivered an ultimatum, starting with the newspaper photo of him and the songstress and from there to the USB drive, which Lin should already have shown Director Jia. But five days had gone by and Yan had heard nothing. He was as frantic as an ant in a heated wok; the throw down had not been intended, like so many ultimatums, to break ties with Jia. But to mend the rift between them.

Now after five days' silence, Yan was made keenly aware that he had always played a passive role in his relationship with Jia, both in the way they became friends and the way their friendship deteriorated. He had no say in how far the deterioration would go or whether it could ever be repaired. If they both wanted a fence mending, that could be achieved. But if only Yan was interested, then the break would be irreparable.

Another lesson he learned was that a rich man was nothing but a prostitute when dealing with the politically powerful. To be sure, a clean break did no one any good, for Jia would not have smooth sailing if Yan's boat was overturned; worse yet, they might come to grief together. If the breakup was meant to lead to mutual destruction, then it was a matter of spite and devoid of any tactical advantage, and that was something Yan wanted to avoid. He would have been a foolish billionaire if he hadn't understood this, and Jia would not have continued the friendship for so long.

The problem was, the billionaire not only had lost all his money, but was in serious debt; he was no longer the Yan Ge of days past, which was why he'd issued the ultimatum. In a way, the threat was akin to cutting off his nose to spite his face, accomplishing little or nothing; he was resorting to the low-blow threat precisely because he had run out of options. That was not like him; he was an upstanding man forced by circumstances to debase his relationship with Director Jia, turning a profitable and amicable friendship spiteful and unproductive. Clearly they had both changed. Yan Ge missed the time, fifteen years before, when he'd borrowed money from a friend and delivered it to Jia, who had grasped Yan's hands with tears in his eyes.

Now, that was true friendship. How had a relationship with such an affecting beginning passed through many stages of transformation only to end up like this? Yan would not have minded so much if it had been merely a question of whether to repair their relationship or not. But his fate was in the hands of Jia, who, in the blink of an eye, could decide whether Yan would regain his wealth or be reduced to nothing, whether he remained a member of the upper class or was sent to prison, even whether he lived or died.

It was complicated. If Yan had caused his own downfall, he would have no one to blame but himself. But in point of fact, Jia was largely responsible for what happened to Yan, and now he was refusing to come to his aid. No matter how Yan looked at it, Jia was the villain, having dragged Yan down to his level. So if Yan fell, pulling Jia down with him would be payback for his refusing to help and for his small-mindedness. Yan had mulled this over for five days and still found the prospect hopeless. He could not stop thinking about it, even though he knew it was pointless, since Jia had to make the first move.

Then, on the afternoon of the fifth day, he was surprised to receive a text message from Lin: Six thirty tonight, Hometown Congee. Yan was outraged to receive a text message, not a personal call, and by the tone, which was a command, not an invitation. But being the one in trouble, the person who needed help, he had no choice but to obey.

He was prepared for two possible outcomes. First, Director Jia had changed his mind and would help him out. Two, Jia would deliver his own ultimatum and use this opportunity to push Yan so far down he would never rise again. There would be no middle ground, now that they had shed all pretenses of nicety. Letting it drag on and waiting to see what happened was not the style of an old fox like Director Jia. Yan knew the smell of Jia's piss. Lin was much like Jia in this regard, but not entirely. Jia was usually unambiguous in handling business, but would at least speak his mind with Lin; but that attitude did not travel through Lin, who was vague and evasive. The emotionless content of the text message gave Yan no clue as to what was on Lin's mind, which meant he could not predict what Jia intended. He would go to the meeting bereft of confidence.

Yan experienced a degree of nostalgia for the time when he'd been poor but free of fear and risk. Fear and risk, however, were less troubling than having to deal with so many ruthless people, people he had to watch out for all the time, some smiling as they practiced their ruthless behavior. The laborers might be hopelessly dense, but at least they were straightforward and never devious. They could not be ruthless even if they wanted to. But if they somehow did want to, they would not know how to go about it.

Yan saw himself as a sheep that had somehow stumbled into a wolves' den. Had he not gone to college, he would have remained in Henan as a rice farmer who rose with sun and rested at sunset, performing physical labor that would not tax his mind. He'd have married a virtuous wife and had a couple of kids; life would have been hard but happy.

Why would he be happy? Because there would be no need to overthink everything. College had screwed him. Idle thoughts about his past and the present were useless in bailing him out of his predicament and were good only for giving him a chance to marvel over the unpredictability of life and fate. His apprehension and agitation caused him to break out in a sweat even as he downed a bowl of cool congee; this failing troubled him. Lin laughed when he saw Yan's sweaty forehead, and after finishing his own steamy congee, calmly offered Yan a napkin to wipe his face, a gesture akin to mockery. Yan had to suppress his anger when he was reminded of the purpose of the meeting; as the saying goes, you lower your head when standing under someone's eaves.

"Director Jia has an idea," Lin belched and said, "about a small business deal."

Yan was surprised; he hadn't expected the negotiations to begin this way.

"What kind of business?"

It was a tactless question, but Lin did not mock him this time. Instead, he lit a cigarette.

"He said he'll help you get a loan of eighty million yuan if you turn over the USB drive."

This came as a surprise, a pleasant one, his earlier distress vanishing on the wind. The threat had obviously worked; the USB drive was more powerful than the photo. Eighty million was not enough to pay off the four hundred he owed the bank, but would serve as a stopgap solution. He could pay the interest and get construction moving again at several sites. Jia's offer was like a nitroglycerin pill for a heart patient. Not knowing how to execute an about-face in attitude, Yan could only express his gratitude:

"That's not a business deal. It's a helping hand from you and Director Jia. I'll never forget you, or Director Jia, and must ask your and his forgiveness for my past mistakes."

He was, of course, referring to the photo and the USB drive, but the gratitude was lost on Lin, who replied woodenly:

"No, helping is what we did in the past. This time it's a business deal."

Yan Ge grasped the two men's intention with absolute clarity. He had shown his hand with the photo and USB drive; they had shown theirs with the eighty million. Help and business are entirely different. Help is murky, business is clear-cut; helping hands can be extended indefinitely, business deals are concluded one at a time. The unspoken message here was: this is where everything ends. The amount Jia offered was precisely calculated as being just enough to rescue Yan from his dire situation; he would neither starve nor be sated. After the money changed hands, they would sever all ties and Yan would have to tackle whatever happened after that on his own. It was an indeed a business transaction, a bank loan in exchange for the USB drive and photo. Yan Ge finally comprehended how crafty the man was. Yet the loan was his salvation, a poison pill he would have to swallow. Knowing what the two men had in mind, he acted decorously this time:

"Thank you, and please thank Director Jia for me."

The deal carried a high price tag: once it was concluded, Yan would lose Jia as a source of wealth he had enjoyed for more than a decade; he would lose not only a person, but a towering tree, not just a man, but a channel for connections he had constructed over that period. Material goods and money were easily obtained; nothing was harder to put together than a channel for connections. It would be like losing a melon and getting a sesame seed in return. For him, at this moment, the sesame seed was the life-saving tonic he had to swallow. He had no choice. As far as their relationship was concerned, Jia had always been in the driver's seat, so it was a business deal when he said it was. If Yan Ge did not go along, the deal was off. That was how Jia's craftiness manifested itself.

No matter what Yan thought, the tonic did help, like a sinking ship being refloated after half the cargo is removed. He felt better and consoled himself that he could take a breather for now; he would worry about tomorrow later. With Director Jia out of the picture, he could find himself another director; all he had to do was pay to re-accumulate the connections. When a cart reaches the foothills a road will open up, and when a boat comes to a bend the river will straighten out. These thoughts lightened his mood considerably, and he wondered if this was how a man became a social outcast.

There was another reason why he accepted the offer—he had made a deal with his wife before coming to the meeting. When he figured out, via Little Bai and Lao Wen, where Qu Li had gone after leaving home, he realized that her disappearance was all tied up with money, which was actually easier to tackle than if it had been another man.

It was much the same as the situation with Jia and Lin, though certainly not simple. When he showed up at the bank, he and his wife went to a coffee shop for a talk, where he learned that she had transferred some money; what he did not learn was how much, where it came from, or where it had gone. Alerted by her action, he pored over his company's accounts. There he learned from his finance director that his wife had had a hand in every business deal he'd made over the past eight years. Yan had employed an informant; so had she. Hers was the assistant manager who had been killed in an automobile accident two months earlier. The man had helped her take a cut of every transaction, not too big a slice to be noticed, of course, but enough to accumulate quite a sum over time. She had turned out to be both clever and ruthless. She'd been plotting against him all along.

But he couldn't figure out what exactly had happened eight years earlier to trigger her mutinous plan. A woman? The need for money? Something he'd done in their daily life? Something he'd said? And what had been her relationship with the dead man? Yan Ge trembled at the thought of how complicated the world and people can be. His thoughts went to her incessant trips to Shanghai. What did she do there?

He began to suspect that not only had she faked her depression, but had intentionally put on weight and turned temperamental. Of course not everything was fake, but she could well have been putting on an act the whole time. His investigation showed that the small cuts she'd taken had netted her more than fifty million, an amount that would not have been of great importance to Yan in the past, but now, when his boat was sinking, was a substantial number. When he brought it up, she did not panic, as if she'd known this day would come sooner or later. What surprised him was the no-nonsense tone she adopted.

"Now that it's come to this, tell me what you plan to do."

Now that it had come to this, he had to make a deal with her, but it did not progress as smoothly as the one he'd made with Jia and Lin. After a prolonged argument and repeated concessions on his part, they finally reached an agreement: one, she would allow him half of the money to help him out, and he would pay her back once his financial troubles were over; two, the loan would cancel out whatever she had done in the past; three, there would be a promissory note for the loan; four, she wanted the loan processed on the day their divorce was finalized, thus severing all ties.

The deal was humiliating to him, because the money, which had been his to begin with, was converted into a loan. Moreover, he had wanted to "borrow" the whole amount, but she would only lend him half. With all her illegal and immoral, behind-the-back maneuvering, she had the upper hand.

Yan believed in the principle that a divorcing couple's property should be divided equally, and that they should share responsibility for a debt accumulated jointly. In their case, however, he was to be responsible for the debt, while she was entitled to their money. Twenty-five million, which would have been nothing to him in the past, was a lifesaver at a moment like this, which was why, after a heated argument, he eventually agreed.

In two days, he had made deals with the two most intimate parties in his life; one from his private life, his wife, the other from his social circle, Director Jia and Lao Lin. Twenty-five million plus eighty million meant he would have over a hundred million, enough to save his business; besides, the deals brought things out into the open, and he now knew where everyone stood.

Except for one thing. He woke up that night struck by such a terrifying thought he broke out in a cold sweat. After they were married, Qu Li had suffered several miscarriages; now that seemed suspicious. If she had planned them she must have been preparing to divorce him one day and, more importantly, cruelly refused to have a child with him. Worse yet, she may have wanted to terminate the Yan family line. And there was yet another possibility: she could have aborted a baby by someone else, perhaps by the dead assistant general manager. The more Yan thought about it, the more terrible he felt, until he had to accept the proposition that the people closest to you can be your worse enemies, as was the case with the late employee, whom he had unwisely trusted.

After the two deals were struck, Yan actually felt much better, more reassured; as the ancients said, no extreme lasts forever. All alone now, he was relieved. After reaching an agreement with Lin, Yan had taken him to retrieve the USB drive, which he had stashed not at home, nor at the stud farm, where he spent time with his horses whenever he was especially happy or really upset. In his view, horses were more principled than humans. No, it was somewhere else, at his Beethoven Villa quarters, which had been vacant for quite some time.

But Qu Li had the only keys, after changing the locks when she'd caught Yan with a movie actress in bed two summers before. He had to admit that he was at least partially responsible for her ultimate betrayal. But that was why he'd stashed the drive there, a place neither his wife nor anyone else would think to check. On the day he went to hide it, he entered by prying open a back window, like a common thief. He could not repeat that with Lao Lin, so he picked Qu Li up in his car and the three of them went to the villa together. This was the first husband-and-wife meeting since their deal was struck, and the soon-to-be strangers were actually civil to each other.

Once inside, Qu Li went straight to the bedroom while Yan went around the living room collecting the six copies he'd made from six spots under the floorboards. No one would ever have guessed the secret under their feet. Watching Yan pry up the floorboards, Lin had to laugh.

"You're quite something."

Yan replaced the board after retrieving the last drive and then walked over to a window and pressed a hidden button. A false panel under the window slid open for him to take out a laptop, which he placed on a coffee table, along with the six USB drives.

"Here they are. All of them."

"Whether they're all here or not is up to you," Lin said unemotionally. "Director Jia often says that being upright is more important than being rich."

"That's so true." Yan was sweating again from all the effort. He wiped his forehead and continued, "I understand." He looked discomfited, but before he could say anything, they heard a scream from upstairs.

"What's wrong?"

They ran up to the third-floor bedroom, where they realized they'd had a break-in. Like Qu Li, they were startled, but a quick check around the house showed them that the thief was alone and that he'd fled by leaping out the window. His loot was hidden in the entertainment unit, so they hadn't lost anything. Yan congratulated himself on hiding the drives under the floorboards and the laptop behind the false panel, both of which a thief would not normally check. Nothing was amiss so long as the drives were not taken; losing the other stuff was no big deal. With the thief's sack in hand, they went downstairs.

"Could he have heard what we were saying?" Lin was worried.

"Don't worry," Yan said. "He was on the third floor."

Someone was banging on the door. Yan opened it and in stormed the security guards. Before Yan could say a word, one insisted on searching room to room for the thief while the other wanted to call the police. Lin stopped them and spoke up before Yan:

"No need for that." He pointed to the sack. "It was a dumb thief. After all that, he left his sack behind."

A light went off in Yan's head.

"False alarm, no need to call the police. We wouldn't mind, but your company would surely be unhappy. Weren't some guards fired after a break-in a while ago? Go on now; it's late and this has been tough on you."

Finally understanding what he was getting at, the guards nodded.

"Thank you, Mr. Yan. Thanks so much."

They backed out of the house, thanking him repeatedly. When they were alone again, Qu Li, dressed in a bathrobe, picked up Lin's pack of cigarettes and lit one, before sitting down on the sofa.

"Who says we didn't lose anything? The thief took my purse."

"It was an expensive purse." Yan looked surprised. "A limited UK edition."

"I don't mind losing the purse, but I'd like to have the contents back."

"How much money could you have had in your purse?" Yan asked with a dismissive wave. "Consider that the price to pay for peace of mind."

"You didn't know this, but there was another USB drive in the purse."

Yan and Lin were stunned.

"What's on it?" Yan asked.

Pointing her cigarette at the drives on the coffee table, she said nonchalantly:

"Same as those."

A second shocker for Yan and Lin, who were speechless. Another light went off in Yan's head, and he slapped his forehead.

"So this was all your doing!" He looked at his wife in disbelief. "Who are you anyway? After all these years we've been together, I don't think I know who you are."

"You cheated first." She blew a smoke ring. "I have to be on guard against insidious people like you."

Lin turned to her.

"Was it password protected?"

"I should have, in case anything happened to it, but I didn't because I was afraid someone might do something to me."

The men were flabbergasted. Yan jumped up to attack her, but Lin stopped him.

"It's all over now." Yan's hands shook in front of Lin, who sighed before breaking into a smile.

"All right, then. Now we're no longer enemies and must join forces." He was suddenly suspicious. "With all these houses in the compound, why did the thief pick this one?"

The anxious look on his face told Yan that Lin might be right in suspecting that the theft was a plot related to the matter with Jia. He tensed up. They did not know that it was not a plot and that it had nothing to do with Jia, even though it was no accident that the thief picked Yan's house. Cao's people had told the thief, Yang Zhi, which one to break in; they'd had their eye on Yan's place for quite some time because of Qu Li's driver, Lao Wen.

Since his affair with the maid had caused a tumult at home, Wen had turned over a new leaf and stopped seeing her, though even if he'd wanted to he could not have, since she was one of two maids fired at the Yan home.

But he could not give up having affairs, and maids were the best he could hope for. He could hardly be blamed; he was still in his forties and his wife no longer wanted sex, so he had to find someone, driven by a different impulse than when he was a younger man. With limited options, he now resorted to prostitutes.

One day, when Qu told him to pick up something at the now vacant villa—they had moved over to the stud farm—Wen decided to satisfy his need for sex by taking along a prostitute. So he cruised the streets in Qu Li's BMW, stopping at a hair salon, where he chose a masseuse. After settling on a hundred yuan, he drove to the villa, where they did it on the sofa.

Afterward, as he was putting on his pants, an argument over the price broke out, since the woman mistook Wen to be the owner of the BMW and the villa, and demanded five hundred. Her greed angered him, but she argued that a hundred was for doing it at the hair salon, but five hundred for doing it elsewhere. Wen could afford five hundred, but was angered by her deception. They got physical.

"I'll call the police and have you arrested," Wen threatened, slapping her and pointing to the phone. "Don't think I won't."

Unable to fight Wen by herself, she sobbed and picked up the money before running out, making sure to remember the man and the house. She had a good friend named Su Shunqing, a masseuse who was in a relationship with a restaurant deliveryman, the same one who had stopped Yang Zhi in company with Baldy Cui. The young man, a high school graduate, was a bit of a pedant, and now, with a prostitute as a girlfriend, he liked to compare himself with the Song poet Liu Yong, with the well-known lines, "Where will I awaken after my drinking binge / The willow-lined river bank / An early morning wind blows over the late moon."

The modern "Liu Yong" always obeyed his girlfriend, never veering an inch from what she wanted. Her profession allowed her to sleep with any man she chose, while he was to remain faithful to her; and she was significantly more high maintenance than girls in other professions. His delivering job did not earn him enough to support her, so he ended up working for Brother Cao as a snitch for extra money.

It so happened that the prostitute beaten by Lao Wen told Su what had happened to her at Beethoven Villa. Su told "Liu Yong," who worked for a restaurant not far from the compound. In fact, he often made deliveries there. Partly to impress her with his connections, partly to punish the owner of the villa, and partly to earn some extra money, he took notice of the house when he made deliveries.

After two weeks, he went to Cao and told him that the house was vacant but fully furnished; ripe for the picking, it would be a shame to pass up the opportunity. And that was how Yang Zhi ended

up burglarizing the place. It had all started with a humiliated prostitute, but the theft seemed so much more complicated to Lin and Yan,
who were ignorant of the facts. Put more precisely, it did not matter if
it had anything to do with Yan and Jia—they were both now involved
in the wake of the theft of the USB drive.

17

Liu Pengju and Mai Dangna

After picking up the purse Yang Zhi left behind, Liu Yuejin took off running, cradling it as if it were spoils. Too ruffled to see where he was going, he ran down several lanes, crossed some streets, and switched buses more than once. He had no recollection of how he made it back to the construction site, feeling as if he'd been chased by hordes.

When he got back, he headed straight for the dining hall, unlocked his little room, went in, and bolted the door behind him before collapsing onto his bed, only then realizing that he was drenched in sweat. He hadn't felt this tired once over the past five days of searching for his pack; now he was exhausted from finding a purse. Obviously, being a thief isn't easy.

Then it occurred to him that he'd left his bicycle in the lane across from Beethoven Villa; he didn't have the nerve to go back for it. It was, after all, an old bike that had recently suffered damage, so it was next to worthless. His only regret was for the second-hand tire that had cost him thirty yuan.

When he finally pulled himself together, he turned on the overhead light, but immediately turned it off and fished a small flashlight out from under his pillow. He turned it on and held it in his mouth to study the purse. It was a shape he'd never seen before, cucumber-like, and the material felt much softer than either plastic or patent. To him, though, it was just a purse and nothing special.

He began to search the contents, believing that he'd had a stroke of good luck, even though he'd spent half the night following Yang Zhi, only to lose him in the end. And he had yet to find his own pack. The purse, which clearly belonged to a wealthy woman, might well contain cash, maybe even a diamond ring, which would surely make up for his lost pack. Why else would Yang pretend to be a delivery man to steal it? It was like losing a goat but getting a horse in return.

So he was sorely disappointed after turning the purse inside out; it contained only a little over five hundred yuan, some bankcards, women's cosmetics, and implements like compacts, brow brushes, and tweezers. There were even a couple of sanitary napkins. Bankcards would be nice if he had the passcodes; but even if he did, the owner might have already reported the lost cards, so that trying to use them would be too risky. He was so upset he could hardly breathe, but his anger was directed at Yang Zhi.

"You stupid fuck. You steal poor people's money, but with the rich you go for women's stuff. Are you some kind of pervert?"

Then he found a USB drive. Liu knew nothing about computers, so he had no idea what it was for. From its attractive rectangular shape, he thought it might be another feminine item, but for what he did not know. As he was examining the thing, someone banged on his door. Thinking it must be the people who were chasing him, he snapped off the flashlight, slipped the thing into his pocket, and tossed the purse into one of the vats that lined the room. After putting the lid back on the vat, he lay down on the bed and pulled the blanket over him.

"Who is it?" he asked in the voice of someone who had been asleep.

"It's me. Open the door."

It was Lao Deng, the man charged with guarding the construction material. Liu felt better knowing it was Deng, but what if he was being forced to bang on the door by those other people?

"Who's with you?" Liu asked to make sure.

"I'm alone. Is that OK?" Lao Deng replied, sounding slightly pissed. "Were you expecting me to bring you a girl?"

Finally feeling at ease, he threw the blanket aside and got up to open the door.

"You were out all night," Lao Deng demanded. "What were you up to?"

"I've been here all along." Liu feigned ignorance before putting on a puzzled look. "I don't often sleep that soundly."

"Someone's looking for you, you know."

"Who?" Liu was surprised.

"Your son. He's called five times in the last hour. He wants you to pick him up at West Station."

It wasn't the people he'd feared, but the news was a bit of a shocker.

"What's that good-for-nothing coming here for? Why didn't he tell me?"

"You know I have insomnia," Lao Deng grumbled. "Well, his calls pretty much ruined a night's sleep. It's that bastard Ren Baoliang's fault. Why did he have to stick the phone in the storage room? I'm going to smash that damn thing."

It was two in the morning when Liu got to the station. Had it been daytime, there would have been a teeming throng. Now, the square was nearly deserted, with only a few people milling around. But there were plenty of people lying on the ground, sleeping this way and that, some with glaring eyes, some snoring loudly, some grinding their teeth, out in the open for all the world to see. There were yet others who were awake, chewing bread on the steps while glancing around shifty-eyed. Others sat on their luggage, carrying on lackluster conversations that were interrupted by an occasional yawn. A couple from who knows where were standing by a pillar, the woman leaning against it in the arms of her man, who seemed to be biting her.

Liu made three rounds of the square but failed to find his son; now he was worried. It was the dull-witted boy's first time to Beijing, and he could have gotten lost, maybe even been kidnapped to be sold. Losing his son would be so much worse than losing the pack. His son had probably come to Beijing for his tuition precisely because Liu could not send it after losing his pack. If he now lost his son, it would be because of the pack, and Liu could not stop cursing the thief as he continued his search.

After reaching the western edge of the square, he was about to turn back when he heard someone next to a pillar cough in his direction. He turned and saw his son standing there. It had only been six months since he'd last seen him, but the boy had grown taller and darker, with a bit of stubble in the space above his lips. The boy was bigger too—tall and big, dark and big. The father kept getting thinner while the son grew heavier. No wonder Liu hadn't noticed him earlier.

But why hadn't the boy spotted him? Why hadn't he come out to greet him? Why make his father anxious?

Liu Yuejin was even more surprised to see a woman next to his son. In her midtwenties, she was wearing makeup in the middle of the night, dressed in a halter top over a pair of pink crop pants and sandals. Maybe his son hadn't noticed his father because he was kissing her when Liu walked by earlier. Liu was confounded by this sudden development, and neither father nor son knew what to say. That turned Liu into a scold.

"What are you doing here? Why aren't you home studying?"

He immediately regretted saying that, wishing he hadn't started their conversation this way. His son had come to Beijing because he'd failed to send him the tuition money, so his question was the same as slapping himself in the face. But Liu was in for more surprises.

"Study?" His tall, big, dark, and overweight son came straight to the point. "I won't lie to you. I quit school three months ago."

The shock quickly turned to rage, as Liu bellowed:

"You quit? Is that it? Without a word to me." He was seething now. "Why did you keep asking for tuition money if you'd quit? To cheat your own father?"

What incensed Liu most was the fact that he'd lost his pack because he'd been on his way to send his son the money. Without the trickery the boy had pulled on him, Liu would not have suffered as he had. If not for the woman, he'd have gone up to give the boy a kick in the rear.

"So what have you been doing now that you're not in school?" he roared.

"Mom told me to go sell liquor with my stepfather."

This son of his was an endless source of surprises that night. Too proud to take money from his ex-wife, Liu had spent six years working like a dog to support his son, and finally when the six-year period was nearly up, his son went over to his mother's side without breathing a word to him. Liu had worked for nothing for six years, and his pride meant nothing. He stomped the ground to give force to his resentment.

"You're switching to your mother's side? Do you know what she's like? She was a worn-shoe, a loose woman, seven years ago." He wasn't done. "And your stepfather? Know what he does? He sells fake liquor and should have been shot long ago."

"That was then. Now he makes the real stuff," his son said coolly. "You don't have to yell like that. I had a row with them yesterday, so I came to see you."

"Over what?" Another surprise for Liu.

"Mom had a baby last month, and they've treated me differently ever since. I wanted to choke that little bastard, but of course I couldn't."

That was the surprise of surprises. His ex-wife and Li Gengsheng had a baby? She was in her early forties and he was likely in his mid-forties. How amazing. Liu was feeling even more distressed now.

"They violated the family planning law. Why doesn't anyone do something about it?"

While father and son were engaged in their heated discussion, the haltered woman quietly tugged on Pengju's sleeve. Getting the hint, he changed his tune.

"Oh, by the way, this is my girlfriend, Mai Dangna."

Putting aside the argument with his son, Liu Yuejin sized up the woman and decided he didn't like her, and not just because of how she was dressed. She didn't seem to care how she looked or what others thought of her; clearly she was not the girl next door. He recalled Yang Yuhuan, from the Manli Hair Salon, who had the same attitude toward herself and the world. For a prostitute, it's okay to have that appearance and bearing, but for his son's girlfriend, that troubled him. Taking his son to the other side of the pillar, he was savvy enough not to refer to the woman as a prostitute.

"Mai Dangna. Why does that sound so familiar?"

"None of your business. Her parents called her Mai Jie, Wheat Stalks, and it was too rustic for her taste, so she changed it, to sound like Madonna."

Liu didn't care about the name enough to pursue the topic.

"When did you two get together?" he whispered.

"Two months ago." His son looked impatient.

"She looks so much older than you." Liu was taking the long way round. "She isn't your girlfriend, is she?"

Ignoring the question, Pengju went back to the girl, followed by his father. She didn't seem interested in the conversation between father and son. When she saw them arguing, she smiled and came up to Liu Yuejin.

"Uncle, Pengju is always telling me how well you're doing in Beijing. He had a falling out with his mother, so we've decided to see if we can get something started here."

"Get something started? What is it you want to start?"

"Aren't you always bragging about sixty thousand yuan over the phone?" his son said. "Well, let's have it." He pointed to the woman. "Mai Dangna can do foot massage, so we want to open a foot massage parlor here."

Liu Yuejin felt like crying. In the past they'd fought over the phone when he couldn't come up with the money the boy wanted. His son would demand to know if his father really did have the money, which was why Liu brought up the sixty thousand. His son had no idea where the money had come from nor did he know it was only a promissory note. Worse yet, the note had vanished along with his pack.

18

Zhao Xiaojun

Liu Yuejin became homeless the moment his son showed up with his girlfriend.

Father and son argued all the way from the train station to the construction site. Liu Pengju kept questioning his father about the money and Liu, unable to explain the intricate details, eventually said,

"Okay, I have it, but I can't spend it yet."

"Why not?"

"It's in a CD and I'll lose big if I cash it in now."

He had said the same thing to his son many times over the phone, which was why Pengju was suspicious in the first place. Liu then grumbled about his son's actions, not about transferring his allegiance to his mother and her fake-liquor salesman without telling him, but about not getting any money out of that no-account couple. How could he have let them off so easily? Why leave empty-handed after staying with them for three months? It was an empty betrayal, or worse, like losing the rice bait along with the chicken you meant to steal.

"So you're saying you refused to send me money in order to force me to live with them so I could get money out of them. Is that what I'm hearing?" his son demanded.

"That's not true." Liu was deflated. "I just realized that you've been exploiting the situation between your mother and me," he added. Then his anger found another target. "So the man no longer sells fake liquor? He's making the real thing now, is that it? So he managed to put one over on everyone and become legit, is that what you're saying? And nobody says a word?"

They went on like that until they reached the site. Liu opened the door and they walked in, luggage in hand. Liu Pengju and Mai Dangna were disappointed by the look of the room, with vats and bottles strewn all across the floor. No one who lived like that could possibly have sixty thousand yuan.

"You've been lying to me all these years," his son complained.

Disheartened, Liu did not respond. He'd begun worrying about the living arrangements. Before he could come up with a solution, his son said gruffly:

"We're staying here, what about you?"

The surprises just kept coming. His son had already decided he'd be in charge; this was his place and now he was asking where Liu Yuejin would stay. What upset Liu most was his son's declaration that they would *stay* in his place, not live together like a couple planning to marry. They were linking up, that was all. Liu was about to erupt when the woman said:

"We don't want to put you out, Uncle. We can get a hotel room."

The concession notwithstanding, they were intent upon sleeping together, which meant this probably wasn't the first time. It was too late for him to do anything about that, and it was very late; he was tired of arguing, so he said darkly:

"You can stay here. I can find a dozen places to spend the night."

Liu was barely out the door when his son locked it behind him. He turned to see his son's arms around the woman, as the light reflected their intertwined shadows on the curtain. Then he saw those shadows fall onto his bed before the light was turned off. Rustling sounds emerged from inside, followed by unrestrained moaning and groaning. Liu froze on the spot, not to eavesdrop, but reminded of how eager he'd been nineteen years earlier as a bridegroom. Instead of feeling his age, he was affected by how things could change so quickly.

Walking away from the dining hall, Liu realized he had no place to go. He could easily find a place to sleep—the construction site, for instance—where he could squeeze in among the hundreds of workers; but he didn't want to go there. He had nothing to say to those men. He'd once been able to shoot the breeze with them, but no longer. They would not be good conversation partners when he had so much on his mind. Besides, they were endlessly inquisitive and had the disagreeable habit of always digressing, either jumping from topic to topic or mixing everything up. The dormitory was no place for him.

But so much had happened in a single day that he needed to talk to someone or he'd burst. If not those workers, who else? Ma Manli at the Manli Hair Salon. It was past three in the morning; she'd surely be in bed and would be upset if he knocked on her door at that late hour. Yet his feet refused to follow his rational train of thoughts and took him up one lane and down another. He could not suppress his joy when, even from a distance, he saw that the lights were still on inside.

By the time he reached the shop, he was in for another surprise; he heard people arguing inside. Through the window he saw it was the same old problem—Zhao Xiaojun, Manli's ex-husband, was having it out with her. They were alone, since, obviously, Yang Yuhuan was long gone. At first Liu thought that Zhao was there for the thirty thousand Manli's brother owed him, but not this time. Flushed and unsteady, Zhao was drunk.

"Just this one time." He had his arms around her and was pushing her toward the room in back. "Just this time."

So he'd come for sex. This was worse. Even drunk, Zhao was stronger than she was; or maybe he was stronger than usual because he was drunk. In any case, he had picked her up. She was kicking out like a little chick, and since she couldn't grab hold of him, she held onto the doorframe.

"No fucking way! We're divorced, so this is rape. Do you hear me?"

"Call it rape if you want." Zhao was barely coherent. "I'm not letting you off this time."

They struggled against the flimsy doorframe, and when he tried to pry her hands loose, they crashed to the floor. On his way down, Zhao bumped his head against a stool, which fell apart under his weight. He lay injured on the floor, while she, cushioned by him, was unharmed. She got to her feet and picked up a pair of scissors from the barber's stand.

"I'll bury this in you if you ever try that again."

Still dazed from the fall, Zhao did not understand what just happened, and when his head finally cleared, he noticed the scissors in her hand.

"Okay, we won't do that, but I want my money."

So it was about money, after all. Manli refused. "I don't owe you any money."

"You're his sister, so now that he's run off his debt is your responsibility."

"He stopped being my brother when he started doing business with you."

"If you won't pay me back," Zhao said as he struggled to get up, "let's get remarried."

"Are you out of your mind?"

Finally getting to his feet by holding on to the barber's chair, he picked up a razor. But instead of pointing it at her, he held it against his own neck,

"I'll kill myself if you won't marry me again."

Liu was dumbfounded, not by Zhao's threat but by his desire to marry Manli again. Liu had always thought that his frequent visits to the salon were motivated only by money, never sensing that he had other ideas. Why divorce her in the first place then? Manli would have none of it.

"Don't just hold it there. You have to open the artery." Then she said, "A tough guy? You don't look the part."

Now that she'd seen through him, his embarrassment turned to anger and he ran at her with the razor while she fended him off with the scissors. Knowing that something terrible was about to happen,

Liu had no time to think. He kicked open the door, rushed in, and wrapped his arms around Zhao, though he had no idea what to do next in the ex-couple's fight over money and remarriage. It wasn't his place to say anything, since intervening had always backfired in the past. All he could do was focus on Zhao's drunken state by shaking the man and shouting:

"Hey, wake up. Come on. How much did you have, anyway?"

Zhao indeed had had too much to drink and Liu's action only confused him even further. He slumped in Liu's arms.

"Who are you?"

Liu didn't know what to say. It should have been an easy question to answer, but not on this night.

"A friend." He was evasive, but inside he was cursing. "You owe me a thousand yuan, you dumb fuck."

Zhao stared at him blankly, unsure what he meant by "friend," giving Liu the break he needed to take away the razor.

"Let's go somewhere and talk this out," Liu shouted into Zhao's ear.

"W-wh-where?" slurred Zhao.

"Somewhere where we can get a drink."

Zhao was elated by the suggestion.

"You mean it? I'm not drunk, you know."

"I know. That's why we'll get something together."

With that, he managed to get Zhao out of the salon, but had no idea what to do next. As he was walking out, he turned and saw Manli throw away the scissors and slump down tearfully on the fallen doorframe. Once he deposited Zhao somewhere, he'd go back to console her and ask about this divorce and remarriage idea. She'd been cool to him for quite some time, making it hard to bring up these questions, but now he had an excuse and maybe she wouldn't be so off-putting this time. Liu forgot about his own troubles as he dragged Zhao out to the main road, where he planned to leave him on a bus bench. That would help sober him up and the location would ensure his safety. But even though he was addled by drink,

Zhao remembered Liu's promise. He glared at him when he realized where they were headed.

"Where are we going? You damned liar." He struggled to turn around. "I'm going back. I've got unfinished business."

Liu had no choice but to keep going. After crossing a couple of intersections, they made it to a 24-hour diner run by a Mongolian. It was called Ordos Restaurant, but had no more than five or six tables. The menu promised Mongolian barbecue, stir-fried beef and mutton, and noodles. Zhao was happy to see that Liu had found a drinking establishment, one that was deserted at such a late hour. The cook was asleep, there were no more hot kebobs or other hot dishes, and the glass case on the counter was home to only some cold vegetarian dishes that were by then tired and wilting. A bow-legged Mongolian girl with bright red cheeks and bloodshot eyes, who'd probably spent half her life on a horse, came up with what food was left and some liquor, after which she returned to the counter and fell asleep. Liu hadn't wanted Zhao to drink any more, but the man wouldn't hear of quitting and downed three glasses in a row. Then he wanted to toast Liu, who had no interest in drinking, as he was reminded of his recent troubles, losing one pack and then finding a purse.

"What's this?" Zhao started to get nasty. "I'm not good enough to drink with you?"

He picked up a stool to threaten Liu, who was forced to drink. After the first glass came a second, and then another, followed by yet another. There was no change in Zhao, but Liu got seriously drunk, fatigued by the five-day search and a particularly tiring night running all over Beijing. He'd always thought that getting drunk was a bad thing, but on this night it helped him forget his problems and actually cheered him. So they had two more toasts, and Liu forgot all about why they were there, as well as his relationship to the man he was with. Having only met a few times, they didn't know each other well, and Zhao owed Liu money. But now they were becoming fast friends. As they talked, Liu strained to remember the question he'd wanted to ask Zhao. Then it came to him—he wanted to ask why

Zhao and Ma had divorced and why he wanted to remarry her. He should never have opened his mouth, because when he did, Zhao broke down and wept.

"I fell into my own trap." He reached out for Liu's hand. "I got divorced because of another woman, a woman with big breasts, unlike my wife, who looks like a man at first glance. Back then I had all the money I needed, so divorce and marriage meant nothing to me. But now, I'm broke and last month the slut ran away. I looked all over for her, but not a trace. So I've lost two women. A huge loss. I have no one. Why? Why me?"

He was not done. "Ma Manli is no good. She and that slut were friends, so maybe they plotted against me." He continued angrily, "She shacked up with someone three years ago and thought she could pull a fast one. Some men favor men in drag."

Liu was confused by the jumbled story, except that Ma Manli seemed much more complex than the salon owner he thought he knew. He was reminded of something else when Zhao mentioned his second wife running away. His own wife had also run away.

"My wife ran away too. You and me, we're in the same boat." He paused, realizing that his wife hadn't run away, that she'd been taken from him. He shook his head. "Not really the same."

Then anger took hold of him, not at Zhao but at the world in general. "Didn't someone steal my wife from me? The thought makes my heart ache; it still hurts after all these years."

"It's pointless to go on living." Zhao shook his head. "I want to die."

The comment was too much for Liu, who shared the sentiment.

"I know what you mean. I was this close to hanging myself six years ago."

The more they talked, the closer they felt to each other. Zhao got up and walked unsteadily around the table to sit next to Liu.

"We're friends." He put his hand out. "How about lending me some money. I make money with every business I start, so you won't regret it."

"I believe you." Liu thumped his chest. "I'll give you a loan." Then he began to cry. "I do want to lend you money, but didn't I tell you it's all gone?"

It had been days since he was able to pour his heart out, so with the help of alcohol, he released his pent-up emotions by telling everything to Zhao Xiaojun, hardly more than a stranger, from the loss of the pack to obtaining the purse, and from there to the arrival of his no-good son with his girlfriend. He told him things he hadn't revealed to his closest friends. But he began to slur his words and became incoherent. At one point he lost the thread of his narration, making him anxious as he tried to get back to where he had been. Finally when he got to what happened that day, it was lights out and he realized that Zhao had fallen asleep on the table. Liu nudged him to wake him up, only to see him slump to the floor like oozing mud.

19

Lao Xing

Lao Xing worked for Worried Wise Men Inquiry Agency as an investigator, what's known as a private eye in the West. It was a profession that had cropped up only recently in China. Originally from Hebei, he was a forty-five-year-old man who looked fifty-four, with a wrinkled face and gray hair that nearly fused with his brows. He'd look like a peasant from the plains of Hebei if he put on a farmer's outfit, and a steel mill worker if he was in overalls. Even when he wore a coat and tie, all he could manage was to look like a migrant worker visiting relatives in Beijing, not an effective and very clever private eye. Which was why Yan Ge was so disappointed at their first meeting. Then he noticed that Lao Xing was given to laughing, not a problem, by any means, except that Xing took pleasure in sniggering. You'd be having a serious conversation and he'd find a hole in your narrative that would make him snigger with his hand over his mouth—infuriating. Yan Ge was talking very fast, given his anxiety over the lost drive.

"Slow down. There's no need to rush."

How could Yan not rush? People's futures were tied to a drive he had used to blackmail others, and which could now be used against him. There were more than a dozen video clips, some showing Director Jia and Lao Lin with prostitutes, which wasn't Yan's concern. Before the scenes with the prostitutes, on the other hand, were recordings of him bribing both men. Taking bribes was a crime, so was handing them out, and in his case, the amount could easily send him to the execution ground. Jia and Lin deserved to be punished for taking money, but Yan, who had given them the money, was also in hot water, and he felt that was unfair. The threat, originally targeted at the two men only, now had the same lethal power against him. A bigger problem for Yan was that it would be easier to find the drive if it had fallen into the hands of certain people than when it involved a thief, whose whereabouts was hard to pinpoint. He had to find the thief.

If whoever stole the purse was computer savvy and saw the contents, Yan would be in more trouble than he could imagine. But if the thief didn't know anything about computers and threw the thing away, he'd be in even more trouble if it landed in the hands of a particular group of people. It had been used purely for a business deal with Jia and Lin to exchange for an eighty-million-yuan loan, which could bring temporary relief to Yan's financial troubles. Now that the drive was missing, he'd lost his leverage, bringing the deal to a halt. His survival, originally in Jia's hands, had now transferred into the hands of the thief. The night before, when Lin heard about the theft of the drive at the villa, he'd laughed over the absurdity.

"All right," he said. "We're no longer enemies and have to join forces."

But then he grew suspicious, unsure if it was yet another scheme. He hurried off after gathering up the six USB drives and the laptop. At five the next morning he phoned Yan to tell him that he'd related the incident to Director Jia, who was giving Yan ten days to find the drive. If it was recovered during that time frame, their deal would go through as planned; if not, there'd be no more need to keep looking and they could just wait for the hammer to fall. Jia's words made Yan break out in a cold sweat, not because he'd set a deadline, which was a sign of apprehension, but because it was ten days. No more, no less. Why would the hammer fall after ten days? Yan could not figure out the importance of the date or what was going on in the mind of the old fox. He was sure only that Jia had his reasons, for their situations were not the same.

Then there was Qu Li, who had also changed after the theft; their arrangement had to be put on hold. Theoretically, since she was neither Jia nor Lin, what was on the drive didn't concern her at all. On the other hand, she was clearly involved, because she was the one who'd instructed the assistant general manager to make the recording. She'd been the one who'd started it all and also the one who'd lost the thing, so she should have been feeling contrite. But no, she wasn't anxious at all. To her this cache of stolen secrets should be made public. After Lin left that night, she sniggered.

"Looks like we're all going down together." She added, "That's all right with me. The sooner it's over, the better."

She went to bed. How someone who could fight with hair stylists could remain calm over something this big amazed Yan. After all those years of marriage she remained an enigma. He had to forget the twenty-five million for now. Besides, if the drive wasn't found, Jia, the big ship, would sink, and her small straw of a loan could not save him, which was why he'd let it drop for the moment. He had to look at the big picture. Once the drive was found, he could resume discussions with Jia and Lin, and with her as well.

He could not get the police involved, which was why he'd decided to use a private investigator; and not just any PI. He recalled meeting the owner of an investigative agency at a banquet hosted by a friend two years before. When asked what case he was working on, the oily-faced man from Tianjin had regaled the dinner guests with a series of outlandish anecdotes, most of which involved affairs and made everyone laugh. When the banquet was over, the man told Yan:

"I made up everything I said back there. I may be engaged in a sordid profession, but it has its set of ethics."

Yan quickly forgot about the man after an exchange of business cards, since he had no need for a PI. But now he drove to the stud farm, where he dumped the contents of a drawer to the floor and found the man's card. He was mildly amused to note the name of his agency: "Worried Wise Men," a take on the saying that a wise man can think of everything and still make a mistake. So true. Yan had to agree.

He dialed the number and the call went through. The man remembered meeting him at the banquet two years earlier. Yan told him he needed a PI on a personal matter, nothing serious but urgent, and he'd like someone who knew a trick or two. Yan was pleased to find the man reassuring, for he did not press him for details. He simply said that a man who knew a trick or two would be there in an hour. When an hour passed, Yan called back and learned that the man who knew more tricks than anyone else at the agency was working on a case in Baoding. He would be pulled off that case and brought back to Beijing without delay. Yan waited.

Around noontime, the doorbell rang, and Yan opened the door to see a man he first mistook as a gardener who had knocked on the wrong door. But when he handed Yan his business card, Yan saw that he was from the agency. He did not look like someone who knew a single a trick. He was bathed in sweat, having rushed back from Baoding, and his suit made him look like a migrant worker. Yan was unhappy with the man for sending someone like this. But after they sat down and chatted for ten minutes, his view changed.

Yan began by beating around the bush, instead of talking about the USB drive. The man, Lao Xing, talked slowly and loved to snigger, but he grasped Yan's main point right off; in fact, he only sniggered when Yan was borderline incoherent. After Yan finished, Lao Xing summarized the key issues in a few words. He may have looked simple but he was shrewd; his working-class appearance could have been the very reason he was perfect for the job of a PI. Never judge a man by his looks. When he was done with the chitchat Yan probed the man's experience.

"What sort of cases have you worked on?"

"What else?" he said as he gazed at the horses outside. "Mostly extramarital affairs."

"How many did you catch last year?"

"I don't have the exact number," Xing said, "but it has to be over thirty." He was not shy about his successes.

"Our society is a mess," Yan said with a sigh. "You probably stir up more trouble than the adulterers."

"You're right, Mr. Yan." Xing nodded his agreement. "I really shouldn't be ruining people's families over money."

"Your work must be interesting, searching for people all day long." Yan studied Xing's face.

"Why would that be interesting?" Xing retorted mildly. "It depends on who you're searching for. It's not like looking up old friends for a get-together. How much fun can it be to search high and low for a total stranger?"

Yan had to agree with Xing. He asked about Xing's past. Xing was obliging. An archeology major in college, he was assigned a job at the National Science Academy Archeology Institute, but it was lonely work, dealing with the dead. As someone from the countryside, poverty held no appeal, especially since his parents could have used some financial help. So, he quit and started a business. For the next ten years he made some money and lost some, mostly lost. Obviously he wasn't cut out for business, but it was too late when he came to that realization, for he owed so much money the business folded. He tried several lines of work before settling on this one.

"As Chairman Mao said, those who aren't content with their lot will suffer. It would have been wonderful to keep digging up old bones for exhibitions and telling visitors that thousand-year-old skeletons are really more than ten thousand. But instead of that, I'm digging up info about the living. I've returned to the present antiquity."

Touched by the statement, Yan was about to say so when Xing checked his watch.

"So, what exactly do you want me to look into?"

Xing was back on the matter at hand before Yan could recover from his sentimental reaction. Yan felt as if he were struggling in the water while Xing had already made it back to shore. He knew that Xing was more rational than he, and he was having trouble regaining his composure.

"I'm not looking for a third party in an affair. I want to find a thief."

Xing gave his reply some thought.

"It must be a special thief if you come to me, not to the police."

"It's a small-time burglar, but what he took was no small matter. It was my wife's purse."

Xing waited patiently for Yan to provide more information.

"There wasn't much money in the purse, and the other stuff isn't all that important, except for a USB drive with all the documents from my company, mostly critical business secrets. I didn't want to call the police for fear of alerting my competitors."

Xing nodded and asked, "Did you have a look at the thief?"

"No, but she did. She said he has a dark mole on the left side of his face, in the shape of an apricot flower. Oh, and he left behind an order form from a delivery service. The box had the name of his restaurant." Yan paused—PI like—and thought before continuing. "Of course, he wouldn't be working at the restaurant now."

Xing nodded his agreement as he opened his briefcase to retrieve a stack of documents.

"I'll take your case. Now we need to talk about fees."

Yan laid his hand on the document.

"This is quite urgent and I'd like to have it back within five days. Longer than that, it would be hard to find, especially if the thief threw it away and someone else found it. So I'll make you a deal. I'll pay you two hundred thousand if you find it in two days, a hundred and fifty thousand if it takes three, and a hundred thousand for five."

Yan had thought that Xing would be surprised by the offer, or at least he'd cover his mouth and snigger, but Xing responded deadpan:

"Don't think of that as an exceptional offer, Mr. Yan. That's pretty much my fee scale anyway."

Yan was visibly shaken.

20

Liu Yuejin

Liu Yuejin slept on the curb till noon, when the stifling heat roused him.

A tall building provided some cool shade in the early morning, but the area turned into a kitchen steamer by noon as the position of the sun shifted. He woke up to find himself drenched, as if he'd just been fished out of water. Then he spotted white sweat stains on his T-shirt and pants. Completely in the dark as to where he was, he finally recalled what had happened the night before. He had gotten drunk, that was all. His head spun when he tried to sit up, so he lay back down.

A sudden thirst reminded him that he hadn't drunk alone, so he reached out to find Zhao Xiaojun. Zhao's spot was empty, replaced by a pile of stomach contents that had dried in the sun into the shape of a snake, an abbreviated snake, since part of it seemed to have been gnawed away by a dog. It was hard to say whose stomach it had come from, his or Zhao's.

Then he remembered that they had fallen into a drunken stupor at Ordos Restaurant, one on the floor, the other at the table, so how had he ended up at the curb? The people at the restaurant, he concluded. They must have tossed him and Zhao onto the curb during their morning cleanup. Those Mongolians are a bunch of rats, he said to himself, when he was hit by another question: How come he was the only one left? Obviously, Zhao woke up first and just up and left without a thought for Liu. That Zhao Xiaojun is a rat too. They'd gotten drunk together, but he'd split after sobering up. The injustice hit Liu when he realized that he'd gotten drunk on account of Zhao, not for himself.

Finally everything came back to him: yesterday his son and his girlfriend had come to Beijing to see him. He'd gotten seriously drunk and slept on the curb till noon, while they remained at his place. After he'd been away the whole morning, his no-good son would probably claim he'd done it on purpose. What he'd gone through over the past few days came to mind; he'd lost a pack and found a purse in return. The purse had nothing, while his pack contained sixty thousand yuan, and he began to rue how he'd been delayed in his search by other people's affairs before his own problem was solved.

As his thoughts returned to the "compensation" he'd had to pay the chicken neck vendor for touching his wife, Liu blamed it all on alcohol. With his mind clear, he went into a minor panic and, despite the dizziness, jumped to his feet. He bought a bottle of water at a roadside shop and staggered back to the construction side, sipping water along the way.

He was in for a shock when he got back to the dining hall and opened the door: his room was deserted and a shambles. The blanket was tossed into a bundle, the desk drawer had been pulled out, and a trunk was open, a sign that the clothes inside had been rummaged over. Every lid on the vat and bottles on the floor was off and lying on the floor. Confused and still under the influence of alcohol, he turned round and round, keeping from falling by bracing with his hands before spotting a piece of paper on the table. Originally used to wrap roast chicken, it now served as a note with a few crooked lines:

"We're going back. You don't have money, you lied to me. I took some travel money—the thousand or so yuan you hid behind the poster calendar—and the purse. You have no use for it and Dangna needed one. After I get home, I'll work hard, make some serious money, and when I have enough, I'll support you in your old age.

Your son, Liu Pengju."

Liu immediately sobered up. His first reaction was to climb onto the bed and remove the movie star calendar from the wall; now there was only a hole where he'd stashed the last bit of money he had. A grand total of a 1,652 yuan, wrapped in a plastic bag to keep it dry, now gone, including the bag. He'd worked hard selling swill to save that amount, which he'd put separately to keep his sources of income straight; it was his emergency fund that he would touch only in the direst situation.

At two in the morning every Wednesday and Sunday he rode his bicycle with a bucket on each side of the rack to deliver leftover rice, buns, and swill he'd saved up over three days to the Shunyi Pig Farm, about eighty li away. The dining hall food wasn't rich enough to fetch a good price, so he had to save one yuan here and eighty cents there, and now it was all gone. He hadn't touched the money even when he'd run a three-day fever of a hundred and three the month before. He jumped off the bed to check the vat for fermented tofu, where he'd stowed the purse taken from Yang Zhi. It too was gone.

"You bastard." He stomped his foot and cursed. "Your father's broke and now you've added insult to injury."

He sat down on the bed with his head in his hands, when he detected a strange smell. A quick sniff told him it was from the woman's cosmetics, as well as the smell from what they'd done the night broke, on his bedding. He pulled his own sweaty hair; it stank.

"I've been looking for a thief. Who's the thief?" he muttered to himself. "My bastard son, that's who."

21

Yang Zhi

After five fruitless days of searching, Yang Zhi found Zhang Duanduan by accident.

He finally realized he should have known the difference between robbers and thieves; the latter had defined territory that must not be encroached upon, while the former moved from job to job, migration being an important characteristic of the profession and the reason behind thieves' distain for them. He had been robbed in a small room in the eastern suburb, which he mistook as their base, thinking they would work the area, like dates not falling far from the tree. That was why he had concentrated his search in the Chaoyang District, including the snack stalls by the Tonghui River, all to no avail.

In the meantime, he'd gotten tangled up with Brother Cao's people, who had sent him to burgle the Beethoven Villa, a job that had ended up with him escaping the complex with a purse that had subsequently fallen into the hands of a man he had stolen from before. Breaking into a luxury house was no small matter, so he decided to hide out in the western suburbs, staying out of sight from the police and Cao's lackeys. Thieves from Yang's hometown had a base in this slum area that offered some potential for small-time crooks.

After fleeing the villa, he came straight to the base, ignoring the greetings from several petty thieves, and went into the back room. When he calmed down, he began to sense disappointment over what had transpired that day—leaving behind a sack of loot and then losing the purse in his flight.

As his thoughts returned to the villa, he was reminded of the trouble between his legs, a more serious matter than losing the loot. Lying in bed, he fondled himself, but not much happened—just a half-hearted stiffening.

Disregarding the scare and fatigue of the night, he went in search of a prostitute, who managed to arouse him along the way; but nothing stirred once they were in bed. Holding her in his arms, he strained to recall the woman at the villa, but what he managed to conjure up was Zhang Duanduan's face and the fright he'd experienced in that small room. It dawned on him that he'd gotten away with a whole bottle of potency pills; he took a few, but half an hour later still no effect. For him it was all over.

After one whole gloomy day, he refused to accept reality and went out again with his satchel to find a prostitute. Looking at the brightly lit world on the main street, thoughts of his impotence and his attempts to solve the problem dejected him; the whole world faded in front of him. He knew precisely where to find what he was looking for, in the hair salons or under nearby trees, but he wasn't sure he should even try, unlike the day before, when he'd first been concerned about his problem.

With a sigh, he squatted down at the curb to smoke, when he heard some people arguing in the wooded area behind him. He didn't pay much attention at first, but he heard a familiar accent and took a closer look. His eyes lit up at the sight of Zhang Duanduan with the three Gansu men, who were quarrelling among themselves while she tried to be the peacemaker. As the saying goes, you wear out a pair of steel-soled shoes in a futile search, but then what you're looking for falls into your hands.

Jumping to his feet, Yang was about to rush them when he realized he'd left his knife behind, whereas these robbers would surely be armed. He wanted to go back to get his knife, but was afraid of losing sight of the robbers, who started to walk out of the wooded area heading east. Yang Zhi, though weaponless, followed, checking to see if there was a shop along the way where he could buy a cleaver, a razor, even a paring knife. Anything would be better than nothing. But all he could see were shops selling soft drinks, alcohol, cigarettes, and condiments. No hardware store in sight. Then he spotted one, but it was closed. They came upon a supermarket, well lit and packed with shoppers. Supermarkets sold household items and might carry cleavers; yet the gang would likely be out of sight by the time he found the shelf, got a knife, and paid. He had to pass it up and settle for a broken brick he managed to pry off a flowerbed. Stuffing it into his satchel, he continued to follow the four, who were bickering the whole time. They argued when they walked and argued when they stopped, which was why they never noticed Yang behind them.

By then he had changed tactics. Instead of direct confrontation, he'd follow them to see where they went and find their new nest. Then he'd either go back for his weapon or get some Shanxi thieves to help him. His plan to kill Zhang Duanduan had expanded into taking every member of the gang, now that even potency pills were no use in helping him to get the thing up. He wouldn't spare a single one of the Gansu men.

When they reached Bajiao Street, they ducked into the subway station; Yang picked up his pace and followed along. They boarded a subway train through the front door of a car, and Yang did the same, through the back door. The car was packed but he managed to squeeze his way up front, closer to the gang, but keeping a three-meter safe distance. As the train rumbled along, the Gansu men stopped arguing. Liu wondered where they'd get off and where they were headed after that, hoping they'd return to their hideout. His thoughts were all over the place when he heard an argument break out again. After hearing them argue all that time, he didn't pay much attention.

The train stopped at Muxidi station. Yang watched them carefully; they showed no sign that this was their stop, so he relaxed. Passengers were piling into the car when one of the men pointed at something on the platform and yelled out, drawing the attention of his companions, and, before the door closed, the four of them fought through the crowd and got off. Caught off guard, Yang sprang into action but was grabbed from behind by someone when he reached the door. Surprised, he struggled and demanded angrily:

"What are you doing? You got a death wish or something?"

The man's hand was clamped onto his arm like a vice. It was a stumpy fellow with a square face and short but powerful arms that, with each slight movement, made Yang's arm crack. Knowing he'd met his match, Yang changed his tone:

"I'm in a hurry, my brother."

The man smiled before whispering into Yang's ear:

"Don't make a move or you'll suffer even more."

Yang took a good look at the man, but couldn't figure him out and decided to obey his order, since he could be a policeman nabbing him for a prior offense.

The stumpy man was not a policeman. He was Lao Xing, from the Worried Wise Men Agency, who had managed to locate Yang with the help of the delivery bicycle left at Beethoven Villa. Yan Ge had said it was useless with the deliveryman gone, but he was wrong. Yang got away, but the real deliveryman still worked at the restaurant, oblivious to what had happened that night with Yang. By looking into the bike, Xing quickly found the place, and the man who looked like a college student. "Liu Yong" feigned ignorance at first by saying that his bike had been stolen. Xing's threat to send him to the police scared him enough to reveal that he'd lent his bike to some people and had no idea what they did with it. Xing told him to take him to see these people. When asked how many there were, "Liu Yong" gave only Yang Zhi's name, on condition that Xing would let him go if he helped him find Yang. It was a calculated move by "Liu Yong," who knew he wouldn't be in trouble as long as he didn't rat on Brother Cao and his people. Besides, Yang wasn't one of them.

Xing agreed to his condition, and they headed to Shijingshan. Baldy Cui had been there a few times to get Yang to pay off his debt, but each time Yang was out working and they never got hold of him.

Xing was in luck on this day, however, since Yang had returned for safety and stayed close to home, only going out for sex. "Liu Yong" spotted him while he was trying to make up his mind about getting a prostitute. He was so intent on watching the Gansu gang he was unaware that he was being followed by Xing, who in turn let the gang get away from Yang.

Xing was civil when he took Yang out of the subway station and found a diner, where he revealed his true identity. Knowing that Xing was a PI, not a policeman, Yang felt better, except for the fact that the gang had gotten away. They ate and drank, including some hard liquor. Yang saw that Xing had powerful arms but was a gentle man who smiled a lot when he talked, though he avoided coming to the point. First he told Yang that he was originally from Hebei and asked Yang where he was from. Then he talked about how hard it was for him to make a living under such conditions. All rubbish. Yang had too much on his mind to beat around the bush and began to lose patience as he looked around the diner.

"Why were you following those people on the subway?" Xing asked out of the blue.

So he knew that Yang had been after the gang. With his tongue loosened by alcohol and no one to talk to about the problems he'd been having, Yang began telling the stranger what he'd gone through, starting with his first encounter with the gang, but skipping the parts about stealing Liu's pack and the botched job at Beethoven Villa. Focusing solely on his stolen pack, he also omitted his impotence and the reason behind it.

"Losing a pack is no big deal," Xing consoled him. "Those people weren't that bad. For a few hundred yuan, the really vicious ones will shut you up permanently."

"That's bullshit!" Yang flew into a sudden rage.

Then he forgot to hide his secret and told Xing about how he'd become impotent from the scare. Xing paused and began to snigger, but quickly turned that off when he saw Yang's face.

"That does sound serious."

"It's all your fault. I'd have killed them all if not for your meddling."

"Killing them now won't do you any good," Xing tried to soothe him. "You need to see a shrink."

That only fanned the flames of anger in Yang, who ran out of patience.

"No more nonsense, all right? Tell me why you were looking for me."

"Take it easy, my friend." Xing gestured to calm him down. "There's no need to get so riled up. I want to make you a business deal."

"What kind of deal?" Yang asked blankly.

"Did you steal something from Beethoven Villa last night?"

His question sent a shock through Yang, who realized that this was why Xing wanted to talk to him. He'd thought he was safe once he'd made it out of the place; who'd have guessed that he'd be found out so quickly. Then suspicion of Xing's true identity crept into his mind and he tensed up; no longer angry, he was tongue-tied as he made one last desperate attempt to feign ignorance.

"What villa? I didn't go out last night."

Xing laughed, immediately deflating Yang's bluster. Knowing he could not pull this off, he came clean:

"Yeah, I did. But I was nearly caught, so I didn't steal anything."

"What about a woman's purse?" He framed the shape in the air.

Another surprise for Yang. Obviously, Xing knew everything.

"I don't care about the purse." Xing gestured again. "But there was something in the purse, about this big, a USB drive." He took out his wallet and continued. "Give me that drive and I'll give you ten thousand yuan, here and now. Not a bad deal, wouldn't you say?"

Yang looked lost as he sighed. "Not a bad deal at all. I only wish I had it."

Now it was Xing's turn to be surprised. "Where is it then?"

"Someone spotted me, so I ran off and tossed the purse along the way. It's probably in some other asshole's hands."

"Who could that be?" Xing stared wide-eyed.

"What's on the drive?" Yang asked. "Is it important?"

"What's on it is of great importance to someone, but insignificant to you and me."

"Who are these people?"

"Who's asking the questions here?" Xing was getting irritated. "Who took the purse?"

Yang could not help playing dumb again. "It was so dark in the alley I couldn't see his face."

Xing knew that Yang was playing games with him, so he simply sighed.

"Obviously, I was wrong to think of you as a friend, because you're not treating me as one." He continued, "Think hard and tell me what he looked like. Once you remember, you'll help me find him and I'll still give you ten thousand yuan. If you can't, we'll be here till you do."

"Okay if I use the toilet?" Yang asked, with sweat showing on his head.

Xing glanced at him and then at Yang's satchel on the table, which was made of synthetic fabric but looked heavy and bulky. Yang might be planning on making a call in the toilet, Xing thought; that was all right with him, since he likely just wanted to check with someone to see if it was a good deal. So he nodded. Yang got up and headed toward the toilet but ran out as he passed the door, leaving his satchel behind. He vanished into the crowd.

Xing cursed himself for his carelessness, like letting a cooked duck fly out of his hand. Knowing it was no use chasing after him, he picked up Yang's bag, hoping to find useful clues inside. He opened it and was greeted by a broken brick, whose purpose escaped him. He threw the brick away and continued to search; in addition to six hundred or so yuan, there were his tools of the trade—picks, pliers, a length of wire. Then, from the inside pocket, he retrieved two colored boxes that contained imported male enhancement drugs. So, Yang had been telling the truth about his impotence; Xing shook his head and sighed, both for Yang's sake and for his.

22

Lao Xing

The loss of Yang as a link to the missing purse made Lao Xing's search for the other thief, Liu Yuejin, much more difficult. Since the cooked duck had flown away, he had to return to where it all started, so he went back to the restaurant the following morning, only to find "Liu Yong" gone. There went another clue. His next stop was the Beethoven Villa, where he began anew his investigation around Yan's house. He blamed neither others nor himself for the full circle he'd made, for he followed a motto he often used on others—no matter what happens, don't lose your calm.

He failed to unearth anything useful around Beethoven Villa; the security guards knew no more, perhaps even less than what was recorded on the surveillance cameras. On the tape, Xing saw Yang Zhi fleeing with a purse; he watched it a second time and Yang was still fleeing, and the same for the third time—utterly useless in finding him again. Besides, locating Yang was no longer essential, since he'd thrown away the purse and someone else had picked it up. The critical step now was to find that other person, but the tape did not show who that was; nor did the guards have anything to share. Lao Xing was troubled by the lack of progress.

Leaving the villa, he went to check out the area near the alley and talked to the residents, which included a bicycle repairman, a vendor of roasted sweet potatoes, a popcorn vendor, a cobbler, and sellers of flatbreads and boiled corn. Not a single one of them had heard anything that night; that made sense and was to be expected, since everyone, the vendors and the residents, should have all been in bed. By mid-afternoon, he had yet to make any headway in his investigation. He sighed and cursed himself again for being so careless at the diner. He'd had Yang right where he wanted him but then had let him slip away. A growing sense of self-reproach made him anxious, no matter how hard he tried to stay composed.

His next stop would be the Shijingshan area, where he might be able to nab Yang again and find the other thief, though it would most likely be an unproductive trip. He'd run out of ideas. Where to go next? He couldn't make up his mind. His indecision caught the attention of a bald old man with a hunched back.

"I've been watching you," the old man shouted, probably hard of hearing. "You looking for someone?"

Xing nodded.

"Not the upright sort, is he?"

It was a vague question and Xing wasn't sure how he should answer. He nodded again.

"I know who you're looking for."

Xing was elated by the glimmer of hope.

"Tell me who that is, Grandpa, and I'll buy you a carton of cigarettes."

The old man pursed his lips and sniggered the way Xing so often did.

"You think I'm a doddering old man, don't you, young man? I figure it has to be something big to have you so worried. If you could take care of this with a carton of cigarettes, you'd be off having a leisurely smoke somewhere. Let's make a deal."

Xing paused; the "nosy old man" had gotten his attention.

"What do you have mind, Grandpa?"

The man held out three fingers.

"Three hundred?" Xing asked.

"Do you want to know or not?" The hunchback was visibly upset.

So he meant three thousand. Xing realized that the old man could not be bought off easily, but that only meant he had valuable information to sell. After a bit of bargaining, they settled on fifteen hundred, after which the man took Xing into the alley. They turned a corner and arrived at the man's house in a large compound with a jumble of buildings, where seven or eight families lived. When they reached the innermost yard, the old man pointed to an old bike by a pile of briquettes.

"Left behind by the thief," the man said. "I have trouble sleeping at night, so I usually go out for a walk. A couple of days ago, I went out and saw someone hiding in the alley. I knew right off he was up to no good. I stayed up after I got home, and half an hour later, I heard people running down the lane. I came out and saw two of them, both thieves, no doubt. I couldn't catch up with them, but I got this bike."

"A bike is not a thief, Grandpa." Xing was disappointed.

The old man smugly retrieved an old newspaper from under the seat and spread it out. In the margin was scribbled, "Lao Li at Shunyi Pig Farm," with a cell phone number.

"I know who the thief is." He pointed at the name and announced, "It's Lao Li from the pig farm."

Taking the paper from the man, Xing looked closely at the name and the number and decided that Lao Li was not the thief. Who writes his own name and phone number on a sheet of newspaper? He put it back under the seat, figuring there must be some connection between the thief and the information on the paper. Finally he'd regained the trail of clues. More importantly, since Yang Zhi had left his delivery bike in the grass outside the villa, this one had to have been left behind by the other thief, the one who'd picked up the purse.

Overjoyed by the new discovery, Xing took out fifteen hundred and gave it to the man before walking off with the bike. He placed a call to the number on the paper once he was out of the compound, and to his surprise, Lao Li answered the phone. Xing said he wanted to buy a pig and had gotten Li's number from a friend. Li, sounding hoarse, gave him directions without asking any questions; the pig farm was at Kuliushu in the Shunyi District, not far, but not especially close. Loading the bike into his secondhand Honda, Xing drove to the pig farm with the trunk open. Li turned out to be skinny as a beanpole. When he asked who'd recommended his place, Xing removed the bike from his trunk and asked Li if he recognized it.

"Isn't that Liu Yuejin's bike?" Li blurted out.

When Xing asked Liu's address, a suddenly guarded Li realized that Xing and Liu did not know each other, and that Xing was not there to buy a pig.

"What do you want him for? And how did his bike end up in your hands?"

"I went to a friend's house last night," Xing said with a smile. "On my way home, I found this bike under Xiaoyun Bridge and on the back seat was a pack filled with stuff that could be important to him. I searched and found a sheet of newspaper under the seat, and written on the paper were your name and cell phone number. So I came to see you." He showed Li the paper and went to his car to bring out the bag Yang had left behind when he ran out of the diner. He showed it to Li, who remained suspicious.

"It's hard to do a good deed these days. People don't even believe you when you want to help. Why don't I just leave the bike and the bag with you, and you can give them back."

That convinced Li, who waved and said:

"You got yourself into this, so you take care it. Liu Yuejin is a cook at a construction site behind the China World Trade Center. The Henan construction team."

Xing drove back downtown, and as he crossed the Guomao Bridge, he saw a large construction site in the distance. One of the buildings, already over seventy stories high, had a safety warning hanging on the side. To Xing's surprise, it was Yan Ge's company. So Yan's wife's purse had turned up at his own construction site. Xing had a laugh over that.

Without notifying Yan, Xing drove straight to the site, but was blocked by Lao Deng, who guarded the materials at night and the gate during the day. Deng would have let him through if Xing had been there to see someone else, but not Liu Yuejin. Deng and Liu did not get along, though they never argued or had money problems. Deng simply didn't like Liu. Worse yet, Deng, an insomniac, was having a terrible day from lack of sleep the night before, when he'd gotten Liu to go to the phone. Xing became the target of his displeasure.

"What do you want with him?" He glared at Xing. "You have to talk to the boss if you want to see anyone at the site."

Instead of showing him where to find Liu, Deng took him to see Ren Baoliang, who was squatting by the date tree in his yard, fuming. He'd just had a row with some troublemakers among the workers over money owed them. He'd have liked to pay them, but had no money, since Yan Ge had yet to pay him. Ren was already unhappy with Liu, had been since the days he was responsible for buying provisions, but mainly after a fall-out two years before, when Liu had spread rumors behind his back. Now he'd asked for a couple of days off, time he spent sneaking around, and Ren could only conclude that he had joined the ranks of the misfits, though he was too preoccupied to worry about Liu. When he saw a stranger coming to see Liu, Ren automatically assumed that Xing was no good either.

"What do you want with him?" Ren asked, without looking up.

Forced by circumstances, Xing claimed Yan as a friend and said he needed to ask Liu about something. Ren's attitude changed at the mention of Yan Ge, but he wondered how a cook could have anything to do with a friend of Yan's. He was more cordial now, though he felt a need to complain about Yan.

"It's been more than six months since anyone was paid. Mr. Yan really shouldn't keep putting it off. If he does, we could have a repeat of the Anyuan workers' riot of 1922. I think I'll go raise hell at his house, like the workers have been doing to me."

"I'll be sure to bring that up with Mr. Yan," Xing said with a smile.

Pleased to hear that, Ren took Xing to see if Liu was in his room. They were greeted by a locked door.

At that moment, Liu was out looking for the thief. Two days had yielded no results. Though he'd devoted much of the previous day to finding his son and his girlfriend, he could justifiably claim he'd spent two days hunting for thieves, since he considered his son one of them. At noon the day before, he'd raced back to Beijing's West Station after realizing his son had taken all his valuables. If he doesn't think twice about stealing from his old man, he fumed, what won't he do out in society? Liu also suspected that the woman was behind it, and he vowed not to let her off easily. At that moment, it was clearly more important to vent his anger against both of them than to get his things back.

The train station was alive with people; the square and the waiting room were so packed he had trouble elbowing his way through the throngs of people. After circling the place eight times and gazing at thousands of faces, he failed to find his son or the girlfriend. Every once in a while, someone would look familiar from a distance, but only then. A few men looked like they could be his son from the rear, but he was disappointed again and again when he checked the faces. They could have gotten on a train back to Henan, or they might not have come to the station at all. His son's theft had shocked him out of his drunken stupor, and now he was suffering from a head-splitting hangover. But headache or not, he had to find them, so he kept at it till midnight, when all the trains had left the station and the area reverted back to a quiet, deserted place strewn with people who would spend the night sleeping in the square. With a cheerless sigh, he sat down on the steps in front of the entrance.

He was back searching for Yang Zhi the next morning, after weighing the relative importance of finding his son and locating the thief. Put differently, recovering the pack he had lost was more urgent than retrieving the purse he had found; or, the money in the pack mattered more than the few hundred his son had taken. Putting his son out of his mind, he went to the post office, the garment market, the bus stop, the subway entrance, and the lane in the eastern suburb. After a whole day, nothing. At night, he returned to the snack stalls along the Tonghui River, where he'd found Yang before. Hoping the man would appear again, he went to the same place. Lamps were, as usual, brightly lit along the river, in which high-rises were reflected—the picture of a flourishing city. After several rounds, he found nothing. Obviously the thief was frightened enough to stay away, and Liu realized that his search was futile. He returned to the work site.

He opened the door of his room, turned on the light and shut the door behind him. It was immediately kicked open with a bang, and in barged two people, Ren Baoliang and Lao Xing, who had been awaiting Liu's return. Seeing that Xing was Yan Ge's friend, Ren had invited to him to dinner, during which time he'd again asked why Xing wanted to find Liu. This time Xing revealed that he was searching for the purse for Yan. He was vague on details, but it was enough to convince Ren.

The presence of a stranger in his room unnerved Liu, but Ren went after him before he could say a word.

"We've known each other for years, Yuejin, but have you ever told me the truth?"

"What's this all about?" Liu was bewildered by the presence of the men.

"You told me someone beat you up, so I gave you a few days off to see a doctor. But did you go see a doctor? Or did you go out thieving? You've been misappropriating dining hall funds all along, and now you've moved into new areas."

Still confused, Liu looked at Ren and then at Xing.

"I'm from an investigative agency," Xing spoke up. "I'm helping a friend look for something. Did you find a purse a couple of nights ago?"

Liu's guard went up at the mention of a purse. It was finally coming to a head; his pack was still nowhere to be found and yet the owner of the purse had found him. It was no longer with him either, however—his son and his girlfriend had taken it—so his first reaction was to feign confusion.

"What purse? You've got the wrong man." He glanced at Ren and then said to Xing, "I lost a pack. I didn't find a purse." Then he turned to Ren. "Besides seeing a doctor, I've been looking for my pack. I didn't steal anything."

Xing waved him off. "No one says you stole anything. The purse isn't that important. There's a computer drive in it, and that's what I want."

Xing had wanted to offer Liu ten thousand yuan for the drive, but Ren's presence made it hard to bring that up; besides, Xing had learned a lesson from dealing with Yang Zhi, who, in Xing's view, might have been alarmed by the mention of money at the restaurant.

On his part, Liu continued to play dumb, for he had no idea what a computer drive was or why Xing wanted it back.

"What's a computer drive?" Then a crafty thought entered his head. "Is it valuable?"

Ren barged in before Xing could answer:

"It's valuable, so valuable that even selling you wouldn't fetch that kind of money." He pointed to Xing and continued. "He's been sent by Mr. Yan, so watch what you say."

Ren's outburst frightened Liu enough to keep quiet about finding the purse. It also seemed that Yang Zhi had taken it from Yan's house. Yan was Ren's boss, so he had to stay out of it.

"I have no idea what you're talking about." He pretended to be confused. "You can search my room if you don't believe me. It's not that big."

He went ahead and lifted the lids off all the vats and bottles, upsetting Ren, who was on the verge of erupting again. Xing stopped them both:

"I'd be wasting my time if I did that. There's nothing of value to you on the drive, just some pictures from Mr. Yan's childhood, precious records that are useless to anyone else."

Liu insisted that he hadn't taken it. Ren set upon him again, not because of the drive or over Liu's penchant for stealing things, but because it occurred to him that Liu might have been the instigator behind the trouble-making workers, since he had once tried to get paid by pretending to hang himself. Liu was getting red in the face as he defended himself, saying he'd been away from the site in search of his pack, so how could he be saying things behind Ren's back? Watching the two men argue back and forth, Xing began to wonder where the truth lay and exactly who had the purse and the USB drive. It could be Liu Yuejin or it could be Yang Zhi, who had lied about the purse. Yes, it was probably Yang; why else would he bolt like that the night before, even leaving his own bag behind?

23

Yang Zhi

Liu was jumpy after Xing and Ren left.

He had faked the argument with Ren, which was inconsequential compared to the existence of the pack and the purse. What bothered him was not what he'd encountered in recent days, but a feeling that the nature of the incident was changing from one thing to something completely different. After locking the door, he squatted against it to smoke a cigarette and tried to make sense of recent developments.

So, here it went: six days ago he'd lost a pack, along with a divorce decree and an IOU for sixty thousand yuan, for which he had plans. In his search for the pack he'd found a purse, which was in his possession only briefly. He went looking for the thief who took his pack, while someone began looking for him because he had picked up the purse. These searches were quite different. He was alone in his, with no help, not from the police or from Brother Cao. In the case of Yan Ge's lost purse, not one, but two people—Ren Baoliang and the guy from the investigative agency—came to see him. Yet there was a similarity: like him with his pack, they were not interested in the purse itself but what was in it.

His son had taken the purse but not the computer drive. Liu had found it while searching the contents of the purse and had slipped it into his pocket because it looked interesting. As Xing said, it had no value to Liu, and he ought to turn it over, except that he did not think it was that simple. He knew that Xing was lying about Yan Ge's childhood photos. Who would go to all that trouble for a few photographs? So it was a pretense to see if Liu had it, and Xing would have something else to say if Liu admitted to finding the purse. Liu's thoughts turned to the bankcards in the purse; they must be looking for the cards, which were now with his son. Without a password, they were just plastic. He might have given Xing the purse, if he had it, that is. To find the cards he had to first locate his son, who could already be back in Henan. Or maybe they were looking for something other than the cards.

No matter what, Liu knew he first had to find his son, something that would delay his own search. In his mind it was clear which item was more important. No matter what Yan Ge and his people were looking for, in the end it had to do with money. Several millions or hundreds of millions meant nothing to Yan, while sixty thousand was a lifeline to him, which was why he'd nearly hanged himself the day he lost the pack. He couldn't let the search for the purse interfere with his hunt for his own pack, and that was why he'd played dumb with Xing, with the full awareness that it wouldn't end there. Now that he was involved, it would only grow bigger and more complicated, so his most urgent task was to get his pack back. But where would he find the thief? He'd found him once; the second time would be harder.

The more he reflected on it the more worried he became. He went to bed but was awake until four in the morning, when he drifted into a troubled sleep with three bad dreams. In the first, he was back in Henan, being chased by a dog, and no matter how hard he ran he could not shake the animal, which followed him up a tree belonging to Second Master. It took a bite out of his leg and he woke up. In the second dream, he was in the water but had forgotten how to swim, so he flailed his arms as his body sank deeper and deeper. None of the people having a meeting on the riverbank saw him struggling in the water, and when he screamed for help, his voice was swallowed up by announcements from loudspeakers. In the third, he was in Beijing looking for the thief. He searched everywhere, going into small lanes and onto main thoroughfares, until he was bathed in sweat, and still no sign of the thief. When he walked by Tiananmen Square, he spotted Yang Zhi straddling the glazed tiles on the square's tower. He was grinning and waving at him. "There's the thief," Liu shouted, and Yang leaped into the Jinshui River, where he turned into a toad and swam off. Liu was yelling when someone touched him from behind. He turned to look; it was none other than Yang. "I've got you!" Liu grabbed the thief. Worried that it was just a dream and that Yang might dream himself away, he held on tight.

"Wake up, hey, wake up," Yang said. "You're hurting me."

Liu woke up and was stunned to see Yang Zhi actually sitting at the foot of his bed. *I must be dreaming*, Liu said to himself, but he looked around and saw that he was indeed in his own room. He stared blankly at Yang. He'd been looking for the man, how in the world had he shown up like that?

Yang Zhi had been trying to find Liu since the day he bolted from the diner, where Xing had offered him ten thousand yuan for a USB drive. The amount was a sure sign that the drive was worth much more, at least a hundred thousand, five hundred thousand even. He dabbled on a computer when he wasn't out burglarizing, and he knew a thing or two about computer drives. There might well be something important on it; Lao Xing was offering ten thousand for a drive worth ten or fifty times more.

Who did Xing think he was, a fool? He'd wanted to ask for more, but Xing was obviously not the type to bargain with. He had grabbed Yang's arm in the subway, which told him that the man could be rough. Besides, without the drive in hand, he was in no position to bargain, so he used the toilet as an excuse and fled the diner, not from Xing but to look for the drive. He'd start over with Xing once he had the drive back. To find it, he had to first locate the foreman who'd picked up the purse in the alley, which was why he became the hunter and Liu Yuejin the hunted. Yang recalled that the man spoke with a Henan accent and had pointed to the construction site by the post office when giving the street singer a hard time. There was more than one site near the post office, so Yang went from site to site, pretending to be selling building materials. When the day was over, he'd checked eight sites without a glimpse of Liu.

He was stuck. Then it occurred to him that Liu had been waiting for him in the alley near Beethoven Villa, which meant that Liu had followed him there, the same way Yang had tailed the Gansu gang. Where had he picked up the trail? It must have been the snack street along the Tonghui River. Yang deduced that Liu must still be looking for him and might even be at the snack stall that very evening. So that's where he went. When he got there, he was elated to see Liu in the crowd, looking this way and that way, obviously searching for someone.

On his part, Liu had decided to try the Tonghui River area again because he'd found Yang there, oblivious to the fact that Yang had also come looking for him after figuring out his possible whereabouts.

Yang had planned to confront the man who'd picked up the purse and maybe go into business together. There was only a little more than four thousand in the pack he'd taken from Liu, while the purse contained something that could be worth a hundred, even five hundred thousand yuan. He was sure Liu did not know about the purse's potential; he'd be happy to tell him and they could square everything away. Now there was Liu, who had no idea he was being watched, which led to a change of heart. Yang decided, instead of meeting with Liu, he'd steal the purse back from him. It would be just him and Xing in a deal for all that money. Hiding behind the river bridge, he waited for Liu to return home empty-handed. Liu was too dejected to notice anyone following him.

Yang had to laugh when they reached the site, a place he'd visited earlier that day. When Liu walked through the gate, Yang scaled the fence and continued to trail him to the dining hall, finally realizing, when he entered his tiny room, that he was not a foreman; he was a cook, and a braggart to boot. Hiding next to a pile of building materials, Yang wanted to wait until Liu was asleep to get the purse; in his view, that was different from stealing. He had stolen Liu's pack by the post office but this was *his* purse, which Liu had taken, so he was merely getting his own stuff back. Totally justified.

To his surprise, Xing and another man barged into Liu's room a moment after Liu went inside. Obviously, whatever he'd had to do to manage, Xing had also found Liu Yuejin; he had been right to be wary of Xing. Now he was worried that Xing might take the purse from Liu before he had a chance to act; then he began to rue his decision of not talking to Liu earlier. Following the sound of an argument, Xing and the other man came out empty-handed, the other man continuing to argue with Liu from outside. Obviously, they'd failed to retrieve the purse. He sighed from relief and continued his vigil, waiting for Liu to fall asleep. More importantly, as he was hiding in a dead-end corner behind the guard's room, Liu needed to be careful not to be spotted.

Finally, around four, when Yang could hear the guard snoring, he sneaked over to Liu's room, where he pried open a rear window with a wire and climbed in. Liu was asleep and clearly dreaming, for he was cursing someone. With a soft snigger Yang began to search the room, from the drawers, trunk, and under the bed to the vats and bottles on the floor, but no purse. He daringly groped around the head of Liu's bed—still, nothing. So where had the cook hidden it? Leaning against the bed, Yang was getting anxious, as it was getting light outside; time was running out, so he decided to wake Liu up. Dazed and realizing that it was not a dream, Liu grabbed Yang's lapel and shouted:

"Gotcha! Now give me back my pack. There's sixty thousand yuan in it."

Liu grabbed so violently that he scratched Yang's chest and drew blood. And, if that weren't enough, the mention of money set Yang off.

"What money? Are you saying that old fanny pack of yours contained sixty thousand? Don't bullshit me. Don't you know how to tell the truth?"

"I don't mean real money." Liu was flustered. "I mean the divorce decree inside."

"What divorce decree?"

Liu knew he was being incoherent, but he couldn't help it.

"Not the divorce decree," he blurted out. "The IOU."

That confused Yang even more. "What IOU? I didn't touch anything but the money, and I didn't get to keep that. The pack was snatched by a gang from Gansu."

Liu fell back down and passed out. Knowing that after all the trouble of trying to find Yang, he didn't have the bag either was too much for him.

Unnerved by the sight of an unconscious Liu, Yang slapped him. "Wake up, I say, wake up. I've something more important to talk to you about. Where's *my* purse?"

24

Qu Li

Yan Ge and Qu Li had a serious talk. As a younger man, Yan had always thought that the scale of a couple's fight was determined by the degree of severity—that is, whether they raised their voices or not; whether or not they cursed each other; whether or not they focused on one problem or brought up extraneous issues, the past, or other trivial matters; whether or not they made sweeping generalizations and used one incident to condemn everything; and whether or not the fight turned physical, with kicking, tearing, scratching, and biting, ending with a fierce ultimatum:

"Damn you, I want a divorce."

He and Qu Li had had that kind of fight when they were younger. She'd been a quiet girl, but was every bit as ferocious as anyone else during a fight. He learned that every couple, including all his friends, fought like that, and only after he turned forty did he realize that it was a "low tactic" quarrel. True severity rarely manifested itself on the surface while, in a minor quarrel, a couple usually forgot why they'd fought so violently when it was all over.

As a couple passed that stage, they no longer fought; instead, they sat down calmly to talk and in great detail go over the problem from beginning to end. The more they analyzed, the deeper their discussion, and the deeper the discussion, the more they trembled from fear. Talking instead of arguing usually produced especially brutal results, like an ocean whose calm surface hides surging currents and threatening eddies.

But everyone has currents and eddies in their daily life. Surface severity muddies the water, while a calm discussion carries concrete goals, which a fight was meant to achieve. People don't argue for the sake of arguing; they argue to achieve an objective. Violent arguments are emotionally induced while a calm discussion is goal-oriented. When a goal is involved, everything turns profound and complex, or it changes its nature. If a man lives a pragmatic life, that is proof that he has evolved. Motivation changes everything.

Yan's argument with Qu Li was unique. They passed both the violent and the calm surface stages and entered a mixture of the two, a combining of the ocean surface and what lay below, to create a unique whole. When she was agitated, Qu cursed, but she no longer kicked, tore at, scratched, or bit him as she had done back then, for the sake of their feelings for one another. Whenever she got word of one of Yan's affairs, or learned that he had a new woman, she had raised hell; now, however, she changed her approach by paying close attention and forming a goal. By maneuvering behind his back, she had stealthily skimmed off fifty million over eight years. To him, taking the money was not nearly as serious as her collusion with the deceased assistant general manager to make the video recordings. At the time, he had assumed that the man had taken the videos to blackmail him. What a timely accident!

Yan was reminded of a day six years earlier, when he was walking along the shore of Beidaihe with Director Jia, who had suddenly muttered, "Everything would be fine if a few people were to die." Back then Yan had been shocked by the comment; now he understood what Jia meant. The assistant general manager had plotted against Yan, but in the end his plan had come to Yan's aid, though of course it took him a while to learn that Qu Li, his wife, the woman who slept beside him, had been behind it. She continued to have rows with him over his affairs, but kept quiet about other matters, stealing his money and taping his dealings with Jia. That was the difference between her former and current selves where their arguments were concerned. Put differently, her actions went beyond the normative relationship between husband and wife, which was why their present argument differed from the previous two types. Put yet another way, she was adept at alternating between the two styles of quarrels, covering her clandestine actions with violent outbursts, hiding what she did behind his back with open confrontations, and concealing their conflicting interests with their status as husband and wife. After the photo of Yan and the pop singer made the paper, Yan's reenactment was, of course, phony, but then so was her on-site investigation. So who could say her illness was not a scam as well?

In any case, none of this was important any longer; what mattered was how she'd ruined things for him at a critical moment. He was on the brink of finalizing the deal with Jia when her purse was stolen, along with the USB drive, thus introducing uncertainty into the transaction. The thief messed up Yan's plan, but ultimately the source of the trouble could be traced back to Qu Li.

It had been six days since they'd lost the drive and, according to Lao Xing, it was nowhere to be found. He had found the thief, who turned out to have lost the purse to another thief, who'd had the purse taken from him by yet a third thief. Yan could not help but be unhappy with Xing; the PI wasn't clever enough to figure out which thief had the drive, even after he'd located two of them. He'd been right in his evaluation of Xing at their first meeting, but the drive had complicated the situation, turning one matter into something altogether different.

On the other hand, Yan was getting anxious about Jia's approaching deadline. Why ten days? He had no idea, except that Jia must have had his reason for setting the deadline; besides, earlier was better than later to Yan. The sooner he retrieved the drive, the sooner he could get his life back. Time waits for no man.

Qu Li, the cause of all these troubles, had reacted to the loss of the drive with indifference. He had originally thought she wouldn't mind if they were doomed to suffer the same fate until he discovered that he'd been deceived again. In the past, she'd covered up her stealthy actions with violent rows; now she performed an about-face and hid her vicious scheme under a composed surface. Luckily Yan had her every move relayed to him by Little Bai, through her driver, Lao Wen. That morning, Bai told Yan he'd learned from Wen that Qu Li had told him to buy a plane ticket for Shanghai, with the express instruction not to tell anyone about it. That was how Yan realized that her nonchalance was a front. She'd been waiting for him to find the USB drive, but after six days, she thought it was lost forever and either was ready to sneak away or might have come up with a different plan.

Yan would not let her get away that easily, not before their business deal was concluded, which hinged upon the recovery of the drive. From his perspective, this was a bad time for her to leave Beijing, even without their arrangement. She might create new complications, but, more importantly, he had accounts to settle with her once they retrieved the drive and concluded the transaction. Given the urgency of finding the drive, he had no time for anything else. But when it was over, he wanted to sit her down and calmly go over things. If she could skim profits and videotape his dealings, how did he know she hadn't done even more?

In all honesty, he didn't care if she left Beijing, but it would be harder to reach her when she was in Shanghai, and besides, she might go somewhere else from there or even go into hiding. How would he find her then? If finding a purse was proving to be so difficult, imagine how much harder it would be to find his wife. He had her whereabouts under control when she was in Beijing, which was why he could no longer worry about exposing Bai or Wen. He walked into the bedroom and told her she was not to leave for Shanghai.

Momentarily taken aback by his command, she quickly realized that her driver had sold her out, but she did not look terribly perturbed. Putting down her hairbrush, she lit a cigarette.

"We're getting a divorce, so we can go our separate ways."

"That was then. Now the drive is missing and we're linked by mutual interest."

She picked up her new purse and stood up.

"You can't stop me if I want to leave."

He had to agree with her. Lao Wen was not enough to keep her under his control; after learning about Wen's betrayal, she'd no longer use him and could simply go out and hail a cab. She'd vanish in an instant, and that could happen in Beijing; she did not have to go to Shanghai to vanish.

Yan blocked her way, so agitated he blurted out:

"You are not going to leave this house."

"Get out of my way." She shoved him aside.

He refused, and they got into a scuffle, as if they'd returned to their younger days. Her cell phone rang and she pushed him away to take the call. As she listened, her expression changed from shock to calm.

"Sure, I'll be there." Flipping her phone shut, she sat down on the bed and looked at him.

"I'll stay in Beijing then. Happy?"

Yan was surprised, not by her change of plans, but by a call that had changed her mind while he could not. Reminded of how she had been meeting people behind his back, he had to ask:

"Who was that?"

"A friend."

She went into the bathroom and locked the door, leaving Yan standing by the bed feeling lost.

The caller was not her friend, but a stranger, a blackmailer. He told her he had her purse and had seen the USB drive they were looking for. If she wanted it back, she must take three hundred thousand yuan to the western suburb at two a.m. and wait by the Sijiqing Bridge on Fourth Ring Road.

"Be there or not. It's your choice."

With no time to think, she agreed to go and the caller hung up. She went into the bathroom to check the caller ID and saw that the call had been made from a pay phone.

The caller was none other than Yang Zhi, who made the call with Liu Yuejin standing next to him. Earlier that day, shortly before day-

break, after Yang managed to rouse the unconscious Liu, he immediately brought up the drive in the purse that Liu had picked up, saying
someone would buy it for as much as five hundred thousand yuan.
Yang told Liu to produce it and they'd sell it together, splitting the
profit. Even if Liu wasn't lying about the amount in the IOU, he'd get
only sixty thousand, while the drive could fetch much more. If they
weren't greedy, they could settle for four hundred thousand, which
would then be split between them. Two hundred thousand was a lot
more than Liu was hoping to get, and he would never have to worry
about retrieving his pack.

Finally everything clicked; Liu now understood why Yang had
showed up in his room. But why had Ren Baoliang and Xing come
to see him? He'd lost a pack and found a purse. He'd thought that
his was more valuable than the one he found and had even cursed
Yang's poor judgment in purse snatching when he searched the contents. Now it was clear that finding the drive was so much better, like
losing a sesame seed and getting a melon, or losing a sheep and getting a horse in return. Who could say what was ill fate and what was
good fortune? He was instantly relieved, a sign to Yang that Liu had
changed his mind and that something could be done.

"The purse was mine to begin with," Yang emphasized.

Liu nodded, though he disputed Yang's claim; he was simply
agreeing to go along with him. If the drive had been worthless, he'd
have handed it over, but now that he knew how valuable it might be,
he had to reconsider. If it was worth so much, why not sell it himself
and forget about a partner? Liu realized that he could manage alone,
whether it fetched four hundred thousand or five hundred thousand.
When everything became clear to him, he nodded and decided to
play dumb.

"That sounds wonderful," he said, sucking his teeth, "but I
don't have the purse."

"Where is it?" Yang could not believe his ears.

"I was trying to catch you, so I left the purse behind, and someone had taken it by the time I came back for it."

Now it was Yang's turn to pass out. When he came to, he told Liu he didn't believe him.

"Those two men who were just here?" Liu spread out his hands. "They came for the purse too, but I don't have it. I'm not a magician." He added, "They told me they'd pay me for it. If I had it, why wouldn't I have given it to them?"

In fact, Xing hadn't mentioned money. But Yang didn't know that and was convinced by what Liu had just told him. He didn't trust Liu, but had searched the place and checked everything inside and outside that small room. Where would a cook put the purse? Besides, a cook like Liu would not say no to money. Yang concluded he'd wasted his time, and since he did not like wasting time, he got up to leave with the idea of finding another solution. Liu stopped him and demanded to have his pack back, or at the very least the 64,100 yuan in it. Yang's mind was on the drive in the purse while Liu cared only about the IOU in his pack. Yang wanted to leave but Liu would not let him go. They got into a tussle.

"Let go," Yang said. "I'll give you your money when I find the drive and get paid."

"Give me back my IOU before you go looking for it."

They resumed their struggle when Yang yelled:

"Stop. I've got an idea."

"What?" Liu paused.

Yang studied his face. "You're a USB drive yourself."

"What do you mean?"

"You said you didn't pick up the purse, but everyone thinks you did, including the two guys who were here earlier and the family in the villa compound. So whether you did or not, it doesn't matter, because everyone says you did, and that means we're rich. The key is you have to stand up and tell them you did."

"What does that mean?" Liu was getting even more confused.

Yang sat Liu down on the bed and explained things to him, their fight forgotten. The drive was gone, but Yang thought Liu could simply buy another one and give it to the owner.

"Will that work?" Liu felt uneasy about the scam.

Yang sighed. "Well, the way things are now, we'll have to try to sell a dead horse as if it was still alive." But then, with a troubled look, he said, "We haven't seen the real drive, so we don't know what it looks like."

Then he pounded Liu's bed with a balled fist. "We'll just have to risk it."

With the drive in his possession, Liu had not wanted to be part of Yang's scheme, but on second thought he realized he could see how Yang planned to sell the fake drive and then sell the genuine one on his own. So he went along.

Before long it was light outside. With Liu in tow, Yang went out to find a pay phone. Back in Yan's house in the villa compound, he had taken a box of Qu Li's business cards, whose unusual triangular shape and hiding place had him puzzled. He dialed the number on the card and it went through. He gave his instructions, including the lowest possible price of three hundred thousand; he could have asked for more and negotiated a better price if he'd actually had the drive. But since Lao Xing and his people were also looking for it, Yang knew he had to act fast and get the money in case Xing found it before the deal went through.

As the saying goes, a long night produces many dreams. The sooner he concluded the transaction, the sooner he could leave the whole thing behind him. Naturally he had no intention of splitting evenly with Liu; he was the one who got everything started, so he deserved the larger share. Put differently, he'd eat the meat and give Liu the broth. The money, which would be enough to pay off his debt to Brother Cao's people, meant he'd no longer be under their thumb; he'd be free. He'd thought that Qu Li would want to bargain, and was surprised when she agreed right off. Now he almost wished he'd asked for more, but at least her response was an indication that the drive really was valuable.

Liu was worried when Yang hung up.

"I didn't know you were going to do that. That's extortion."

"What's extortion? If you kidnap someone and demand a ransom, that's extortion. But here we have something to sell and someone who wants to buy it. That's a business deal." He took Liu to buy a USB drive.

Yang picked the most expensive drive, one that cost nearly a thousand. Liu knew it wasn't the right type—the wrong shape and blue instead of red. It was a fake, but the scam was real, which had Liu increasingly on edge; there was no going back, it seemed. In his view, the deal was unsound and he would definitely not have done it that way if he'd been alone. But he wouldn't be able to make any deal on his own without Yang. He consoled himself with the thought that he'd hand over the real drive once the money changed hands. That wouldn't be cheating, would it? Yang was pretending the fake one was real, and Liu would replace the fake one with the real one, at least if everything went smoothly. If there was a problem during the exchange, he had a way out and would not lose anything. He was no longer worried.

That evening, the two of them took the subway, then switched to a bus before arriving at the Sijiqing Bridge, where they hid and smoked at a peddlers' market east of the bridge. All was quiet now that the peddlers had gone home. At two in the morning, a cab drove up, stopped, and out stepped a woman with a purse. As she walked toward them, Yang could tell it was Qu Li, whose naked body he'd once seen. The purse looked heavy.

"We're rich." Yang slapped Liu.

He surveyed the area for half an hour, and, seeing nothing suspicious, told Liu it was time to move. Petrified by the imminent action, Liu got to his feet unsteadily and said, his eyes on Qu, who was waiting by the bridge:

"We could go to jail if this falls apart." He was gripped by a worrisome question: "I'm just trying to find my money, so how did it turn into extortion?"

Yang gave him a punch. "Don't be such a coward. Take a good look. There before you is money, not prison." He added, "Who doesn't get his money this way in this day and age? You have to take risks if you want to be rich."

Liu had a change of heart. "You go on ahead. I'm staying here."

Yang glanced at Liu, then at Qu, who was still waiting by the bridge, and then around them to make sure nothing was amiss.

"Sure, I can go by myself, but when I get the money it's not going to be fifty-fifty anymore. It'll have to be seventy-thirty." He continued, "This will work better actually. I won't show her the fake drive in case she gets suspicious. I'll tell her you have it."

Then he grabbed Liu.

"But don't even think about double-crossing me. Everyone knows you have the drive, so you'll have to step up to show her when I call out to you."

Realizing there was no turning back, Liu nodded weakly while looking around to make sure he could get away if the deal fell through. If everything went smoothly, he'd hand over the genuine USB drive, since he had no use for it anyway.

As he walked toward the bridge, Yang also had a change of heart. He'd lied to Liu earlier. Instead of driving, Qu Li had taken a cab, which left after she got out, a sign of good faith. It also meant she did have money in her bag. She was a woman and he was a man. At this point, he was no longer interested in extortion; instead he planned to rob her, like the Gansu gang. It was a tactless move, but the circumstances called for drastic action, which would work better with a fake drive, since he wouldn't need to deceive her, and they wouldn't have to negotiate. When he got closer, he'd zero in on the bag, snatch it and run. Like all thieves, Yang was a fast runner, and a woman like that would not be able to catch him. As to the cowardly Liu Yuejin, he'd leave him behind; it was neither nice nor righteous, but he had no choice. Liu would just have to continue searching for his fanny pack.

With the plan all thought out, he felt energized, his muscles and joints ready for combat, like a ball player before a game. Imagine his shock when several brawny guys leaped out from behind a bridge pylon before he even had a chance to run off with the bag. Led by Yan's driver, Little Bai, they pounced on him and wrestled him to the ground. The shock on Qu Li's face told Yang that the ambush was not her idea. On her part, she knew that Little Bai's group had spoiled her plan, which meant that Yan Ge was behind it. So he had had her followed in order to get to the drive first.

As Yang continued to struggle, Qu Li went up and slapped Little Bai.

"Get out of here. This is my business."

But none of them moved. Bai took his revenge for the slap out on Yang by kicking and hitting him savagely. Soon Yang's nose and mouth were bleeding and a piercing pain told him he had a broken rib.

"Give me the fucking drive!"

Yang knew he'd been had, not by the woman, but by someone else. At this point, it really didn't matter; he had a broken rib and no USB drive.

"I don't have it."

Another round of savage beating followed and another rib was broken. He decided to show them the fake drive.

"It's not the right one," Bai and Qu said in unison.

"Who are you, anyway?" Qu demanded.

Bai and his friends kicked Yang again. He began to cry and, looking in the direction of the market, he cursed:

"That damned cook."

Following his gaze, the men saw a figure leap over the wall and run down the alley; they took off in the same direction, leaving one man to guard Yang.

25

Ma Manli and Yuan Datou

Ma Manli was involved three years earlier with Lao Yuan, a thirty-seven-year-old man from Zhoushan, Zhejiang. A peddlers' market two blocks from the Manli Hair Salon was where Yuan sold seafood, mostly ribbonfish, but also yellow croakers, mackerel, frozen shrimps, small white clams, kelp, and seaweed. Manli visited his stall often because of her love for fried Zhoushan ribbonfish, while Yuan came to her place to have his hair washed and cut. Soon they got to know each other well. She still frequented his stall because of the ribbonfish, but, as he revealed to her after they were together, he came to the salon not for grooming purposes but for her. He liked everything about her, her willowy waist, for instance, though he found her eyes most attractive. Manli's eyes were not big, and no one had ever said they were pretty, no one but Yuan, who agreed that they were small—most of the time. But when she got angry and raised her brows, those eyes, so-called phoenix eyes, were beautiful.

"You call these phoenix eyes?" Manli was doubtful.

"Of course they are," Yuan said decisively.

Yuan proceeded to tell her that, in addition to her eyes, he loved the way she looked at people. At thirty-seven, he'd seen enough people, men and women, young and old, with all their different expressions, yet found they all had one thing in common. That was, the eyes began to turn clouded beginning at the age of eight, since everything we experienced was retained in our eyes, even after it vanished from our brains. So after we turned thirty, our eyes were basically like a bowl of congee and quite unattractive. Manli's eyes were similarly clouded, but a ray of bright light returned when she looked at people, which was uncommon. Manli would have none of it, so he added that he really did like her expression, but he also liked to hear her sigh. When they were engaged in a conversation she would suddenly sigh. People normally sigh when they have something on their minds, and most do so for a specific reason with a clear purpose. Her sigh, on the other hand, lacked a goal; when she sighed, it was usually not about whatever it was they were talking about, but more like she was reminded of other troubles. It was a deep and complex sigh and utterly intriguing. In his view, you could learn a lot about a person simply through a sigh. Then, as if that were not enough to convince her, he continued to say that besides her sigh, he also liked the way she walked, her voice, the way she smiled, and her changing manner at various times. In other words, he liked everything about her, because she was different from all other women. Finally convinced, she assumed he knew a lot about women and, about her in particular; he might even have known more about her than she herself did. Her husband, Zhao Xiaojun, was the opposite; he noticed nothing in her that Yuan saw; all he ever spotted were her shortcomings, such as her small breasts.

"What do you have to say for yourself? You're a man in drag." Zhao would say whenever they had a fight.

Manli did not like Yuan for the same reasons he liked her. Yuan had a big head and thick neck, which was why he was nicknamed Yuan Datou, Big Head Yuan. He was not tall, had a long torso and stumpy legs, and was not handsome, unlike so many Zhejiang men. If Yuan liked everything about her, she liked him for his conversation, but not because he always said what she wanted to hear, though; she was not that self-centered. He captivated her whenever he talked, in particular for his sense of humor. He'd say the same thing as everyone else, but the effect was different. She'd met other witty people who made her laugh the moment they began to talk, but Yuan was not like them. When they were face to face, she might not find what he was saying funny, but she'd burst out laughing later when she thought about it. Then she'd laugh a second time as she recalled what he'd said, but for a different reason. It became clear to her that Yuan's humor came from his wit, while others just told jokes. For instance, during her first ribbonfish purchase at his stall, before they were acquainted, she disparaged his merchandise as a ruse to bargain for a lower price.

"What nerve! You want five-fifty for a fish as thin as a shoestring. Over there, a big one like a blade of a knife only costs four-eighty."

She'd made up "over there" to support her claim, of course, and if it had been any other fishmonger, she'd have been mocked and her lie exposed. "If it's cheaper over there, buy it over there," they'd say.

Yuan did not poke a hole in her claim, nor did he refute her exaggerated description of his ribbonfish. Instead, he said:

"Don't blame me. It's the fault of whoever named the fish in the first place. It's called a ribbonfish, so it has to look like a ribbon or a shoestring. Those over there, thick as a knife, I'm afraid they're puffed up because they suffered from diabetes."

Since she was focused on bargaining with him, she paid no attention to his retort, but on her way back with the fish, she recalled what he'd said and burst out laughing. And later, while frying the fish, she laughed again.

Or take his first haircut, for instance. By then they knew each other pretty well. A haircut cost five yuan, but she said:

"For others five yuan, for you, ten."

Yuan knew she was referring to his oversized head.

"If you're going to charge by size, you should run a pet shop."

"What do you mean?" Manli asked.

"The last time I was in a pet shop I saw that they charged two hundred to shave off all the hair on a dog the size of my fist."

She made a coquettish sound before starting in on his hair. After he left, she burst out laughing at the sight of a fist-sized dog walking on a leash, and she laughed again that night as she lay in bed and recalled his comment about shaving off all the hair. Yuan was one of those who could say something dirty without sounding filthy.

Another example. The first time they went to bed, Manli was shy about taking off her bra because of her husband's complaint about the size of her breasts; so Yuan helped her take it off. Her breasts did look unusually small to him, but instead of commenting on their size, he felt them and said:

"Function over size."

Then after putting his mouth over one of them, he added, "Too big. I can't hold it in my mouth. Really big."

She laughed out loud, then began to cry.

Her husband was diametrically different from Yuan, and if not for Zhao, she wouldn't have gotten involved with Yuan. During her six-year marriage, they had six months of happiness, and after that everything went downhill. That had nothing to do with money, though they were poor. Yuan was a fishmonger, not a millionaire, but they got along beautifully.

At five feet ten inches, Zhao had long limbs, big eyes, fair skin, and nice features, all of which put him far above Yuan. She'd married him for his looks, and quickly learned that his good looks could only sustain their marriage for half a year, after which problems cropped up. Zhao was a reseller, buying from one city to sell in another; some resellers made fortunes, particularly when they had the right merchandise. But not Zhao; he was good at what he did, but he wanted to get rich so fast he never stayed with one kind of merchandise for long. Whatever he wasn't peddling at the moment always seemed better to him. Sometimes, he might be about to strike it big, but didn't have the patience to stay with whatever it was and lost money, while others made fortunes. He'd then complain about how others did so well. All in all, he'd sold cigarettes, liquor, rice, furs, and pets, even came close to human trafficking. He made some money and lost some money, which was normal; the problem was, he was never himself. Either arrogantly overbearing or dolefully miserable, his reactions were exaggeration personified, overblowing every little thing.

He wore a Western suit all year round, drenched in sweat on a clear summer day and spattered in mud when it rained, as if he were the busiest man in the world.

But neither of these bothered her as much as the way Zhao talked. He talked about everything in a matter-of-fact manner and was always straightforward, with no subtlety, let alone humor. You could say he was humorless. To be sure, there are plenty of people like him; the problem for her was, when they argued, he stopped being matter-of-fact, twisting one thing into another or confusing two matters. It was hard to tell whether he'd been born with an addled brain or was doing it on purpose. How was she supposed to have a good argument if he refused to stay on topic? It was a different kind of quarrel, to be sure, but the core of their problem—money—usually surfaced quickly. They might have started arguing over something else, but eventually it all came down to money. When they got into bed, the core issue of their sex life—her small breasts—came up in a similar fashion.

"Did I just have sex with a woman?" he'd sigh after they were finished. "It just felt like being with a man."

On it went, and their life together lost its spark. It took her a while to realize why—not money, nor her breasts, but the absence of fun, like an ungreased machine whose gears grind and grate against one another. Obviously they didn't like each other, the only difference being that he disliked her because of her breasts, while she was turned off by everything about him. There was simply nothing about him she found attractive.

Then, three years before, he fell for someone else, another woman from the north named Dong Yuanyuan, an acquaintance of Manli's. She said she was a nightclub accountant, but no one really knew what she did at night. Unlike Manli, she had big breasts, like a pair of bowling balls, or a couple of melons.

By rights Manli should have been upset and had it out with her husband over his affair, but she did not; instead, she felt liberated. Zhao liked big-breasted women, and now that he'd found one, Manli figured she was entitled to a relationship of her own. She might have gotten involved with Yuan out of spite, since Zhao shouldn't be the only one having an affair; in the end, however, she recognized Yuan's attraction. He was the first person whose conversation interested her, and she went to bed with him just so she could hear him talk, which was a first for her. Later on, she wondered how she'd done it.

She got pregnant once during their first two years together. It was aborted, since their relationship was secret. After her divorce, they could be open about it, but not to the point of getting married, because Yuan had a wife and children back in Zhoushan. In the beginning, she had no interest in marriage, since she'd already had a failed one with Zhao, and they were still fighting over money even after the divorce. Without marriage between them, she could enjoy simple, uncomplicated conversation and sex with Yuan. But after a while she began to care about marriage because of her age. Now in her thirties, she wanted to be married, and that did not scare him away.

"Which is easier, getting married or getting divorced?" Yuan asked her once.

"Divorced, of course."

"Wrong. A couple gets divorced when they can't get along, but you need to find the right person to marry. So, which one's easier, finding the right person or marrying the wrong one?"

Now she understood what he meant and laughed over his reasoning, not his humor. "So when are you going to get a divorce?"

"If not in one day, maybe two. If not two days, then a month. Maybe six months."

They agreed on six months, but he vanished before the half year passed. It turned out he was a con man, and he didn't vanish because Manli wanted him to divorce his wife and marry her. He was taken away by the police, for he'd conned just about everyone, Manli included. Three years earlier, he'd illegally raised funds in his hometown from over a dozen poor families, since it was hard to get rich people to hand over their money. The scam was exposed before he got much, so he fled to Beijing to be a fishmonger, while a warrant for his arrest was posted online. After three years had gone by, he thought he was safe, but someone from his hometown spotted him when he went to pick up a shipment of fish at the train station. The man, one of the people Yuan had conned, had come to Beijing to look for work. That night, the police arrested Yuan while he was taking an inventory of his fish. He had told Manli he came from Zhoushan, which was a lie; he was in fact from Wenzhou. Everything about him was a lie, including where he came from.

Manli's mind went blank when she heard the news, but instead of feeling wretched over the deception, she burst out laughing. She'd thought he had a great sense of humor, and the funniest thing about him was his fund-raising con game. As the saying goes, he tried to steal a chicken with a handful of rice and ended up losing both. Then she began to cry.

Considering that it was a modest amount, the court sentenced Yuan to a year in prison; he got lucky for not trying to steal more than just a chicken. During the twelve months, Manli never once went to visit him in prison, considering him as good as dead; whenever her thoughts turned to Yuan, she would sigh, not because of their relationship, but because she hadn't known the real him.

One day late at night, Yuan showed up at the Manli Hair Salon after serving his prison sentence. His hair was gray and he looked old. She barely recognized him. He'd turned into an old man who looked more like an old pig. His long torso and stumpy legs made him look like a giant penguin as he shuffled into the salon. He even talked differently now, as he told her that he'd just gotten out and wanted to resume his fishmongering business at the market or maybe sell freshwater fish, which would be brought in from Miyun, a lot closer than Zhoushan. Penniless, he had no place to go and wondered if he could stay with her for a while. He faltered, his former witty self seemingly erased by a year in prison; now he talked matter-of-factly. When she realized who it was, Manli felt a mixture of sorrow and joy at first, but that turned to resentment after listening to him. She was upset not because she'd been conned into a relationship and had even had an abortion for his sake; she was outraged that he was actually asking to stay at her place. There was no shame in asking to stay with a friend, but he was no longer the same person. She didn't care that he was down and out or that he might be conning her again; it was just that nothing about him reminded her of the man she'd known. In her mind, it was someone else pretending to be Yuan, the biggest con man of all.

"Get out," she demanded.

He looked around and was about to pester her when she repeated herself:

"Get out!"

He walked out, realizing that she was no longer the Ma Manli he used to know.

After he left, she sat down, steaming, though she wasn't really angry. She was feeling low as she recalled what had happened between them when she heard a knock at the door. She ignored it, assuming it was Yuan coming back to her. But the knock turned into loud bangs, sounding more and more urgent, so she went up, unlatched the door, and opened it with a savage push.

"Get lost. Did you hear me?" She shouted into the street, frightening the man outside the door.

It was not Yuan, it was Liu Yuejin, with whom Manli had a different relationship. Liu often came to her salon, but the two of them had never slept together; he had wanted to but had no idea how to make it happen. Unlike Yuan, Liu was not witty, but then he never deceived her either, at least not where important things were involved. He was crafty, but not enough to strike it big or bring down anything. He would like to have struck it rich, but, as with his desire to sleep with Manli, he didn't know how. In a word, he was a simple cook. On the other hand, maybe that's just how she saw things; he might have had a different idea. He could have held the conviction that the two of them would end up in her bed sooner or later; otherwise, he wouldn't have spent so much time at the salon. He told her everything; she never reciprocated, even though he felt they could talk about anything.

When he showed up at the salon that earlier night, she had immediately sensed something different about him; he seemed lost and needed someone to talk to. But she was so busy trying to get rid of her ex-husband that Liu held back, and in the end it was Liu who got her ex-husband to leave. Liu's action made her cry. He was nowhere to be seen after that until now, when he showed up, looking even more lost than that night. She was shocked to see him sweating and panting.

"Did you just mug someone? Or were you robbed?"

She was joking, but he confirmed her comment.

"You're right. I did rob someone and then someone else mugged me."

After pushing her back inside, he shut the door, locked it, and turned off the light before taking her to the back room. Believing he was going to try something, she struggled while he held her still and told her everything that had happened over the past seven days, from the thief stealing his fanny pack all the way to what had just taken place at the Sijiqing Bridge. At times he was so flustered he was incoherent, which, compounded by the complexity of the matter, confused her to the point that she was only sure of his agitation.

"I missed something. Start over," she said.

"There's no time." He was growing impatient. "There's nothing you could do even if you didn't miss a thing."

He took out the USB drive. "You know what this is?"

"A USB drive." She nodded. "I used to chat online when I was in a bad mood, though I've lost interest over the past six months."

"Great!" He clapped. "Hurry, let's take a look and see what's on it."

"I sold my computer to Dahao."

Liu had met Dahao, the owner of a carwash a block away from the Manli Hair Salon. Originally from Jiangxi, Dahao was a fleshy, overweight man with eyes that all but disappeared into rolls of flesh on his face. Knowing that Dahao was an avid mahjong player, Liu wondered why a carwash man needed a computer.

"Not to chat online. He's into porn sites."

"I don't care what he's into." Liu was on edge. "Let's take a look."

After she put on a jacket, they left the salon in a hurry and crossed the street to the carwash, where it was obviously too late for any customers. The building had a gaping hole for a door that was now facing deserted streets. Putting aside the porn sites, Dahao had gone out for a game of mahjong that night. Ma's old computer was sitting on a desk in the carwash, covered with grease, including the keyboard. Dahao's nephew, Xiaohao, was watching the place and wouldn't let them use the computer, claiming that Dahao would beat him if they messed it up. Then he grumbled that he was hungry, which told Liu what he needed to know; he handed him ten yuan. Elated, Xiaohao ran across the street to enjoy himself with a bottle, leaving the computer to Liu and Ma.

They inserted the drive and opened a file, but the screen was a blank. They could hear people talking, intermingled with giggling. Ma and Liu had difficulty understanding what was being said, for there were too many people talking about things alien to them. Then a video clip came on the screen, showing a room that looked to be in a hotel. The first person to appear was Yan Ge, to Liu's surprise. He was handing out gifts—jewelry and calligraphy scrolls—always to two men, one old and the other middle-aged, whose attire and expressions indicated that they were officials. The gifts were handed out separately; the two men never appeared together. In addition to jewelry and calligraphy, the gifts also included canvas bags, some-times one and sometimes three or more. Once, when Yan bent for-ward to unzip a bag, the contents, visible on the screen, appeared to be money. The middle-aged man usually got one bag while the older man got three or as many as five, and the gift-giving took place more than ten times, as marked by the time stamps in the lower corner of the screen.

Liu Yuejin and Ma Manli were flabbergasted, unable to even guess the total amount in several dozen bags. What stunned them more was what followed on the screen. The two men could be seen separately engaged in sexual acts with non-Chinese women in the same room, and it happened more than ten times, as indicated by the time stamps. Liu and Ma were speechless. Before watching it, Liu was only aware that it was a valuable computer drive; now he realized what was involved.

They walked out of the carwash and headed back to the salon. When they reached the corner butcher shop, which was closed, they stopped and squatted on the step. The sign in front flapped in the wind, advertising "Trouble-free pork you can eat with ease of mind."

"Those were big bags. They could easily contain millions each, don't you think?" Liu said. "So several dozen bags means billions, doesn't it?"

"What do you call taking that much money?" he continued. "It's major corruption. A cause for execution."

A light went on in his head. "Now I know why so many people were eager to get this back. It's not about money, it's about their lives."

Ma Manli stared at him blankly. Her face slowly drained of color while Liu went on with his indignant outburst.

"I make a few yuan selling swill to Lao Li's pig farm, traveling twenty miles each time. They don't have to lift a finger to receive all that money. They're not humans. They're wolves, man-eating wolves."

Manli, still gaping at him, stammered:

"Don't talk about them any more. You have to think about yourself."

"What about me?"

"You found something you shouldn't have kept, and now they know you have it. I'm afraid you're in big trouble."

Enlightened by her comment, he broke out in a cold sweat.

"You're right. Didn't I tell you about the thief being beaten up under the bridge?" Then he jumped to his feet. "I thought they wanted this, but no, they want more."

He was back on his haunches as he grabbed her hand.

"Now I know. They want the drive to do away with all the witnesses. The thief was beaten to death and I'm next." He slapped his hand on the ground. "It's bad enough to lose a pack. Who'd have guessed it could be so much more complicated and so much worse?"

"I've seen what's on it," Manli said, "so that means I'm in trouble too." She nudged Liu. "Promise me that if they catch you, you won't mention my name. I've got a daughter back home."

As the saying goes, once the limit is reached, things go in the opposite direction. With a major disaster looming over his head, Liu said, "Great. Now we're in it together, for better or for worse."

Manli reached out and put her hands around his neck.

"I'm going to throttle you, damn you."

26

Han Shengli

Han Shengli received a beating from Lao Lai's people.

Lao Lai was a Chinese from Xinjiang, though he looked like a Uighur, which was why anyone who met him for the first time asked, "Are you a Uighur?" He started out explaining that his parents, who were from Shanghai, had been sent to develop the border region fifty years earlier. By living like a Uighur and regularly eating meat, he'd grown to look more Uighur than Chinese. After repeating his background story too many times, he gave up and simply admitted that he was indeed a Uighur.

In Beijing, people from Xinjiang tended to congregate in Weigong Village, to the north of Zizhuyuan Park in the Haidian District of Western Beijing. They sold lamb kebabs, Xinjiang hats, tambouras, a Central Asian musical instrument, and Uighur knives. The merchandise was fake; the trade itself was a front for their real profession of thievery. Lao Lai, in truth a Han Chinese, was their ringleader, a position he had fought hard to attain after several bloody battles.

Soon after taking over, he implemented many new measures. For instance, he no longer allowed the gang to rob people. They were thieves and they stole; if they robbed they would be bandits. Thieves stole with their hands, while robbers used knives, and sooner or later they'd end up killing someone. Anyone who wanted to stick around Weigong Village had to obey the rules and not cross the boundary into killing.

Another change had to do with observing territorial limits. In the past, the gang plied their trade wherever they went, resulting in territorial fights with other thieves. Lao Lai told his underlings to limit their activities to Weigong Village, and he would not tolerate any other gang violating their territory. The gang members paid lip service to his rules and then did whatever they pleased behind his back, rendering the rules ineffectual and him gloomy.

Han Shengli came to Weigong Village one day to see a hometown friend, after which he took a stroll in a nearby market and did a little pilfering. His target was a well-dressed, bespectacled, middle-aged woman with her nose in the air, giving him the impression that she must be rich. He went into action, took her purse and slinked out of the market to check the contents. Not even four hundred yuan. The purse bulged, not with money, but with a thick stack of business cards, and Han knew he had misjudged her. Rich people don't wear glasses; only the poor intellectuals do that. She was not aware that Han had snatched her purse, but his actions were spotted by members of the Xinjiang gang, who nabbed him while he was bemoaning his latest misstep.

Stealing outside one's territory was a major offense, according to the protocols of their trade and Lai's rules. The Xinjiang gang rarely respected territorial lines when stealing, but when someone crossed into their territory, they stuck to the rules and beat him bloody. They also demanded that he cough up twenty thousand, some sixty times what he'd stolen. That was unreasonable. He tried to explain that to the gang, which further incurred their wrath. But he wouldn't stop arguing his case, so his argument-averse captors took him to a basement, where they tied him to a pipe. They would let him go only if he agreed to pay the so-called fine; if not, he could expect an unpleasant death from starvation in the basement. Frightened by rats scurrying around his feet, he wrote out an IOU for twenty thousand to be paid in ten installments, two thousand a day. To make sure he didn't skip out on them, they needed a guarantor from the neighborhood, so he took them to see the friend from his hometown, Lao Gao.

Gao, also from Luoshui, Henan, ran a diner specializing in a Henan specialty, stewed noodles in a spicy soup. Gao clearly had a steady income, the Xinjiang gang noticed, so they let Han go. He went first to the hospital, where his injuries received eight stiches, and, with his head still bandaged, he started working again, stealing now for the Xinjiang gang. Han had been a thief for a very long time, with little to show for it, not because he was faint-hearted, but because he made mistakes in judging targets, locations, and timing. Stealing the purse of a poor intellectual he mistook to be rich was only the latest example of his tendency to miscalculate. Misjudging a target was less serious than stealing in the wrong place and at the wrong time, for that often resulted in being caught in the act. Thievery is an art form. Timing is everything. Han liked to deal in probabilities, and timing was invariably his undoing. By the time he realized that his timing was off, a favorable situation turned unfavorable. In his case, seven attempts out ten were foiled, and he had to flee. The only gain from his flawed thievery was the ability to run fast; he got away about seventy percent of the time. Twenty percent of the time he was caught and beaten or arrested. In a word, he succeeded in only one out of ten attempts, but even that success did not always bring in high-quality loot.

Han worked doubly hard since being caught by the Xinjiang gang. When he was stealing for himself he could work when he felt like it; now he had to go out every day to bring in two thousand yuan and pay off that day's debt. But his ability to judge did not improve with diligence, for he now spent thirteen or fourteen hours on the street yet failed to make more than when he was at it for seven or eight. In the past, he considered it a successful day if he managed to pick up five hundred, and it was not unusual to find no victim after roaming the streets all day. Low productivity hadn't been a problem then, but now it came at a price; he never fulfilled his daily quota and the gang gave him a couple of kicks each time he went to pay them what he could. With Gao as his guarantor, Han was not a flight risk, so they told him they'd do a tally when his deadline was up.

At moments like this, Han directed his anger only at Liu Yuejin, neither at the gang nor at himself, for Liu had paid back only two hundred of the thirty-three hundred he owed Han. As Liu was just a poor cook, Han had thought it pointless to demand his money back, until he learned that Liu had been carrying forty-one hundred in his bag. As Han saw it, Liu preferred having his money stolen over paying him back, which was infuriating. Under normal circumstances, he wouldn't have minded so much, but Liu seemed unfazed by Han being beaten by the debt collectors, a character flaw that went beyond the love of money.

To be sure, thirty-four hundred would not have been enough to pay off the Xinjiang gang, but it would have served as emergency relief on days when he came up short and would have spared him applications of their feet and fists. After getting mad at Liu, Han turned on himself. The Xinjiang gang and Liu Yuejin were both more ruthless than he, a thief who was undeserving of his reputation. He'd been wrong to treat Liu decently, and now that Liu had lost his money, it was useless to be harsh. In order for Liu to pay back his debt, Han had had to help him find his pack by taking him to see Brother Cao, and what had he gotten in return? Liu went behind his back and received a beating at Cao's shed and then complained that Han had taken him to see the wrong people, costing him the deposit and two days of searching for the thief. Seemingly entitled to his anger from that beating, Liu pointed at his own bandaged head and said to Han:

"Quit griping. You're not the only one who got beaten up."

What could Han say but,

"That's where you're wrong. We were beaten for very different reasons. But let's not talk about that. What about my money?"

"I'm as good as dead if I don't find my pack, and you can't stop talking about your money."

There was nothing Han could do with someone like Liu. He had no time to deal with the man, not when the Xinjiang gang was after him for their money; besides, Liu was penniless now and nothing

Han did would get anything out of him. Five days had gone by, and Han hadn't once managed to hand over all two thousand, so they began to show up at Lao Gao's diner and put pressure on him. Frightened of the gang, Gao pressured Han, who offered his advice:

"Why hold on to that little diner? You flee and I flee and we'll both be free."

Gao was incensed. "I wouldn't have helped you out if I'd known this. It may be a tiny diner, but it requires a high rent, and I've already paid three years lease, a total of seventy-two thousand. Why would I want to lose seventy-two thousand over your twenty?" He glared at Han and continued, "I had to borrow to pay the lease."

At the end of seven days, Han had paid the Xinjiang gang something over three thousand, with three days to go. For him to have stolen nearly four thousand counted as an uncommon feat. But the gang thought he was trying to wriggle out of the debt, and that changed the nature of their dealing with him; it was about more than money now. On the seventh night, with Lao Gao as their guide, they came to his place and gave him another beating, bloodying his head again. They said that was just a warning. If he handed over the sixteen thousand he still owed by the tenth day, they'd leave him alone. If not . . . one of them unsheathed a knife and pointed it at Han.

"We know you'll run, so nothing will happen to you." He then pointed the knife at Gao. "Instead, we will cut out the tendons on *his* son's legs to make barbecue."

Gao was so alarmed he yelled at Han, despite the man's bleeding head. "You heard that, Han Shengli. You have to keep me and my family out of this."

After the gang left with Gao, Han went to the hospital again, and then went out to work the following morning with new bandages on his head under a baseball cap. The beating was much more severe this time, causing wounds that required fifteen stitches. One of the cuts was on his forehead, and the bandage peeked out from under the cap no matter how low he pulled the bill. It goes without saying that an injured man is ill-suited to be a thief, not because the injury is too severe to work, but because it will draw too much attention. Sure enough, everyone turned to look at Han when they passed him on the street. Of course there was no reason for them to assume that he was a thief, but it made it hard for him to steal from anyone. Everything—the target, location, and timing—could be in perfect harmony for a kill, but the opportunity would vanish with a single glance from a passing person. In the past, it was his misjudgment that had led to missing the right moment, but now his attire was to blame.

After a day of hard work, he carried out three attempts. He was discovered twice and had to run for it, leaving the loot behind. The only success was a middle-aged man leaning against an advertising sign, fast asleep, cradling a satchel. Han took a look around and, seeing no one, grabbed the satchel and took off. Technically speaking, it was a robbery, not a theft. When he stopped in an alley to check the contents, he was disappointed by what he saw—not a cent, only a jumble of receipts. The man was engaged in the illegal resale of used receipts. Han had inadvertently ruined the man's business. He fared better the next day, taking in over five hundred yuan, but that was still far less than the gang demanded.

On the morning of the third day, the deadline, he got up early and sat on his bed, worried sick. How in the world was he going to steal sixteen thousand in one day? No way, not unless he robbed a bank, but he did not have the nerve to do that; even if he had, he wouldn't know how to go about it. In the end, he decided not to go out, since he could never manage to get that much. He thought of skipping town and leaving Lao Gao to deal with the aftermath, but being from neighboring villages in Henan, Gao knew where he lived. Han might be able to run, but he couldn't hide from Gao forever unless he changed his name and never went home again. It wasn't worth it, not for sixteen thousand yuan. His anger turned to Liu Yuejin again for not paying him back, but that was also useless, since Liu himself was still looking for *his* pack. Besides, Liu owed him less than four thousand, which was a fourth of what the gang wanted. The more he reflected upon the situation, the more wretched he felt, when he suddenly remembered someone who just might save him.

That was none other than Brother Cao, who controlled the Chaoyang District, an equal of Lao Lai, the head of the Weigong Village gang. Han hoped that Cao could mediate on his behalf with Lai to get a one-month extension. When he arrived at the shed, everyone, including Baldy Cui and Little Fatso, were busy slaughtering ducks, while Cao was reclining in a rattan chair listening to the radio, as a recent cold made it hard for him to read the papers. Cao listened attentively to a news report on the conflict between Israel and Palestine, suicide bombs on one side, air attacks on the other, so Han cowered at the entrance, afraid to interrupt, until Cao snapped off the radio when the news was replaced by celebrity gossip.

"Brother Cao," Han called out by the door.

"Who's that?" Unable to recognize the voice, Cao twisted his head to look.

"It's Shengli, from Henan. I'm here to ask a favor."

"Him again." Cao thought Han was there about Liu's missing pack and said with a frown, "That friend of yours has no sense."

"It's not about that. It's something else." Han walked up and gave Cao a quick rundown of what had happened. At one point he began to tear up, but he held back, knowing that Brother Cao hated weepy people.

"It's your own fault," Cao said. "You can't blame the Xinjiang gang."

"I know. I shouldn't have done it." Han nodded, knowing that Cao was referring to working outside his own area. He continued, "It's not only me who will be in trouble if I don't pay up today. It's Lao Gao I worry about; his son is only six." He relayed the threat to Cao.

"Weigong Village is on the other side of the city. I don't know this Lao Lai you're talking about."

Han's heart sank. "You enjoy great prestige, Brother Cao. He surely has heard of you even if you don't know him. A word from you would be a great help." He added, "I'll pay them back. I just need an extension."

Without responding, Cao lay back down and closed his eyes. After ten minutes, Han thought he must be asleep, which could only mean he didn't want to get involved. Han could not force the issue. Looking around, he saw that all the others were busy dispatching ducks and no one paid him any heed; he knew he had to stay clear of them. It was hopeless. He decided to leave when Brother Cao opened his eyes and called out:

"Lao Cui."

Cui threw down the duck he was working on and wiped his bloody hands on his apron before rushing to Cao's side.

"How much do you owe them?" Cao asked Han.

"I have over five hundred with me, so that makes it sixteen thousand."

"Go see these people," Cao said to Cui, "and take sixteen thousand with you."

Cui was shocked. So was Han, who never imagined that Brother Cao would solve his problem this way. He didn't know the man that well. Baldy Cui stared blankly at Han while Han teared up again.

"Brother Cao."

"It's all right now, Shengli. Go on home."

Han got down on his knees, drawing a frown from Cao, so he quickly got to his feet. He didn't dare say too much, so after expressing his deep appreciation, he left. Still filled with gratitude toward Cao on his way home, Han was now also aware of his empty stomach; and that reminded him of his head injury, which had begun to bother him. Over the past two days he'd been too focused on thievery to pay it much attention. He went to the hospital to have the wound cleaned and rewrapped after a new application of medicine.

On his way home he was seized by the realization that he was done with the Xinjiang gang once Brother Cao paid them back for him, but would then be in Cao's debt, even if Cao was willing to forgive the sixteen thousand. From now on, when he went out to steal, he would be stealing for Cao. It all became clear; Cao was not helping him out of the goodness of his heart. He was much more calculating than Han, that was for sure. But on the other hand, if Cao hadn't intervened, this would be Han's day of reckoning. The help did not come without strings, but it did help him out, at least for now. He'd have to wait and see what happened next between him and Cao.

He didn't have to wait long. Cao sent Little Fatso to summon Han the very next day. When he got there, he saw a man with a face swollen black and blue lying on a bed against the wall. Han was stunned by the bandages all over the man's body and his labored breathing. He walked up to get a closer look. It turned out to be someone he knew, a man from Shanxi known as Yang Zhi, who had run afoul of Cao's people. Han wondered whether Yang had been beaten by Cao's people or by someone else before concluding that it had to be someone else, since Yang was lying in Cao's shed. The severity of the injuries showed how vicious the attackers had been.

"Who did this?" Han blurted out.

Cao ignored his question and took him to the side. "Shengli, I have a favor to ask."

Thinking that Cao wanted him to take part in a fight between the gangs, Han was scared by the prospect of bloodshed, but he couldn't say no, not after the help from Cao just the day before.

"As long as it's something I can do."

"I'm not asking for your help simply because I helped you out yesterday," Cao said with a nod. "I'm not that short-sighted. It's a coincidence and I have no one else to turn to."

An expansive sentiment rose up inside Han, who quickly said:

"I'll do anything, Brother Cao."

"The man, Liu Yuejin, who came with you last time. Is he a good friend of yours?"

Han was mystified by the sudden turn of events and how even Liu was involved.

"He owes me money."

Cao waved. "Let's not talk about that now." He pointed to Yang. "That friend of yours took his purse. I'd like you to go see your friend and get it back."

With enormous relief Han agreed readily. "I thought it was something serious. It's just a purse. No problem at all."

Cao interrupted him with a gesture. "It's not that simple. It's no ordinary purse, and in fact the purse itself is not important. There's a USB drive in it and that's what we want. Bring that drive to me and that will even out what took place yesterday."

A sixteen-thousand-yuan debt erased—what a terrific deal. He could hardly believe it. Thumping his chest, he assured Cao:

"Liu Yuejin owes me money, so he'll have to do what I say. Even if he doesn't want to, he will when I mention your name."

"That's the point." Cao frowned. "If I could get it back myself, why would I ask you? So make sure my name doesn't come up, or you'll alert him."

"I see. We're not going to force him. We'll trick him."

Cao nodded and frowned again, implying that Han was right about the plan, but that it should not be openly talked about like that.

"Go on. It has to be done quickly. Make sure no one else gets there first."

"I'll go see him immediately." Han got up and left.

He discovered it wasn't that simple when he got to the site. Liu had vanished the night before and Ren Baoliang was looking for him.

27

Lao Lin

"Out of control. This is totally out of control."

That was the first thing Lao Lin said when he saw Yan Ge at Lao Qi's Teahouse. Qi, a moon-faced native of Beijing, was on the heavy side. Like Yan, he had adopted a vegetarian diet after turning forty. Yan was pretty casual about the diet, simply preferring to avoid meat, while Lao Qi went all in, and that, strangely, only made him fat. Before the age of forty, he'd been a well-known hooligan in the Houhai area of the city, engaging in every possible vice—booze, women, and gambling. With the change of diet, he also became a devout Buddhist, which, according to him, was the reason he put on weight.

"Amitabha," he would put his palms together and say. "When your mind is at ease, you relax and your body widens."

Yan saw things a bit differently, but had to agree to a certain extent.

Lao Qi's Teahouse, located on a busy corner of Beixinqiao, always smelled of Tibetan incense, with mind-clearing effects on whoever walked in, particularly with the additional chanting of Buddhist sutras piped in. Instead of such ordinary teas as Dragonwell, Oolong, Iron Buddha, or Pu'er, Qi offered only high-mountain holy teas from Tibet, like Zhufeng, Red Hawk, and White Eagle. When asked why, Qi simply replied:

"For the pure land, not for the tea."

At other places, a pot of Dragonwell could be had for under three hundred, while Qi's tea was far more expensive, with a pot of Red Hawk costing seven eighty; White Eagle was eight eighty, and Zhufeng twelve eighty. White Eagle and Zhufeng, when steeped in a pot, did not look much like tea; the leaves were huge with lots of twigs, accompanied by a muddy odor. Which was perhaps why ordinary folks did not frequent his shop. Put more aptly, he had no poor people as customers. The place was usually quiet during the day, but the private rooms on both floors were filled at night. Latecomers had to take a number. Lin had known Qi for eight years, while Yan had gotten to know Qi through Lin.

Lin often joked about Qi's tea. "You call this tea? You say it's tea from Mount Everest, but I think it's more like tree leaves from Mount Fang."

Qi laughed and held his palms together.

"Amitabha, you're right. I'm not here to sell tea, but to rob the rich to help the poor."

Everyone had a good laugh over his response.

In addition to selling tea, Qi told fortunes on the side, though people said that was not connected to his conversion to Buddhism, since he had done that before the age of forty. When you sat down across from him, he surveyed your face and, without recourse to a close scrutiny, told you what had happened thirty years in your past and what would happen thirty years into your future, all together sixty years, an exceptionally arcane gift. Many people came to his teahouse for fortune telling, not for the tea. But he would not tell the fortune of someone who came only a time or two; you had to be there often enough for Qi to know you well before he would impart his knowledge. He explained that this was not a ruse to get people to drink more of his tea. Without knowing someone well, it was hard to determine how much he should say about a person's fortunes.

Lin had come with a friend eight years earlier and, as a favor to that friend, Qi had told Lin's fortune at their first meeting, on the condition that he would focus only on Lin's previous thirty years.

Even at this first meeting Qi was able to see all the important events during that period and gave Lin such a thorough analysis that he was more frightened than impressed. Six months later, he returned for a prediction for the next thirty years, which was equally spine tingling.

Once, on an inspection trip to Inner Mongolia, he and Director Jia were chatting in the hotel when Lin mentioned his experience with Lao Qi. Jia found it very interesting. Following a banquet after their return, Jia asked Lin to take him to Qi's teahouse, where, owing to Lin's connection, Qi agreed to read Jia's fortune. After taking a long look, Qi remained silent, but when urged by Jia, he put his palms together and said:

"Amitabha. Such a terrific fortune, there's no need to even talk about it."

"What game are you playing, Lao Qi? The director is too busy to return ten times for your tea."

Qi just smiled and said, "Heavenly secrets must not be revealed."

They spent the night drinking tea, with no fortunes told. Later Lin brought Yan Ge over, and after ten visits, Yan asked Qi to read his fortune. He received two cryptic lines:

"Spring comes on the sixth nine-day cycle / A drizzle moistens the ground."

The lines were simple enough but impossible to decipher, and Qi refused to explain. To alleviate Yan's concern, Qi said simply:

"It is good."

That stopped Yan from further inquiry. Lin and Yan's early visits had involved the telling of fortunes, but after that they returned mostly because it was quiet in the day and lively at night. As time went by, it seemed natural to come this way whenever they had no dinner plan or after they'd eaten. "Where to?" "Lao Qi's Teahouse."

So that became their favorite meeting place, especially now that they were anxious to locate a USB drive that had reunited them after a near terminal fall-out. It had taken a week to find the thief, but no USB drive. Then another thief was caught, and still no drive. In turn they were contacted by a blackmailer. When Liu Yuejin ran away from the Sijiqing Bridge, they discovered that he was the one with the drive, but it was too late, because he vanished. Everyone, including Yan and Lin, even Lao Xing the private investigator and Yang Zhi, who had been severely beaten, was kicking himself for not sensing early enough that the real thief was right under their nose.

"You found him but let him get away," Yan grumbled to Xing. "How fitting is that for an agency that calls itself 'Worried Wise Men'?"

"I know what you mean." Xing sighed. "I never imagined that a cook could be so good at keeping his cool." Then he tried to console Yan. "But worrying about it now is a waste of time. I'll keep looking for him."

Yan was so mad he could cry. "No need to worry? It'll be too late if he delivers the thing to the wrong place."

Obviously he had hired the wrong PI and had only himself to blame.

Upon hearing that a cook had the drive, but no one could find him, Lin was worried for reasons different from Yan. They agreed to meet at three o'clock at Lao Qi's Teahouse. Yan got there first to find the place peaceful and quiet and the owner nowhere in sight. Lao Qi had told everyone that he stayed home to read sutras in the day because his evenings were taken up running the teahouse, but his wife said she never saw him reading a sutra. He was always sleeping.

"Well, you sleep when you're tired. What's wrong with that?" Qi argued.

Lin arrived shortly after Yan and started complaining about how everything was out of control as soon as they sat down in a private room. "But then again it's not a bad thing that the cook has disappeared."

The surprised look on Yan's face made Lin hasten to add, "At least we know the drive is with him, and not someone else."

Yan nodded his agreement.

"The problem is, we don't know if the cook has seen what's on it. Your wife said it's not password protected. If he hasn't opened it, all we need to worry about is getting it back, but if he has, then so much more will be at stake."

Alerted to something he hadn't thought of, Yan was petrified, but his dismay quickly turned to fury.

"I can't believe she'd do something like this to me." He pounded on the table. "I could kill her."

When he finally calmed down, he said, "A cook probably doesn't know a thing about a computer drive."

"Don't rely on luck for things like this. We have to be prepared for the worst."

Wiping the sweat from his forehead, Yan nodded and said:

"Since we're here, why don't we get Lao Qi over to see if he can help us locate the cook and maybe even tell us when we can get the thing back."

"Lao Qi's tricks work only for people without problems." Lin shook his head. "He's useless when you're in trouble. Just about everybody knows of the drive by now, so there's no need to drag him into this."

"You see things more clearly than I do," Yan said, obviously impressed.

"I wish that were true!" Lin sighed. "It's like closing the gate after the sheep are gone. A clear thinker would have slaughtered the sheep and be gnawing on bones by now. That's what's troubling Director Jia."

Lin went on to tell Yan that Jia had flown to Europe five days earlier and would be back in five more days. They had to find the cook and retrieve the drive before his return. Yan had been given ten days and would be given an extension of five days. If they could not recover it, they'd perish together when the contents went public; even if that didn't happen, Jia would decide what to do and Lin could no longer help Yan out. From the look on Yan's face, Lin knew that Yan thought Jia had gone abroad to avoid possible fallout.

"Director Jia went abroad to avoid other problems, not this one," he corrected him.

Then Lin complained about the useless investigative agency Yan had engaged, in particular the unreliable PI. With someone like him, they'd be better off not finding the drive. They had to get personally involved now that it had reached this point.

"Are they here?" he asked Yan.

"They're here, waiting in my car."

Yan placed a call, and a moment later his driver walked in with two men, Ren Baoliang, who had been asked by Brother Cao to look up Liu Yuejin at the site, and Han Shengli, who had been detained by Ren. Liu was nowhere to be found. Once Yan knew that he had the drive, he'd called Ren and told him to find the cook within two days. If he was successful, Yan would give Ren the construction funds; if not, Ren would be fired, since he had hired the cook, and was responsible for the theft. But how was he supposed to find Liu if he didn't want to be found? He might still be in Beijing, or he could have gone back to Henan or some other place. Ren had no idea where to start.

When Han came on his own looking for Liu, Ren detained him, but not because he thought Han knew where Liu was. In Ren's reasoning, the cook and Han were close friends, and that was where the problem lay: Liu had been an upright person before meeting Han, whose negative influence had turned him into a petty thief who stole from the dining hall. Worse yet, he'd now evolved into a thief who had victimized Mr. Yan. So Han should also be held responsible. Ren had forgotten that Liu had not stolen Qu Li's purse; he'd found it. He believed that all thieves thought alike, so Han ought to be better at guessing what was going through Liu's mind and figuring out where he might be. In fact, Han was completely in the dark. He hadn't known about Liu finding the purse until Brother Cao told him only moments before, and it wasn't until he came to the site that he learned of Liu's disappearance. In a word, he knew less than Ren. But Ren would not let him off the hook, forcing him to hunker down and think.

"I know where he's hiding," Han finally offered.

"Where?" Ren was overjoyed. "Show me where I can find him and I'll give you a thousand yuan."

That was unexpected. A thousand yuan wasn't a lot of money, but something was certainly up. Brother Cao would cancel his debt of sixteen thousand if he found Liu, and now someone else was offering him money to do the same. Prior to this, Han had only managed to get two hundred after coming to see Liu daily for the thirty-four hundred he was owed. Who'd have thought he'd be given money once the cook disappeared? Liu had actually brought him good fortune, a much better deal than stealing. In the meantime, he was aware that the vanished cook was no longer the person he once knew; that one was a shrimp of a man and the new cook was a big fish, all because of the purse he'd found. Han had been in the thievery business for many years; why had he never found a purse like that? The unfairness led to another thought: Now that Liu was a big fish, it would be wrong to give him up too easily. A thousand yuan was not going to do it.

"I was just talking." Han pretended to look troubled. "It's hard to say if we can find him or not."

Seeing that Han was obviously not going to take him to find Liu yet, Ren raised the offer to two thousand. He still refused to go, making Ren suspect that Han might not know Liu's whereabouts and was simply trying to con him. Han got to his feet, but Ren would not let him go, fearing that Han might really have the information. Eventually he decided to call Yan Ge, who then relayed the news to Lin. Lin took it seriously and asked to meet with Han. Yan told his driver to pick them up and bring the pair to Lao Qi's Teahouse, where they were to wait in the car until summoned by Yan.

Neither Han nor Ren had ever been to a teahouse before. After ushering them into the private room, Little Bai turned and left, leaving the pair to deal with Yan and Lin alone. Han looked at the men before him, both wearing glasses, but one fat and the other skinny; their attire told him that they were rich and probably powerful. Ren did know one of them, as he pointed at Han and said to the skinny one:

"Here he is, Mr. Yan. At first he said he knew where Liu was, but then he denied it. I think he could use a good beating to straighten him out." He continued, "Not long ago, he came to see Liu Yuejin every day. Liu wasn't a thief until he met this guy."

"Who are you talking about?" Han cut in. "I don't know if Liu Yuejin steals, but I certainly don't."

Ren was getting worked up. "Every man, woman, and child in Henan knows you're a thief. If you didn't steal anything, why'd you get such a beating?"

They were starting to get into it, so Yan stopped Ren. "You can go on back now. We don't need you here anymore."

It was embarrassing to be dismissed like that, after bringing Han over, but he had no choice but to follow Yan's order. Dragging his feet, unwilling to go quietly, once he was out the door, he turned to say:

"Mr. Yan, what about the construction funds?"

"Next week," Yan said with a frown.

With Ren gone, the fat man told Han to sit beside him.

"You're a good friend of Liu Yuejin?" the man asked Han affably.

This being his first time in a place like this, Han did not know what to do or say, but he could tell that the two men were also looking for Liu. A quick count told him this was group number five, and they were clearly high-class people. The matter was getting more serious by the minute. It seemed that Liu was not just a big fish; he was a shark. Han was frightened by the ever-growing scale of the search and began to backtrack.

"Ren Baoliang made it all up." Han decided to play dumb. "I do know Liu Yuejin, but we're not friends. We're enemies. He owes me money."

"It's great he's your enemy." The fat man laughed. "You always work harder when you're trying to find an enemy."

Han hadn't expected the fat man to have anticipated his lie and even have a response ready, which told him that he was no match for the fat guy.

"Liu didn't tell me where he was going to hide out."

Ignoring him, the fat man continued:

"Go find him and get the purse. I'll give you twenty thousand if nothing is missing from the purse."

Twenty thousand! That was more than he owed Brother Cao. This was the third time someone had offered him money, and that really scared him. He was reluctant, not because he was afraid he might be in big trouble if the matter got even more serious, but because he wasn't sure he could find Liu. He had a pretty good idea where he might be hiding, but if he wasn't certain, he'd likely end up paying, even with his life, for something he couldn't accomplish or for money he shouldn't have accepted. He was reminded of the theft in Weigong Village that he should not have carried out; he'd learned his lesson well. More importantly, he'd gone looking for Brother Cao, who had helped him out and would erase his debt once Liu was located. In Han's view, Brother Cao and his people were harder to deal with than the others, and that went beyond money owed. On the other hand, he couldn't say no to these two men, who could also cause him trouble, so eventually he found a way out.

"I can help you find him, but based on our code, you have to give me a ten-thousand-yuan deposit."

He'd hoped that they'd refuse, worried that Han, someone they'd never met before, would flee with their money. If they refused, he'd be free. To his surprise, the skinny man, Mr. Yan, reached for his satchel and took out a stack of money.

"I'll give you another ten when you bring me the purse," Yan said as he tossed him the money, "plus another ten as a bonus."

Han was bowled over. People had been after him for money; that was bad enough. Now people wanted to give him money. Owing money was a real dilemma. So, it seemed, was receiving it.

28

Lao Qi

Han Shengli left after they were finished. When Lao Lin and Yan Ge reached the stairs, Lin said to Yan:

"You go on ahead. I need to use the toilet."

Yan walked down the stairs, while Lin went to the men's room, where he took out his cell phone and dialed a number.

"Follow him."

It was unclear whether he was talking about Han or Yan. Then he turned to use the toilet; after a feeble attempt at what he came to do, he walked out and ran into Lao Qi, who had just come from home, sleepy eyed, shuffling along with a book in his hand. Lin thought it must be a Buddhist sutra, but it was a thread-bound volume of *Dream of the Red Chamber*. Lao Qi, a Master Practitioner of Buddhism, should not be reading a book like that, Lin said to himself. But he had no time to deal with that. Reminded of Yan's suggestion to ask Qi for information on the thief and the USB drive, which Lin had rejected, now that he was alone it wouldn't hurt to go ahead. He stopped Qi and led him back into the private room, where he told Qi about their search.

"As the saying goes, everything is nothing and nothingness is everything." Qi cast him a glance and said, "Why bother to look for it?"

Everything and nothingness, two words from the *Heart Sutra*. Lin felt like laughing. A popular saying? Really? But he said with a straight face:

"I'm not joking, Lao Qi. We have to find it."

Qi glanced at him again and said casually, "It'll be over soon."

Knowing that Qi was not serious, Lin nonetheless was relieved to hear that it would be over soon, like a sick man who will go see any doctor. Later, when it was indeed all over, Lin would recall what Qi had said and break out in a cold sweat.

29

Liu Yuejin

Brother Cao's people caught Liu Yuejin, but not because of Han Shengli.

Han had never been sure whether he could find Liu, though he did know two places Liu would go if he decided to stay in Beijing. If Liu left the city, then there was no way he could find the man again. After agreeing to search for both Cao and Yan, Han now had two "masters" to serve, and he worried himself sick over which one to deliver Liu to even before he found him. Since he could not get out of the deal with either side, he forced himself to start searching and wait to see what happened; under the assumption that Liu was still in town, he went to check out those two places. He'd decide who to hand him over to later.

The first place that came to mind was everyone's first choice—the Manli Hair Salon. Back when he was badgering Liu for the money owed, if he wasn't at the dining hall, he was sure to be at Manli's place. Han had always wondered if there was something going on between Liu and Ma, and after some furtive and careful observations, he reached the conclusion that they were not involved. If they had been, he wouldn't have been going to see her all the time, and Han had had a secret laugh over Liu's fruitless effort. Which was also why, in Han's analysis, Liu would not now be hiding there. Too obvious, too close to the work site, and everyone knew he'd been seeing her. Liu couldn't be that stupid. And, given the lack of a relationship, she wouldn't let him stay there.

On the other hand, nothing had been progressing logically, so Han decided to pay her a visit, just to make sure. After leaving Lao Qi's Teahouse, he got to Manli's Hair Salon after one subway and three bus rides. It was late in the afternoon, about dinnertime, so the salon was empty except for Yang Yuhuan, who was lying in a chair texting, her chubby legs resting on the barber's stand. Nothing seemed amiss in the quiet shop. Han got an idea for something else and went into the back room after signaling Yang with his eyes. The ten thousand from Yan had stiffened his back and more; it went smoothly for him. When they were done and she was getting up, he roped his arms around her naked body and asked in a feigned casual air:

"Has Liu Yuejin been here lately, Yuhuan?"

He knew that she disliked Liu for hanging around the hair salon and scaring away her clients. She wouldn't cover for him, he was sure of that. Pushing him off, she got up and started getting dressed.

"No, I haven't seen him."

"Do you know where he is?"

"He's not my boyfriend, why ask me?" She glared at him. "Go to the dining hall."

Her retort told him that she knew nothing about what had been happening to Liu. He got dressed, and when he came out into the shop, Manli stepped in with a bag of chicken necks.

"I wonder where Liu Yuejin is." Han pretended to look lost. "I found the thief who took his pack."

He stole a glance to see if she reacted differently when she heard Liu's name, but she ignored him and walked to the sink to wash the necks, seemingly unconcerned. That could only mean one thing: Liu was not there. Besides, it was a small place, with two rooms; where would he hide, anyway?

The other place, known only to Han, was Lao Gao's noodle shop in Weigong Village. Lao Gao was the man he'd talked into being a guarantor after he was caught stealing by the Uighur gang. The three of them, Han, Gao, and Liu, were all from Luoshui, Henan, and Han knew that Liu and Gao were close, for he'd run into Liu many times at Gao's diner. It usually took Liu two hours, changing buses five or six times, to get there on weekends when the traffic was light; on weekdays, the trip would take at least three hours, and sometimes five. Han had seen Liu at Gao's place even on weekdays, which told him that the two were unusually close. Moreover, they could be smoking side by side without saying a word, and yet Han could tell they knew what the other person was thinking. If Liu was there at night, he'd get up around ten to catch the last bus, and Gao would walk him to the door,

"Be careful crossing the street."

"I won't be here next week," Liu might say before striding off.

If he was there on a busy day, he would toss away his cigarette and help out in the kitchen. Han had thought they got along well because they were both cooks and from the same city. Gao contradicted him by saying that he and Liu had worked for a restaurant back in Luoshui, but had never seen eye to eye. Once, when half a bucket of cooking oil went missing in the kitchen, Gao and Liu suspected each other and had an argument, after which they didn't speak for two weeks. Later they left for Beijing one after the other and worked at different places; they missed seeing and talking to each other if they stayed away for ten days or a couple of weeks. Now they both laughed whenever the incident at Luoshui came up. Lao Gao's noodle diner was the only place left for Liu to hide; he might even be cooking noodles for Gao at the moment.

After leaving the Manli Hair Salon, Han headed straight for Weigong Village. For over a week, he'd dreaded the thought of the area because of his debt to the Xinjiang gang, but now that Cao had taken care of the money, he felt he could come with his head held high. Gao was out buying groceries, Han was told. So he first checked the place out and saw no sign of Liu inside or outside the diner. Gao might have hidden Liu elsewhere, he said to himself. When Gao saw Han, he threw down a bunch of celery and, before Han could ask about Liu, began to rail at him about the Xinjiang gang.

"Wasn't that taken care of already?" Han was taken aback.

"Yours, yes," Gao glowered at him, "but my troubles are just beginning."

Since agreeing to be Han's guarantor, the Xinjiang gang visited Gao every time Han failed to pay on time; the gang's children pestered Gao's son. In addition to selling Uighur knives or shining shoes on the street, these young Uighurs now took on the extra job of stopping Gao's son for money. If he had none, they'd beat him up; if he had less than twenty yuan on him, they'd beat him up. He'd suffered five beatings so far, and he wouldn't leave the house if he didn't have twenty yuan in his pocket, even after Brother Cao had paid off Han's debt. The adult affair had been resolved; but the children refused to put on the brakes. The day before, when Gao's son went out to buy a lollypop, he was stopped and beaten again, so scaring him he didn't go to school today.

"This is outrageous." Han was incensed. "They breached our agreement. I'm going to tell Brother Cao."

Gao had no idea who Brother Cao was.

"You're the one who brought me all the trouble," he said. "So starting tomorrow, you walk my son to school and pick him up afterward. You don't have anything to do anyway."

"I'm awfully busy," Han muttered.

He told Gao it was all Liu Yuejin's fault. If Liu hadn't owed Han money, Han would have been able to pay the Xinjiang gang and they wouldn't be harassing Gao and his son. His scenario was, of course, far from the truth, for Liu only owed him a portion of what he had had to pay the Xinjiang gang. He was eager to find Liu, which to him was more important than the abuse of Gao's son, so he took out two hundred yuan and slammed it on the table.

"Here, give this to your son. Two hundred, enough to get out of ten beatings, all right? If they keep at it, I'll use a knife to show them what I'm made of."

Gao stared blankly at the money, confused by Han's move.

"Go find Liu Yuejin and tell him to pay me back. If he does, I'll give you a thousand as compensation for your mental anguish. You'll not be my guarantor for nothing."

Convinced that Han was okay, Gao fell for his ruse.

"You wait here. I'll go get him at the construction site."

Gao took off his apron to leave, which told Han that Liu was not hiding at Gao's place. In fact, Gao didn't even know that Liu was missing. Obviously Gao knew less than he did and was totally useless.

"When was the last time he was here?" Han stopped Gao.

"More than two weeks," Gao cried out when he thought back. "But he owes you money, so why is he hiding from me?"

The look on Gao's face showed that he truly was in the dark. Deflated, Han scooped up the money from the table and walked out.

So Liu wasn't at Manli's place or at Gao's diner. Han concluded that Liu had fled Beijing, which was fine with him. Everyone, including Brother Cao, the two upper-class strangers at Qi's Teahouse, and Ren Baoliang, was in a hurry to find Liu, but not him, not Han Sheng-li, because he benefited from a missing Liu Yuejin. He had already been paid by two parties and would spend the money as he saw fit. In fact, it would only bring him more trouble if he did manage to locate Liu, since he wouldn't know who to deliver him to.

Han relayed his failed search to both Brother Cao and Yan Ge, who seemed to get even more on edge. He went along, knowing full well that the two parties were eager to find Liu for different reasons, knowledge of which he would keep to himself.

And yet, Liu Yuejin was caught, but by Brother Cao's people, not Han Shengli. It was the injured Yang Zhi, whose life was spared because the USB drive was a fake, who found him. As Little Bai and others were chasing Liu at the peddlers' market, Yang struggled to flee but was stopped by one of Bai's people left to guard him.

"He's a con man. No point keeping him around," Qu Li had said and saved his life.

Yang dragged himself away and fled in a taxi. He was enormously grateful to the fake USB drive and to the woman, and his two broken ribs led to unexpected results. First, they helped him make up his mind to work for Cao, though he couldn't go out to work with broken ribs for a while and needed a place to recuperate. He could have gone back to the Shijingshan area and stayed with the Shanxi gang for a while. But that was a small place with few prospects and, taking a long view, he knew he had to aim high if he was looking for the best locale to pin his future on.

That said, it really didn't matter which side he went to. The critical factor was which side was better at helping him find the genuine drive, which had proved to be a valuable commodity from his extortion attempt. It was a profitable enterprise he couldn't pass up, and those few petty thieves from Shanxi wouldn't be much help in locating the cook and the USB drive. Brother Cao was the man to go to when a major deal was involved, not to mention the fact that he owed Cao's people a gambling debt. After serious consideration, he decided he'd help them search for the USB drive and reap the reward, with a percentage for him. He'd be able to pay off his debt.

So he went to Cao's shed, where he stayed in bed to recover, during which time he sensed a stirring between his legs. It must have been the beating that helped him forget his problem, or it could have been that his problem was driven away during the beating. In any case, the thing seemed to be working again, a pleasant surprise for Yang, who now thought it was worth all the injury. To him it was more important than locating the drive, for he was himself again. Though he was laid up, his mind began to work once more, and he started to ponder Liu's whereabouts. Finally, early one morning, he came up with a place.

First, he determined that the cook was still in Beijing, but not because of the USB drive. From his experience working with Liu on the extortion attempt with Qu Li, Yang could tell that the cowardly cook was more worried about his pack and the IOU. He was, in a word, someone who focused on trivial matters and ignored the big picture. If he could tell what was important, he would have been able to see that the drive was the reason Yang had been assaulted. Left alone, he was not brave enough to continue the extortion. To be sure, he would flee Beijing to avoid capture, but precisely because he only worried about insignificant matters—the IOU and the sixty thousand—he would stick around to look for the pack. Cowardly in critical matters and daring in the trivial—cowardly where others were concerned but fearless when it was about himself. After a detailed analysis, Yang knew what was going on in Liu's head, making it easy to figure out where he'd find him.

Yang was right. Liu hadn't left Beijing, but, as Yang had surmised, had stuck around to search for his pack. After watching what was on the drive that night, Manli had told him to clear out of the construction site and the city of Beijing, since what was on it could cost them their lives. For his sake, as well as for herself, she advised against returning to Henan; someone might trace his roots back to his hometown and catch him there. But Liu did not heed her advice, at least not all of it. After parting with her, he changed his mind, only taking half of her suggestion to slip away from the site. His worry over not finding the IOU and the likelihood that Li Gengsheng would break his promise trumped his fear of the potential harm from the drive. If he hadn't known who had his pack he might have given up and skipped town, but he had the tenuous clue that the Gansu gang had taken it. From following Yang Zhi, he also knew where their den was; it was simply too good a chance to pass up. Which was more important, his life or the pack?

He thought long and hard and struck middle ground; he had to look for it, but not for too long. Three days. He'd give himself three days; whether he found the bag nor not, he'd have to leave after three days.

With that settled, he needed a place to stay for the time being. Like Han, he had thought of Manli's place and Gao's diner, but he decided against these two options, even though he didn't believe Manli or Gao would sell him out or that Manli would be upset with him for not taking her advice. It was simply because Liu was a different person now, and his life hung in the balance. Neither place was safe. So where would he be safe? Not at a friend's place, but somewhere no one would think of, and there had better be a crowd.

Where else but the train station? He could hide among the swarm of passengers and shout for help if something happened. That was why he ended up sleeping among strangers at West Station at night when he was not looking for his pack.

It was not, however, West Station where Cao's people caught him. Yang Zhi, like Han Shengli, had considered many places, but not the train station. He had, however, thought of one place Han had not thought of; like Liu, Yang recalled the place he'd been robbed by the Gansu gang. Liu had followed Yang to the little room and, not knowing that the gang had moved to a different location, would want to go back there to wait for them. Yang relayed his speculation to Brother Cao, who then told Baldy Cui to take some men to that lane in the eastern suburb. Cui knew the area well, as it was where he had stopped Yang and forced him to make the delivery to Beethoven Villa.

Yang guessed right. At night, Liu slinked over to the little room, only to be greeted by a locked door. Disappointed but unwilling to give up, he was about to hunker down to wait when Cui and his people ambushed him. Caught off guard, Liu thought that Cao's people had come after him for something else. He'd have told them not to interfere with his business if he hadn't noticed that they were ordered not to talk to him. He decided he'd better not cross them.

When they returned to the shed and Brother Cao mentioned the USB drive, Liu realized that there were yet other people searching for it. Known for his meticulousness, Cao took his time detailing to Liu how his capture had come about, stressing that the purse was not important. All he wanted was the USB drive. Everything would be fine if Liu would just hand it over.

It was now clear to Liu that Cao had not seen the drive; he wanted it for money, obviously unaware of its lethal contents. It was not a drive; it was a time bomb. But Liu did not know how to tell that to Cao or describe his own predicament; how could he tell the man that it was for his own good that he should not have the drive? If he did, it would be like strapping a time bomb on Cao. It wasn't that Liu was afraid Cao would be in big trouble; it was just that he knew he'd suffer collateral damage once people knew that the USB drive had come from him.

He decided to play dumb, telling Cao he hadn't found a purse, let alone something called a USB drive. Cao did not believe him, naturally, and told him to think harder, so everyone would come out fine. Liu continued to lie, saying that, with so many people after the drive, he would have turned it over if he had it. He was a cook and a computer drive was useless to him, he added. Cao sighed and walked out with his hands behind his back. With him gone, Cui and others hung Liu up and tried to beat an answer out of him. Han Shengli joined in, hitting Liu harder than anyone else, for no other reason than he'd lost face by misjudging Liu's intention.

Liu had not fled Beijing, and so Han had failed the first task entrusted to him by Brother Cao, which was almost as if the payment to the Xinjiang gang was made for nothing. Brother Cao didn't say a word about it, but Han felt uneasy, so he gave Liu extra kicks and slapped him a few more times than the others to vent his anger and make up for his oversight. The viciousness shocked not only Liu, but Cao's people, who knew that Han and Liu were good friends.

"That bastard has no regard for old friendships." Baldy Cui could not hide his amazement.

Liu was beaten black and blue, with blood over all his face, but he held fast to his original story, that he hadn't found a purse, let alone a USB drive. Cao's people were left with no choice but to keep up with the torture. Han even began to enjoy himself and picked up a board to strike Liu when Cao strode in and stopped everyone. Still suffering from a cold, he came up to Liu to size him up with his watery eyes. Liu cowered instinctively as he thought Cao was about to hit him, but Cao simply patted him on the cheek.

"You'll have my respect if you stick to your story after we hang you up overnight." He wiped his eyes with a tissue and said to everyone else, "It's getting late. Go home and get some sleep."

"You stay here to watch him," Cao ordered Little Fatso.

The others left, all but Little Fatso, who objected to the task Cao had given him. Unable to do so openly, he vented his anger on Liu by picking up a rag from the chopping board and stuffing it into Liu's mouth.

30

Little Fatso

Liu Yuejin passed out.

It was the fourth time in his life he'd done that. The first was in 1960, when he was two, and many people in his village had died of starvation during China's worst famine. Liu had a maternal uncle, a thief, who was the sole reason Liu survived. The farmers guarded what little was left in the fields like hawks, so his uncle was not always successful in finding food, and Liu had fainted from hunger. The second incident occurred after Li Gengsheng beat him when he caught his wife in bed with Li. That was the result of anger. The third time was a few days before, when Yang Zhi told him that his pack had been taken by the Gansu gang; the tension was too much for him. Now in Cao's shed, he lost consciousness after they hung him up from a beam in the shed; with his body suspended and circulation cut off, he began to gasp for air, especially with the rag in his mouth.

Not wanting him to scream for help, Little Fatso had stuffed his mouth with a rag used to wipe the cleaver after slaughtering ducks. The stench of rancid blood knocked Liu out. Strangely, he had a dream in which he seemed to have returned to years before his divorce. He and his wife were walking in a marketplace with their son, who was five or six at the time. It was thronged with people, and they lost sight of the boy; then, even his wife was missing. He panicked, but his feet refused to move; he wanted to call out but no sound came. Finally when he woke up, he had no idea where he was. It took him a while to recall that he was in Cao's shed and slowly pieced everything together to get a grip on his current situation. The lights were on in the shed, and Little Fatso was snoring away in Cao's rattan chair. Next to Liu was the cage where Cao's mynah bird had been jumping up and down because, with its ears sealed, it had night and day all mixed up. Finally tired of leaping around, it stuck its head through the slats to observe Liu and, when it saw him wake up, greeted him:

"Happy New Year."

Liu was startled by the greeting, but he had no time for the bird; instead, he kicked his legs hard and tried to scream through the rag, finally waking up Little Fatso, who came up to remove the rag.

"Water," Liu said, breathing hard. "I'm dying of thirst."

Little Fatso looked at him and picked up Cao's mug to give him some water. Liu gulped down as much as he could.

"I need a toilet," he said when Fatso was about to stuff his mouth again.

"Go ahead. There are only the two of us here."

Obviously Little Fatty would be happy to see him pee in his pants.

"Number two," Liu said, and added, when Fatty looked at him, "I'll do it here if you don't mind the smell."

Fatty gave Liu's comment some thought before untying the rope to lower Liu. He pulled down Liu's pants after bringing over the plastic basin used to catch duck's blood.

"What about my hands? Do you want to wipe me when I'm done?"

"What if you run away?"

"How would I run in this state?" Liu continued, "We've gotten to know one another and I wouldn't get you in trouble after you tried to help me."

After thinking it over, Fatty got a knife from the chopping board, freed Liu's hands, and pressed the knife up close to him.

"Don't get any ideas or I'll use this on you."

With his hands free, Liu knew that Fatty was no longer a threat, so he leaned forward while pulling up his pants.

"Tell you the truth, little brother. I don't want to live any more, so come on, do me a favor, kill me now."

Fatty backed off, his face bright red from irritation.

"Don't push me. Or I'll do it."

Liu snatched the knife out of Fatty's hand.

"Who are you kidding? You can't even kill a duck, and now you're going to kill me?" He wasn't done yet. "In the state I'm in, I could kill anyone, you included."

He kicked Fatty to the ground, tied him up, stuffed the rag in his mouth, and hung him up by the birdcage. Then he took off his bloodied clothes and put on a set of Cao's clothes that had been draped over a rope. When that was done, he reached into Fatty's pocket and came out with a couple of hundred yuan, which he stuffed into his pocket. He tucked away the knife, cautiously opened the door, and looked around to make sure he was safe before taking off running.

He had no idea that at the moment he escaped, Baldy Cui and two of his lackeys crept out from behind the shed and began to follow him.

31

Fang Junde

Liu Yuejin ran to Manli's Hair Salon, not for a place to hide, but to tell her that, after the beating at Cao's shed, he realized he had to stop looking for his pack or he'd lose his life along with it. The people who caught and beat him belonged to one group, and who knows how many more groups were out there looking for him. He had thought his lost pack was more important than the purse he'd found, which was why he'd stayed in Beijing. Now it was clear that whatever was in the purse trumped the stuff in his pack. Objects are like people; you can think what you want about yourself, but only other people can validate your worth. Now he truly regretted not taking Manli's advice; had he left Beijing earlier, he would not have experienced the hairy episode at Cao's shed, but he wasn't going there to confess his regret. He wanted to talk to her about the drive.

Cao and his people would discover his escape soon enough; if they caught him again, they wouldn't stop at hanging him up. More likely, they'd kill him. He was going there in spite of the danger to give her a message. Back in Henan, he'd learned the phrase "deliver the message despite the danger" in local drum narratives. The story settings were normally a battlefield, an imperial palace, a prison, or the execution ground in pre-modern China. Who could have predicted that he would be in a similar situation during peaceful times in the modern era? He could only say he was destined for something extraordinary.

After the physical abuse he'd suffered at the shed, he wasn't thinking clearly, and the flight only confused him more; he actually ran down two lanes before realizing he was heading the wrong way. When he turned to double back, he saw shadowy figures in the next lane over and ducked into a neighboring lane to hide. He broke out in a cold sweat at the realization that he'd grown a tail when he left the shed. Earlier he'd congratulated himself on getting away, but was puzzled over how Cao would let him escape so easily by leaving only the worthless Fatty to guard him. He'd been in too much of a hurry to get away to give it much thought at the time; now it all made sense. It was a setup. Cao had meant for him to slip away, so they could follow him to the drive.

An idea crept into his head: he'd pretend not to notice the tail and continue running. If they knew that he knew that they were following him, they'd grab him and take him back to the shed, but he could still be on the lam if they thought he was unaware of them. He'd think of something on the way to get out of this jam. After leaving the lane, he made a sudden change of direction and, instead of heading for Manli's place, ran onto a busy street heavy with late-night traffic. He went straight for a bus stop, where people waiting for the bus gave him a degree of protection. A bus arrived just as he got there; he jumped on and headed toward West Station.

He made it to the station without a hitch, not because he was alert enough to discover his tail or clever enough to pretend he hadn't seen them. From the moment he jumped onto the bus to his arrival at the train station, he changed buses three times and each time ran the risk of being caught by Baldy Cui and his lackeys, who had wanted to seize him when they saw him getting on the bus. They did not know where he was going, but it seemed obvious that he was going to retrieve the drive, and more than once they had a chance to catch him when he changed buses. When he first sprinted out of the alley, the bus and he arrived at the stop at the same time, but the same timeliness did not prevail the next time, and he had to wait for the bus. He waited for half an hour the third time and there was still no bus, so he hailed a taxi, afraid that the longer he waited the more likely he'd be caught.

On their part, Baldy Cui and his lackeys could have grabbed him any time they wanted. They could have done it even on the bus; with a knife pressed against him, he wouldn't dare make a sound, and the driver and ticket seller would keep their mouths shut as well. Liu made it safely to West Station, not because of his own cleverness but because of a man called Fang Junde.

Like Lao Xing, Fang was a PI from Nothing Amiss Investigative Agency, but unlike Xing, who focused on extramarital affairs and marriages on the rocks, Fang specialized in personal vendettas, breaking arms and legs. Xing's agency was publically registered, while Fang's was an underground operation. Like Cao, Xing and Fang had both been hired to find the drive, Xing by Yan Ge and Fang by Lao Lin. When they learned that a cook had the USB drive, and no one could find him, Lin was unhappy with Yan for hiring the wrong PI, so he got Han Shengli to look for Liu, while privately engaging Fang Junde to follow Han Shengli, bypassing Yan Ge to get to Liu Yuejin first. He did not want Liu and the drive falling into Han's hands. It was a complicated scheme that involved even more people than before, but Lin would not be under anyone's thumb if the double-cross succeeded. In a word, the upside outstripped the downside. It was like the Chinese story in which a mantis trying to catch a cicada is unaware of an oriole lying in wait.

By following Han Shengli, Fang Junde located Cao's shed and had the place watched day and night. Eventually that paid off. Cao's people nabbed Liu Yuejin with the help of Yang Zhi, but, not knowing much about Cao, Fang decided to stay hidden. He had a chance to go for Liu when he escaped, until he saw Baldy and his lackeys following Liu, which told him that Liu had been set up. He had to stop Baldy's group before they could get to Liu. So, while Liu was busy changing buses and Baldy's group was about to run out from under a bridge to pounce on him, Fang and his buddy blocked their way. It was apparent to Baldy that the two men did not mean well, but he mistook them as muggers who should have known better. Too preoccupied with catching Liu, Baldy did not bother talking to them before whipping out a knife, the sight of which brought out pistols from Fang and his buddy. Overwhelmed by superior firepower, Baldy froze. Knowing he'd met his match, he put the knife away and said:

"Tell us if it's money you want. We have a job to do."

"We don't want money; we want him," Fang said, pointing at Liu, who was waiting at a bus stop.

It was another group after Liu but, of course, Baldy had no idea on whose order.

"We're all in this together, so can't we work something out?"

"No way." Fang shook his head and pointed the pistol at them. "Now get lost."

Baldy Cui had been around long enough to know that Fang was no soft touch, even though the man did not raise his voice or show any emotion; he was clearly someone who meant what he said. So Cui and his buddies left with their tails between their legs.

32

Lao Xing

Liu Yuejin walked into the West Station waiting room, where all the seats—even the floor—were taken up by sleeping travelers. He knew he was safe when he saw a policeman on night patrol yawning grandly as he paced the place. Like a startled rabbit returning to its warren, Liu finally managed to calm down. But the policeman noticed Liu's panicky, bloody face and grew suspicious. He ordered him to stop from across the way. Threading his way through the sleeping crowd, he strode over and sized Liu up.

"What happened to you?"

For Liu at that moment, police meant a safe haven, but he didn't dare breathe a word about his situation. He'd lost a pack and found a purse with a USB drive in it, for which he'd been chased, beaten up, nearly killed. But he'd also taken part in an extortion scheme, which added more complications to an already convoluted story, one he couldn't possibly explain coherently. Besides, he had business to take care of, and had to keep avoiding the men stalking him. Talking to the cop would only create further delay. Yet he had to account for his injured face; he had a brainstorm.

"My wife ran away and I've been looking for her for two weeks. Last night I found the two of them at Wangfujing, but damned if the guy didn't beat me up. I can't let that be the end of it."

He wasn't lying, technically, except for the time and place; everything he said had happened to him, and talking about it now brought back the sad memories. Compounded by what had happened over the past few days, it no longer felt like lying.

"Help me get them," he said, grabbing the cop's hand. "I want revenge."

The cop was unprepared for Liu's story, but with his misery-laden face, he didn't look like a thief or worse.

"Let go of me." He tried to shake off Liu's hands. "It's a domestic affair, not serious enough to get the police involved."

He yawned again and waddled off.

Liu bought a phone card to make a hurried call to Manli, not to talk about the USB drive, but about a canvas bag he'd left at her place the day he fled the construction site. It contained his belongings, including a Western suit with a business card in the pocket. Lao Xing had left Liu his card the day he came with Ren Baoliang and Liu denied finding a purse. Liu remembered Xing and the card when he was at West Station waiting for an early morning train back to Henan. Manli had advised against staying in Beijing or returning to Henan. Liu did not heed her first suggestion and was nearly caught by Cao's people, yet he ignored the second half and chose to go back to Henan. He planned what he'd do back home, which was why Xing came to mind. It was still about his lost pack.

In Liu's reasoning, Lao Xing had seen the thieves who took Liu's pack, first Yang Zhi and then the Gansu gang. Now that it was gone, along with the IOU, Liu was afraid that Li Gengsheng would deny ever writing a promissory note. Xing seemed to be the ideal person to bear witness for him, so Liu hoped to get Xing to return to Henan with him; he'd tell him about the computer drive once he got his sixty thousand yuan. Since he did not have the thing on him, using it to lure Xing back to Henan with him would amount to trickery, a deception. But not entirely, at least in Liu's mind, since the purse had been taken back to Henan by his son and Mai Dangna.

The call went through and threw Manli into a panic, since it was so late at night. Before Liu had a chance to mention his suit and the card, Manli asked about the drive, telling him she'd packed up all her valuables, ready to flee if the whereabouts of the drive was discovered. She even told him she was sticking to her original plan of never returning to her hometown. Liu's possession of the drive was known now, because several groups of people were looking for him, but he thought they were safe as long as it didn't fall into any of their hands. In order to calm her down, he lied, saying he was still in Beijing because the affair was winding down. He told her he'd seen the Gansu gang the night before, but they'd slipped away; he needed help finding them again from Lao Xing, who knew what they looked like. Manli dug up the card and read Xing's number to him.

Xing was surprised to receive a call from Liu Yuejin. After Liu had lied to him about the drive, Xing had turned to looking for Yang Zhi, which had cost him two days before he realized that the cook did have the drive and that he'd disappeared with it. Xing wanted the drive for reasons different from everyone else. For one thing, he'd lied to everyone about his profession; he was, in fact, a police officer impersonating a private eye. Like everyone else, he wanted to find Liu because of the USB drive, but he was looking for something more, something pivotal, and yet he did not know what was on the drive or whether locating it would prove to be more consequential than finding something else. He deceived Yan Ge, but the real targets of his investigation were Lin and Director Jia; in a way, Yan was a point of entry, which he hoped would lead him to his targets, someone even higher than Lin and Jia. In a word, you could almost say that Xing's target was a watermelon, while Liu Yuejin and the USB drive were nothing but a sesame seed on Xing's chessboard, though a ready-made opening to a larger case he could not afford to ignore.

Which was why he impersonated a private eye and also why he was not as anxious as the others in looking for Liu and the drive. He was patient and methodical to begin with, and there was another reason he took his time. Over the past decade or so since joining the police force, his main task had been searching for people, a job description much like a private eye. But unlike a private eye, who rooted out third parties in extramarital affairs, he ferreted out murderers and the like, who were never in short supply, yet he slowly tired of that and became less motivated.

Another reason had to do with a career path that seemed bumpier than that of his peers; some who'd been at the police academy with him were now section heads or bureau chiefs while he was still a sergeant. It had nothing to do with his competence; in fact, he'd made more arrests than anyone else in the bureau.

But success at arrests was useless in promotion, which required personal influence. Those who were good at making connections bribed their superiors with money and were soon promoted as section heads or bureau chiefs—in a word, Xing's bosses. By the time he realized that promotion had nothing to do with hard work, it was too late for him, as all those positions were filled. After the promotions, the section heads and bureau chiefs were now in a position to receive bribes.

In contrast, Xing was still on the street, a mere homicide detective, and the disparity in wealth and status grew ever greater, which naturally made him indignant. He was trying to arrest all the criminals out there, while in fact they were all around him. It depressed him not being able to apprehend the criminals he knew. Why was he always arresting total strangers? Why couldn't he get some of those in power?

But when he looked around he saw the same thing happening everywhere; it had taken more than a couple of people and a few days for society to get to this state. There were plenty of criminals out there. In fact, the world was filled with them. All crows, as the saying goes, are the same color. He began to have doubts about his job of catching one group of crows for another group. He could not comprehend the logic of how this vast world worked. No matter how hard he tried, he simply couldn't.

He'd gotten help from the head of the Worried Wise Men Inquiry Agency, a former colleague who had quit his job over similar doubts. Using his talent and experience, the former colleague had opened the agency, specializing in extramarital affairs. When Xing next saw the man, he'd put on weight, spent money lavishly, had moved into a villa, and drove a Mercedes. Xing felt a different kind of indignation; his friend made a living by undertaking investigations for clients while Xing did the same thing, but for the crows. It made sense to do it for money and no sense to work for the crows.

For the past two weeks, since beginning his impersonation, he'd been tempted to quit and take up the same line of work as his friend. When he first met Yan, he'd told Yan that he'd become a PI after failing in business, which was a lie, but a genuine expression of his sentiment. In his conflicted state, he lost his zeal and his judgment suffered, which was one reason the search for the USB drive had been such a convoluted process, though no one else knew that. He was not fully aware of the importance of the drive until Liu vanished and Yan turned panicky.

This might be a more critical opening than he'd realized, he told himself, and he regretted being sloppy. But it was too late to go back and search for Liu. This was not the first time he'd missed an opportunity, and he'd just have to accept the reality. In the end, he was not as anxious as Yan and the other searchers; one day he'd quit and open his own investigative agency. He had no trouble sleeping at night.

Liu's call came at five in the morning, reigniting the fire of passion in Xing, particularly after hearing what Liu had to say. He talked fast and in a Henan dialect, so Xing only got half the story; but that was enough for him to learn what had happened and why Liu needed to go to Henan. Liu told him he wanted to get rid of the purse as soon as possible, otherwise he wouldn't have called. Xing had to go with him to Henan in case someone tried to grab him again along the way. Xing fell for the half-truth in Liu's story. He even felt energized, though not because the vanished clue had appeared on his doorstep; his curiosity was piqued—he would really like to have a look at the contents of the drive. He agreed to make the trip.

"How do I find you?" Liu asked. "I don't want to run into those people again."

Xing was tempted to tell Liu to go to the train station precinct, but he sensed that he might make Liu suspicious of a private investigator telling him to go to the police, and would likely vanish again. He couldn't tell Liu to wait at the train station either, not with people following him. What if someone grabbed him before he could get to him? While his mind went through various options and their respective permutations, Xing began to laugh. Who'd have thought a cook at a construction site could be so important to so many people? Liu Yuejin might turn out to be quite an interesting character, Xing mused.

In the end, he told Liu to buy a ticket to Shijiazhuang and call him with the schedule. Xing would ask a friend to pick him up there while he would drive up to meet him, and from there they would go to Henan together.

33

Liu Yuejin

After boarding the train, Liu Yuejin looked around to make sure he wasn't being followed and finally felt somewhat at ease. Even had there been people tailing him, they would not have been able to take him off a moving train with crowds of passengers and transit police patrolling the aisles. And if they tried, he'd simply cry for help. Leaving Beijing was fleeing from danger; still, he wistfully gazed out the window at the receding scenery. Six years earlier, he'd left Henan for Beijing to make his fortune and, more importantly, get away from the reminders of sadness in his hometown. He'd known no one in the city, but after six years it had become a home away from home. At night he dreamed more about Beijing than about Henan, though he always thought he'd leave one day, whether he had a successful life there or not. But he never imagined he'd be escaping from the city, now that it had become unhealthy to stay there.

On second thought, the possible fatal ending to his Beijing sojourn had nothing to do with his life over those six years; it was all a result of what had happened over the past two weeks. After losing a pack and finding a purse, one thing had led to another, and then to something else altogether. Changes like that were not unprecedented in his life, but mostly they had been trivial matters turning into something major or vice versa. No matter how they changed, they were still the same matter; or, in Liu's down-home analogy, an ant turned into a different ant or, at most, a fly.

But now an ant had suddenly transformed itself into a tiger that pounced on him, a first in his forty-odd years. He could not comprehend how a lost pack could threaten his very existence. No one had cared when he lost it, but disaster had struck after he picked up the purse. People—lots of them—were after him.

Lucky for him, one of them was Lao Xing, whom Liu hoped would serve as a witness. He did not trust Li Gengsheng, a man who would not hesitate to sleep with another man's wife. If he failed to get his sixty thousand, Liu would lose on every front—his wife, the money, and maybe even his son. But what if Li refused to pay up without the IOU, even with Xing present? What could Xing, a private investigator away from his territory, do for him? What then? With no feasible solution, Liu decided he'd just have to wait and see.

Then his thoughts turned positive: if Xing managed to convince Li, then Liu would get his sixty thousand yuan and everything would change. He'd be able to carry out his grand plan. After the clamor over the purse died down, he'd return to Beijing and open a diner. In the past he'd thought of doing that, but had neither the money nor the connections; now after six years, he knew quite a bit about the business.

Lao Gao, who ran a Weigong Village diner, wasn't as good a cook as he was, and Gao told him he made over ten thousand a month. With Liu's skill, conservatively speaking, he could easily make twenty thousand a month, over two hundred thousand a year. He'd be rich.

But making money was not that big a deal; more important for Liu was the prospect of being able to hold his head high, and no more bullying from others. When that happened, his ex-wife would see what Liu Yuejin was made of, and his son would know that he hadn't lied about having money.

Cheered by these positive thoughts, he was reminded of Ma Manli, who was unaware of his flight from Beijing. When he opened his diner and started making money, he'd bring her over to be the boss lady, though he wasn't sure she'd want to. Money didn't seem to matter to her, not compared to friendship, though she had no time for penniless men either, since poverty could be a sign of a man's feck-lessness. She hadn't thought much of Liu when he was a cook, but she might change her attitude once he became the owner of a diner.

And there was her preference for a good talker. He wasn't articulate, not now, because, as a hired cook, he'd had to hold back and watch his step; as a boss, he'd gain confidence and might even become silver-tongued.

With a jumble of thoughts running through his head, Liu experienced an emotional rollercoaster, sad one moment and elated the next. After passing Fengtai, the train stopped at Zhuozhou for five minutes before continuing south.

When a dining cart selling boxed lunches came down the aisle, Liu realized he was hungry. Since the night before, when he was on the run, he'd had no time to worry about his stomach, but now that he felt safe he asked the price of a box of rice with a thin layer of bean sprouts plus two pieces of fatty pork. Five yuan. Way overpriced. He knew that the ingredients cost no more than fifty cents and they were asking five yuan. These people were unconscionable, taking advantage of passengers who could not get off the train to eat. He had more than a hundred yuan left from the money he'd taken from Little Fatso, after spending twenty on a cab ride and thirty for the train ticket.

Not knowing what he'd need to spend money on, he decided not to buy lunch and wait till they reached Baoding, where boxed lunches were sold on the platform. There he asked the price: two-fifty for the same thing, rice with bean sprouts and two pieces of fatty pork. Also a rip-off but cheaper than what he could get on the train. So he got off, handed over the money and picked the box that looked fullest. He had begun to eat on his way back to his seat when some-one came up to him.

"Got a match?" the man asked, a cigarette dangling from his mouth.

Liu took out his lighter.

"You're Liu Yuejin, aren't you?" the man whispered while light-ing his cigarette.

Liu tensed up; a sense of foreboding made him hurry toward the door to his compartment.

"I don't know you."

The man laughed and fell in behind him.

"If you're going back to Henan to see your son, you can forget about that. We've been to your place and he's not there."

"Who are you?" Liu stood still.

"It doesn't matter who I am. What matters is that we know your son isn't in Henan, and we also know your plan to go see him about a purse. We have it, but what we're looking for isn't in it."

Liu could feel his hair standing straight up.

"Where's my son?" he asked in a panicky voice.

The man smiled and continued to puff on his cigarette, without responding. It finally dawned on Liu that his son had been kidnapped, a far more serious matter than losing the pack and the IOU. The tiger was now a crocodile intending to eat him, and his son as well. It was clear that the man was from yet another group, though he had no idea which one. Then he wondered if they indeed had his son or if it was just a scam to blackmail him. As if he could read Liu's mind, the man whipped out his cell and punched in a string of numbers before handing the phone to Liu.

"Who is this?" Liu barely got the question out when he heard weeping on the other end.

"It's me, Pa."

It was his son.

"What did you take from the purse, Pa?" he asked angrily. "Why have they locked us up in a dark room?"

Liu heard a noise that sounded like a slap, followed by Liu Pengju's beseeching voice. He was begging someone else, not his father.

"Please don't hit me any more, good uncle," his son begged. "I don't have it."

Then came Mai Dangna's sobbing.

"Please let me go, Elder Brother. I have nothing to do with this."

The lunch box slipped out of Liu's hand and hit the ground with a thud. His face ashen, Liu looked at the man, who sniffled and put his phone away. After all that had happened over the past two weeks, Liu had learned to read a person's face. Those who smile broadly while they carry out heinous acts are the most merciless and evil, like the man in front of him.

"What, what do you want?" he stammered out of fear.

It was a pointless question. The man draped his arm around Liu's shoulders as if they were best friends.

"Give me that object and I'll tell them to let your son go."

"I don't have it with me." Liu knew he had to tell the truth now.

"On the train?" The man pointed to the train.

"It's still in Beijing," Liu confessed.

"Go get your things," the man said calmly. "We're going back to Beijing together."

34

Lao Xing

Along with two Shijiazhuang policemen, old Xing spent the afternoon searching the area around the train station, but failed to locate Liu Yuejin. The policemen, also in plainclothes, told him that Liu was not on the noon train. When they didn't see him get off, they went looking for him, causing a ten-minute delay of the train's departure. They searched every car, but he was nowhere to be found. Xing had his phone on the whole time, and Liu did not call; Xing could not contact him either.

After thanking his colleagues, Xing searched on his own, with full knowledge that it was fruitless. If he wasn't on the train, he could not be at the station. He'd lost Liu again. But he refused to admit defeat; there was a sliver of hope that Liu might have switched trains and would arrive in Shijiazhuang later. Train after train came and went; he finally gave up at nightfall. Liu Yuejin would not be coming to Shijiazhuang; he'd either deceived Xing or something had happened to him. If it was the latter, where could it have happened, in Beijing or along the way? If it was on the way to Shijiazhuang, then the problem was with the rendezvous point; too far from Beijing, it had given whoever it was a chance to intercept. But Xing had chosen the place, so he only had himself to blame. He'd been in high spirits when he set out earlier, and now he'd cooled off, though he wasn't actually upset. He went to a restaurant near the station, where he ate two fried cakes stuffed with donkey meat, before driving back to Beijing.

35

Liu Yuejin

Liu Yuejin chatted with his son's kidnapper all the way back to Beijing. The slim man, who was in his thirties, had a driver, so he and Liu sat in the back. Having been on Liu's tail for twenty-four hours, he knew what had happened at Cao's shed the night before and had followed him onto the train.

"Lao Lu followed the train to Baoding." The man pointed to his driver.

Lao Lu, expressionless and wordless, drove on.

The man had nothing against Liu; he'd kidnapped his son for money, nothing else. Since they both knew what had happened, they could talk frankly now that things were coming to a head. After a while, they realized they liked each other and might have become friends had they met under different circumstances.

"May I ask your name?"

"No need to stand on ceremony. You can call me Lao Fang," the man said.

Liu asked him how he'd thought about looking up Liu's son and where he'd found him. With a laugh, Fang told Liu everything, starting with how he'd been hired to look for the drive, which, everyone learned once Liu disappeared, was with him. While others searched for Liu in Beijing, Fang adopted a two-prong approach, telling his people to look for Liu in Beijing while he took people to Luoshui in case Liu returned to his hometown.

When he got there, he discovered that Liu was not there, so he decided to find Liu's son instead but learned that he had left for Beijing ten days earlier. At first he hadn't planned on kidnapping the young man; he just thought he'd lead him to his father. Pretending to know Liu from the construction site, he tracked down Pengju's friend, who gave him the young man's cell number. Then, using a pay phone to impersonate someone from Luoshui, he called Pengju and asked where he was. After telling Fang he was in Beijing, Pengju asked who he was, but Fang said it was a wrong number and hung up. Upon returning to Beijing, he called Liu's son from another pay phone to tell him his father had been in a car accident. When Pengju rushed over, Fang nabbed him and found out that the young man hadn't seen his father for days, didn't know he'd vanished and, in fact, knew less about his father than Fang did.

It didn't take much to frighten the young man. Impersonating a policeman, Fang told Pengju that his father was wanted for a stolen purse. Since they were unable to find Liu, they took him instead, and would let him go once they found his father and the purse. That was enough to get Pengju to come clean about the purse, which was now with his girlfriend, who had left him five days earlier after a fight. He had been looking for her, which was why he was still in Beijing. She had a cell but would not answer his calls. Using the same trick and sending a text message from his own cell, Fang told the woman that Pengju had been in a traffic accident and that he'd gotten her number from Pengju's phone. When she rushed over, Fang grabbed her and the purse. He turned the purse inside out; there was no drive. Now he had to keep Liu's son and his girlfriend while searching for Liu.

Fang's story told Liu everything he needed to know, but his first reaction was not concern for his son's safety, since that was pointless. Instead, Liu was incensed over his son's lie.

"That little bastard lied to me again. He said he went back to Luoshui, but he's still in Beijing. Kidnapping is too good for him. I never imagined that my own son would steal from me. I hope he's learned his lesson."

"The purse was in your possession, and he's your son." Fang disagreed. "Which means he took it; he didn't steal it."

Liu was still fuming. "I could tell at first glance that his girlfriend was no good. It must have been her idea to steal from me."

"She was right, though." Fang laughed. "Do you know how much the purse is worth?"

"How much can a purse be worth?"

"It's a famous brand purse and they only make a few. It's worth over a hundred thousand renminbi." Fang added, "But your son's girlfriend didn't know that either."

Liu was beyond disbelief. When he found the purse, he'd actually cursed Yang Zhi for being a lousy thief. He often stole money from the poor, but when it came to stealing from the rich, he managed only to get women's things. Liu had paid little attention to the purse when rummaging through its contents, even though he wouldn't have been able to tell its value either, for it looked like an ordinary purse. Obviously the rich spend their money on very different things. If he'd known, he would not have had to search for his pack after finding the purse. The pack did contain an IOU, but it was for only sixty thousand, while the purse itself was worth more than a hundred thousand. Life had played another trick on him; it was as if he'd found a horse after losing a goat, but didn't know it was a horse. Obviously, Yang hadn't known the purse's worth either.

Fang laughed again at the rueful look on Liu's face. With the long-winded story as a preamble, Fang now felt it was the right time to cut to the chase.

"Where have you hidden the drive?" he asked nonchalantly.

The question brought Liu back to reality now that the purpose of their chat was revealed. At this point, he knew he had no option but to tell him everything.

"In Brother Cao's shed."

It was Fang's turn to be flabbergasted. He had thought the cook would hide the drive at the construction site, at a friend's place, or anywhere other than a place belonging to the very people who were

after him. Fang didn't believe him, but instead of getting angry, he
asked for details.

"How did you manage that?"

"I carried it with me wherever I went. After they nabbed me
last night, I tossed it into a basket of duck feathers when they weren't
looking."

"Why didn't you take it with you when you escaped last night?"

"I was afraid I'd be caught again. The thief's den is the safest
place, the last place they'd look."

Fang fixed his gaze on Liu.

"I've told you the truth. You can believe me or not; it's up to
you," Liu said.

After some consideration, Fang still thought it didn't sound logical, which was precisely the reason why he had to believe Liu.

"You're no ordinary cook."

That said, Fang was not totally convinced of Liu's story. On the
other hand, he had Liu and his son, so Liu wouldn't lie to him, but if
he did, he had ways of dealing with them. One thing was certain—he
wouldn't be so amicable if and when Liu's lie was exposed.

They were still talking when they arrived in Beijing, where
they discussed how to retrieve the drive, agreeing that, it being Cao's
place, they had to get it through wit, not force. Daytime was obviously no good. Armed with pistols, Fang was sure they'd overpower
the people in the shed, who carried only knives, but an open fight
would draw too much attention. They had to wait until after dark.

"Is the place guarded at night?" Fang asked.

"I have no idea. They might be working, they might not."

Fang decided they had to act that night to retrieve the drive,
whether the place was occupied or not. If no one was there, they'd
simply sneak in and get it; if there were people, they'd have to
take it by force. At two in the morning, they drove to the peddlers' market, where they stopped to size up the shed. It was dark
inside and deadly quiet, apparently deserted. They argued over
who should go in. Fang and Lu were not familiar with the place, so

Fang thought that Liu was the ideal person to do it. But Liu was reluctant.

"It may look deserted. But what if they're in there? They carry knives, you know. I told you where the drive is, now you'll have to get it."

"Don't worry. We'll be here if they find out and you get into a fight," Fang tried to reassure him. "The sooner we have the drive, the sooner we'll let your son go. And you and I will go our separate ways amicably."

The mention of his son got Liu into action, though he took his time getting out of the car. Lu grabbed him before he was out.

"What if he runs away?" Lu asked Fang.

"He's a good man; he'd never abandon his son," Fang said with a smile.

That put Lu's mind at ease. Liu got out, crept over to the shed, and pressed his ear to the door. After listening for enough time to smoke a cigarette, he heard nothing, so he quietly walked around to the back, where he pried open a window and jumped inside.

In the car they waited for half an hour, but no sign of Liu. Lu was getting anxious.

"Let's give him a little more time." Fang looked at his watch and said, "Maybe someone moved the basket and maybe the cook is stealing other stuff."

Fifteen minutes went by, and Liu was still inside. Fang finally sensed that something was wrong. They were about to get out for a look when a group of people stormed over like a whirlwind, led by Baldy Cui. Fang and Lu took out their pistols, only to see two rifles trained on their windshield. The night before, Fang had overpowered Cui with his pistol, but now Cui overwhelmed them with greater numbers.

Fang put his pistol away and rolled down the window.

"How did you know?"

Baldy laughed while pointing his rifle at the shed.

"The cook's in there. He alerted us."

Han Shengli, who was part of the group, took out his cell and said smugly, "He called me."

Fang realized that Liu Yuejin had been hatching a plan as they chatted on the way back to Beijing. He'd also put on an act of not wanting to enter the shed. Fang shook his head and said to Baldy with a smile, "He's no ordinary cook."

Liu had sided with Cao not because he was a better man. In fact, it was his people who had hung him up and beaten him that night, while Fang was a good conversational partner. But Fang and Cao, both members of the underworld, meant pretty much the same thing to Liu. With the son in his clutches, Fang was a bigger threat than Cao, but, not knowing much about the man, Liu Yuejin was worried he might want more than just the drive; what if he planned to kill Liu after he got what he was looking for? It made no difference to Liu who got this drive, but if Fang wanted it more, then all three of them—Liu, his son, and his son's girlfriend—would be done for.

On the way back to Beijing, Fang had told Liu he wanted the drive for money and would let Liu's son go once he got it; but he smiled when he talked about killing, which seemed to mean nothing to him, and that aroused Liu's suspicions.

Cao's people, on the other hand, were only after the money. Liu learned that they had no idea what was on the drive when he overheard Cao's conversation with his people the night before. He was even worried for Cao's sake. By coming over to Cao, he'd ensure his own safety first before carrying out the next step. He'd get Cao to help him capture Fang and Lu to exchange for his son and his son's girlfriend, after which he would negotiate a good price for the computer drive to make up for the amount on the IOU. He recalled there was a phone in the shed, so he'd have his chance when he went in to get the drive. That was what had been on his mind on their way back.

Baldy Cui took Fang and Lu into the shed and turned on the light, giving Fang a view of the phone on the chopping board. Liu was crouching on the floor smoking. Without getting up when they entered, he told Baldy what he had in mind. To his surprise, Baldy would not agree to anything.

"You've got things turned around." Cui pointed to Fang and Lu. "Those two and your son have nothing to do with the drive. We're not going to screw this up over them."

"I won't turn over the drive if they're not taken care of." Liu was determined.

Surprised by his forcefulness, Baldy hesitated. "Give me the drive and we'll talk about the exchange."

"Exchange first, then the drive," Liu insisted.

As they began to argue, Fang Junde said to Baldy, "I know where it is."

Baldy looked at Fang.

"You'll let us go when you find the drive?"

Cui nodded.

"He told me on the way back that it's in a basket of feathers."

Baldy told his men to turn over all the baskets. They found no drive after searching through piles of duck feathers. Fang and Cui then knew that Liu had tricked them both. Cui picked up a knife from the chopping board and came up to Liu.

"Where's the drive?"

"I threw it away." Liu played dumb again. "It looked useless to me."

Cui pressed the knife against him, but he didn't flinch.

"Go ahead, kill me if you want, but I don't have it."

Putting the knife away, Cui patted Liu on the shoulder.

"Let's go see someone, and you'll sing a different tune."

"Who's that?" Liu gasped.

36

Ma Manli

Ma Manli was strung up in a dark basement room.

No one had thought of her at first; it was Han Shengli's idea to catch her in order to find the drive. Han had had nothing to show since coming over to Cao's side and failing to find Liu after searching for two days. Cao was visibly unhappy when someone intercepted and nabbed Liu after Cao intentionally let him escape. While they were all scratching their heads for a lack of ideas, Han suddenly recalled Manli. Liu did not have the USB drive with him when brought into the shed, which could only mean that he'd left it with someone else. Manli appeared to be that person. Beijing was a big city, but Liu did not have that many places to hide something like a drive. Yang Zhi had searched one of the likeliest places, his room at the site. That left Manli's hair salon and Lao Gao's diner, but both places had turned up empty. After Cao's people caught Liu, Han went over the searches in his head, trying to decide which one, Gao or Manli, had lied to him. Gao had appeared to be telling the truth; his long friendship with Liu told Han that he was not that good an actor. So it had to be Manli, a woman who had gone through a great deal and was no spring chicken.

Cao had to agree with Han's analysis; besides, they had to give it a try, so Cao told a deflated Cui to get Manli. They would either find the drive at her place or she'd lead them to Liu Yuejin. Han breathed a sigh of relief when his idea was accepted.

They seized Manli at one in the morning. Cui drove a canopied truck to the hair salon, where he pried open the window and jumped in. Before she knew what was happening, her mouth was stuffed with a rag and her hands and feet were tied. She was then dragged out of the salon and tossed into the back of the truck. After closing the tailgate, they took her to the basement room. Without a word, they hung her from the heating pipes and beat her before asking about the drive. No matter how they beat her, she insisted she'd never seen the drive, let alone hidden it for Liu. She told them she didn't even know that Liu had found a purse. Her steadfast denials had nothing to do with her ability to withstand physical abuse; it was simply because, after seeing the drive, she knew she could die if she breathed a word about it.

So Cui asked her about Liu Yuejin's whereabouts. As with the drive, she denied everything, saying she hadn't seen Liu since he lost his pack. After three rounds of beating, they still could not get anything out of her, leading Cui to suspect they'd gotten the wrong person. Since it had been Han's idea to capture Manli, his screw-up delayed their search for Liu. Cui was about to assault Han when his cell phone rang. It was Liu Yuejin calling from the shed; that saved Han from further abuse.

Now Cui refused to exchange Fang and Lu for Liu's son, since he did not want to alert the other parties and complicate the matter even more. They were at an impasse. Instead of beating Liu, Cui took him to the basement room in Fang's car. Manli had been in bed when Cui's lackeys grabbed her, so she'd had no time to put anything over her lingerie, which was now in tatters after the beatings. Her face was bloodied and she had bruises all over. Liu was so shocked he dropped to the floor. Manli was trying to say something but, with the rag in her mouth, he couldn't understand a word. This visit was not meant for them to talk, and Baldy took Liu back to the shed after he had a chance to see what was happening to Manli.

Cui told Liu that Manli had confessed to seeing the USB drive and had also said Liu had it. They'd taken him to see her so he'd have a chance to change his tune and hand over the drive. If he continued with his antics, they'd hang him up and beat him again, and this time he would not escape. Liu fell for Cui's trick. Back in the basement, he'd thought Manli was asking him to save her, though in fact she was telling him not to show them the drive. She was telling him she hadn't confessed and he mustn't either, or they could end up dead. Since Liu did not understand what she was saying, he told Cui where he'd hidden the drive, more for his son's sake than for Manli's. He had to believe Cui now after what he'd seen; besides, even if his son and Manli were safe, he could not take another beating himself.

37

Brother Cao

Liu Yuejin had hidden the USB drive in the seat cushion of the number three tower crane at the construction site. The operator of a crane that could lift material fifty stories had no inkling he was sitting on something so valuable. When they learned the hiding place, Baldy Cui and Fang Junde could not hide their admiration. Han Shengli offered to recover the drive in Fang's car. It was five in the morning, hours before work resumed at the site; he returned an hour later with the drive. Fang examined it to make sure it fit the description of the version and color he'd been given. Cao came to the shed when he heard the news. Cui could not wait to tell him how the drive was recovered, but Cao stopped him to shake hands with Fang and Lu, before shaking Liu's hand.

"Good work."

Pointing to Fang and Lu, Liu Yuejin said:

"Now that you have the drive, Brother Cao, please tell them to let my son go." He continued, "And the woman from the hair salon."

Then he added in a timorous and hesitating voice, "You can't go back on your word."

The last phrase drew a frown from Cao, who hated people going back on their word. Knowing that Cao was piqued, Baldy was about to show Liu his displeasure when Cao stopped him.

"Do you know what I hope to get out of this?"

Liu Yuejin considered the question and replied, "Money."

"You're right and you're wrong." Cao sighed. "I'd be just another thief if it was only about money. Besides money, I also want to solidify our base."

What did that mean? And what was Cao's base? Liu did not know, but he was not in the least interested in finding out, for he was concerned only about getting his son back. In the meantime, Cao picked up the drive and brought it up close, like reading a mahjong tile.

"I have to get a good price in order to solidify our base." He then patted Liu on the shoulder. "I'll give you your son back once it's sold."

Finally at ease, Liu urged, "Then hurry up and sell it, Brother Cao. Someone else might try to get it if you wait too long."

Cao clapped his hands.

"You're right. I'll sell it without delay."

Cao had Liu taken to a three-room apartment rented by him and his Tangshan gang. Yang Zhi was there, recovering from the beating.

After Liu was taken away, Cao got down to business. He could sell the drive to Yan Ge through Han Shengli or to the other party through Fang Junde. Who that other person was Cao neither knew nor cared to know; he was simply pleased that Fang had brought them another buyer, making the merchandise much more valuable once a bidding war began.

First he told Baldy Cui to give Yan a call, since he did not trust Han Shengli, who felt a great loss of face, but did not dare complain. Using Han's cell, Cui called Yan and said he was Han's friend and that he had recovered the drive. He asked Yan to name his price. Yan paused momentarily over the new scenario, but quickly deduced that the caller wanted to negotiate a figure on behalf of Han Shengli, to whom Yan had offered twenty thousand as a reward.

Unsure what Cui was about, Yan told Cui to name *his* price, which Cui did by asking for five hundred thousand. Now Yan knew that Cui was no small-time crook; he was dealing with an experienced gangster, not a petty thief like Han Shengli. Yan countered with two hundred thousand, knowing he should give Cui the respect he deserved. After a few rounds of back and forth, they settled on three hundred and fifty thousand. Yan could easily afford that, since he'd told Lao Xing he'd pay him two hundred thousand if the USB drive was located in two days.

The deadline had come and gone, and the price for the drive should have gone up accordingly. However, not knowing who Cui was, he had to be prepared for the possibility that Cui did not have the drive. He was also worried that the other party might want more if he offered too much. To him three hundred and fifty thousand was the right amount, low enough to stop the other party from hoping for more, but high enough to keep him interested.

The exchange would take place at eleven that night, at the Tie-jiangpu traffic circle, five miles west of the Beijing-Kaifeng highway Xihongmen exit. After Cui hung up, Cao let Fang have his cell phone back so he could call Lao Lin. Fang asked Cao his bottom line, to which Cao responded with a finger gesture—seven hundred thousand. Fang protested, saying it was double the earlier amount, unfair even in a bidding war, but that was not meant to save Lin money. Fang was simply afraid that Lin would reject the offer outright and Cao would sell the USB drive to Yan Ge. Lin had offered him eighteen thousand to find it, so he might not want to pay so much for the drive. Fang knew his fate was in Cao's hands and, as a player in the underworld, was also aware that life and death decisions like this were often made in the blink of an eye.

"Forget it, then." Cao knitted his brow.

Cao's casual dismissal struck fear in Fang's heart, prompting him to call Lin right away. When Lin picked up, Fang told him someone else had the USB drive and was asking seven hundred thousand. To his surprise, the amount did not seem to bother Lin.

"Have you seen it?" Lin asked.

Fang looked at Cao and then at the drive. "I have."

"Is it the real thing?"

"It was hidden under the operator's seat of a tower crane. It has to be genuine."

"All right then."

That sealed the deal, to Fang's astonishment. Lin had readily agreed to the price not because he was free with his money; in fact, he was more miserly than Yan Ge. He just wanted to get hold of the device before anyone else did. Besides, he'd been instructed by Jia, who had phoned from Europe, to take care of another matter. Once the price was settled, both sides agreed to complete the exchange at one that night at Lao Qi's Teahouse.

It was seven in the morning when Lin hung up, so he went straight to work. At noon he went to the bank and withdrew the money, which he put in the trunk of his car. Later that evening, he had a business dinner. At midnight, he drove to Lao Qi's Teahouse, where he received a phone call as he waited in a private room. After listening to the caller, he went quiet for a moment before saying:

"All right."

38

Yan Ge

Yan Ge had asked to have the exchange near the traffic circle. The location, not far from his stud farm, was convenient. Moreover, it was quiet and remote, surrounded by vegetable gardens, with little vehicle traffic at night.

By ten that night, Yan had Little Bai and others hide in the vegetable field and be ready to intercede if anything went wrong with the exchange. He himself got there at half past ten, but no one showed up. A few cars and trucks came his way, but none of them slowed down. By eleven thirty, still no sign of the other party. He tried calling the person who had contacted him earlier that day, as he'd seen the phone in Han Shengli's hand at Lao Qi's Teahouse. But Han's phone was off. Sensing that something was not right, he waited until twelve and then decided to go see Ren Baoliang, hoping to find the caller through Han. He drove away, too preoccupied to give any thought to Bai and others. His phone rang when he was on Five Ring Road after getting onto the Beijing-Kaifeng Expressway. A pleasant surprise from the caller, he thought, but it was from Bai.

"Should we continue to wait, Mr. Yan?"

"No, go on home," Yan said.

After hanging up, he thought he should call Ren instead of going to the site, since Ren might not be there that late. But the call went through and Ren was at the site. He told Ren to find Han Shengli so he could locate the other party. When a confused Ren asked who the other party might be, Yan raged at him.

"Would I have called you if I knew?"

Yan was too focused on the conversation to notice a Land Rover on the tail of his Mercedes. It was after midnight, a time when Five Ring Road was taken up by semis from the northeast, Inner Mongolia, Shandong, Hebei, and Shanxi, since they were not allowed to go through Beijing during daylight hours. They waited outside Five Ring Road till nighttime, when they roared down the road, making it busier than in the daytime. Yan's car was caught in the flow of traffic. He was still railing at Ren as he neared an overpass, where the Land Rover suddenly sped up, caught up with his car, and rammed into his rear fender. Caught off guard, Yan lost control of the car and slammed into the base of a pylon. His car bounced back, hit a semi loaded with coal from Shanxi, and rolled across the divider, landing in the opposite lane. A truck transporting sheep from Inner Mongolia plowed into Yan's car and sent it flying off the road and into a tree. It bounced off the tree and came to rest in a roadside ditch, while all around him sheep were falling like rain. Inside the car, Yan was a bloody mess, his head on the steering wheel, twisted to one side. He was dead. His phone, which had fallen under the passenger's seat, was still on, and Ren's voice could be heard.

"What was that? What just happened?"

Behind the Mercedes on the road, cars and trucks were slamming into each other in both directions, creating a huge pile-up.

39

Lao Lin

It was an easy decision to do business with Lin, who was paying seven hundred thousand. Cao had never gotten that much since starting the duck slaughtering business, ever since changing the shed into a thieves' den for the Tangshan gang. The decision to send Yang Zhi to steal from the house in Beethoven Villa had been his, but he never expected such a big payoff, as no one would stash that much money in a house. It was not until a severely injured Yang showed up at the shed that he realized the value of the drive. Since the villa fell into his area of control, he reasoned it was within his right to take it from Liu and sell it to the highest bidder. His asking price was accepted. Seven hundred thousand was a lot of money; it would build the foundation of his enterprise and further its growth.

But money was not the key here; what he wanted was to solidify his base, and for that, he had Yang Zhi, Han Shengli, Fang Junde, and the cook Liu Yuejin to thank. Without them, this new beginning could never have seen the light of day. It was a group effort that helped pave the way for a new state of affairs. The thought so elated Cao that he abruptly recovered from his cold.

When Fang Junde led Baldy Cui and the others to Lao Qi's Teahouse, Lin was waiting in a private room, a weighty duffle bag to his side. He said nothing and looked no one in the eye. He merely handed the bag to Fang, who tossed it to Cui, who counted the contents, seven one-hundred-thousand-yuan bundles. After zipping it up, Cui took out the USB drive and handed it to Lin, who took a laptop from another bag, booted it up, inserted the drive, and froze when he clicked on the icon.

It was blank. Lin's mind went blank too.

He was stunned by the blank drive, but, more importantly, earlier he had ordered a traffic accident to kill Yan Ge when he was convinced of the drive's authenticity from Fang's assertion that it had to be the real thing. It had been Director Jia's idea to kill Yan. He had wanted Yan dead since the day the photo was published and Yan revealed the existence of the drive; he had waited so long because Yan had the drive. Jia was not an evil person, nor was he angry at Yan for blackmailing him; he just wanted him gone so he could have a clean break and be spared future troubles. It was like saving someone who has fallen into the water. You have a bamboo pole in hand and try to save the person closest to shore. But if it's a leaky fishing boat in the middle of the ocean, you don't lend a helping hand, because the drowning person might drag you into the water, where you'll drown alongside him. The best course of action is to push his head down and drown him yourself; you rid yourself of a burden and no one will know how the boat sank. Everyone dies sooner or later, so the earlier he died the better for others and the sooner his rebirth. Which was what he'd had in mind when he'd said to Yan at Beidaihe:

"Everything would be fine if a few people were to die."

Of course he meant more than that.

Lao Lin was against killing Yan at first, but not because he was fond of the real estate tycoon; he was simply wary of worse consequences than an exposé from the drive. It was no small matter to plan someone's death, after all. Later he consented because of what was on the drive. The video clips showed not only Lin accepting bribes and sleeping with prostitutes, like Jia, but also enjoying his share before Jia did. Lin managed to hide the contents from Jia by focusing the latter's concerns on the lost drive, even after Yan gave him the laptop along with six USB drives. The lost

USB drive had given him the break he needed, but not for long. Yan knew all about his actions through the drive. Lin was worried that Yan might seek revenge when he recovered from his business troubles and repaired his relationship with Jia; Lin would be in serious trouble if Yan told Jia everything. Hence, he decided that Yan must die after the USB drive was recovered. He would destroy all copies, or, better yet, save one in case he needed it as leverage against Jia.

What Lin had not expected was the timing of Yan's death. They were into the fifth day of the search for the USB drive when Jia left the country with the express instruction that it must be retrieved within ten days, at which time Yan would have a traffic accident. Jia would still be abroad, an airtight alibi, which meant that Lin would be the only suspect if the scheme was exposed. He was impressed by how ruthless and cunning Jia was. Yan Ge, of course, was in the dark, and even on the day he died he could not understand why Jia had given him ten days to unearth the USB drive and later given him a five-day extension.

Now they had the drive, except it was a fake, while the genuine one was still out there somewhere. Lin picked up a teacup and splashed hot tea into Fang Junde's face.

"It's a fake, you idiot."

With his face burning, Fang's mind went blank, as he faced the consequences of his con game. Ignoring the pain in his face, he turned, thumped Baldy Cui, and said to Lin:

"I'll keep looking."

He turned to leave as Lin leaned back against the chair and sighed.

"It's too late."

It was too late not because the drive was still missing, but because Director Jia was returning from Paris the next day, and Lin did not know what he could say to him. The fake drive was the right model and color, which could only mean that it was a swindle. He had been suspicious when it was stolen from Yan's house in the villa compound. Now he had his proof, though it no longer mattered. The drive was obviously in the wrong hands and, more importantly, Yan was dead, when he should have died *after* the drive was recovered. Now the sequence of events was all jumbled up.

40

Liu Yuejin

Lin was not in his office the next day when Xing went to arrest him. At his home Xing was by told by the maid that Lin had left for work early that morning. He must have fled the area, Xing surmised; they should have moved sooner, but it was not Xing's fault. He had wanted to arrest everyone at Lao Qi's Teahouse the night before, but his boss, the bureau chief, told him to wait a day after listening to his report. Why? The chief did not elaborate, and now Lin was gone.

News came that night from the Xijun Hotel, the only six-star hotel in Beijing. Lin had not left town; instead he'd gone to the hotel, where he'd committed suicide. The front desk register showed that he'd checked in early that morning. That evening, a housekeeper rang his room and got no answer. Thinking the guest was out, she opened the door and went in. She noticed a strong alcohol smell and spotted two empty Maotai bottles on a table by a chair. Ignoring the bottles, she went to clean the bathroom; she pushed open the door and fainted at the sight of a man hanging from the showerhead. Whatever he had thrown up in the tub had already dried and crusted over. When she came to, she screamed, drawing the attention of hotel security; they took him down but he was long dead. He'd used his pajama belt. Security called the police, who found his work ID in his briefcase; they then called Lin's office and notified the bureau.

Lin's death meant that the case was closed, partly due to Liu Yuejin's help. Two nights earlier, when Fang forced Liu to steal the drive from the shed, Liu also called Xing. He did not know Xing's true identity, he just wanted more people to know what had happened to him, an exit strategy if things did not pan out with Cao. He confessed to Xing about the trip to Henan, adding that he was not lying this time, as his life was in danger. He told Xing the computer drive was hidden in Beijing. If he failed to call Xing again by noon the next day, Xing should go to Cao's shed to save him, and he'd turn over the drive. He did not tell Xing that he had an additional demand—he would turn over the drive only after Xing helped his son, his son's girlfriend, and Ma Manli.

After receiving the call, Xing rushed back to Beijing from Shi-jiazhuang, but did not wait till the following day. Instead, he told some plainclothes policemen to meet him at Cao's shed; he did not free Liu right away, however, because he wanted to have everyone leaving the shed followed. Baldy Cui and Fang Junde were tailed as they headed to Lao Qi's Teahouse. Completely in the dark, Liu was getting nervous when he could not get Cao's people to make a deal, which was why he told Cao where he hid the drive. It was a fake, of course, but a good way to buy time. Liu had gotten the idea when Yang Zhi bought a fake one for the extortion scheme. Since he had the genuine one, Liu was able to buy an identical blank USB drive, which he then hid under the seat of the crane. He had not expected it would come in handy so soon.

Where was the genuine drive?

It was hidden in a place only Liu could think of. After watching what was on the drive with Manli, they were both frightened, but had no idea how best to hide the device. Prior to that, he'd had no qualms about carrying it with him, but now it felt as if he was walking around with a ticking bomb. The dining hall was out of the question, that was for sure, since so many people were trying to find him. Han Shengli was right when he concluded that Liu would not ask old Gao to keep it for him; Liu trusted Gao but did not want so many people to be involved. The fewer people who knew about it, the better. Manli's Hair Salon was his next choice, but she would not go along.

Like him, she was terrified after viewing it and, besides, everyone knew that Liu was at the salon all the time. They put their heads together but came up with nothing, until they parted ways and Liu hit upon an idea—the public toilet behind the salon. It was not a hiding place anyone could easily guess and was close enough to Manli that he could count on her help if worse came to worst. So he sneaked behind the salon, where he had to choose between the men's and the women's toilets. He decided on the women's side. It was midnight and the place was deserted. He entered the third stall from the left and hid the USB drive between the fifth and sixth bricks from the top, and between the eighth and ninth bricks from the left.

41

Brother Cao and His Myna Bird

Lao Xing failed to catch Lin but encountered no problems taking
Cao and his people into custody. That night when he talked to the
bureau chief, the chief agreed to arrest only the Cao gang. Cao had
been waiting for Baldy Cui to return with seven hundred thousand
yuan. At four in the morning Cui showed up, followed by a swarm of
policemen. It was totally unexpected, but Cao knew better than to
resist, so he surrendered.

"How did you know?" he asked Xing.

Instead of telling him about Liu Yuejin's call, Xing looked into
Cao's turgid eyes and said:

"Isn't slaughtering ducks good enough? Why branch out into
the underworld?"

Cao ignored him and focused on his own question. "A small
gang can't outwit a big one," he said with a sigh.

Xing was wondering what he meant when the mynah bird
cocked its tiny head and chimed in angrily:

"Go to hell."

Xing and Cao were surprised. Cao had sealed the bird's ears
with wax to prevent it from learning curse words after teaching it
three pleasant phrases. Maybe the ears had not been sealed completely, or maybe they had been but the wax had loosened up. In
fact, the bird heard everything and had learned all the curse words

it could manage; it was clever enough to keep its mouth shut. It turned out that even the mynah bird was playing dumb with Cao, who, instead of getting angry at the bird, gave it a nod and said, "Nicely said."

42

Lao Xing

Lao Xing received a commendation from the bureau chief, but ironically it was because he had failed to arrest the guilty party in a timely fashion and hence delayed solving the case, which in turn kept everything under wraps without alerting the one they really wanted. If the case had been solved earlier, Jia, who had been out of the country, might have got wind and decided to stay abroad. Since it dragged on for fifteen days, nothing was resolved until the day before his return. Xing apprehended all the others with the sole purpose of catching Jia, because only that would count as truly solving the case. And that was why the bureau chief had told him to wait a day before going after Lin; it was too bad Lin committed suicide before Xing got to him, but they managed to catch the big fish, Jia.

With him out of the country, the police encountered less interference, even though the progress of their investigation was entirely under their control the whole time. With the opportune delay, Jia remained in the dark, giving the police time to gather evidence for his arrest before he could make a move. So when he returned with the delegation, he was picked up at the Beijing airport the moment he stepped off the plane.

Apprehending Jia meant the police were just getting started on the real case, which was to catch someone or some people above him. The case would remain open and Xing would follow leads in Jia's network to see who else was guilty. He found these people intriguing; this was the kind of police work that interested him. But out of the blue he got an order to stop his investigation. The case was considered closed.

Who exactly issued the order was never made clear to Xing or the bureau chief. But no matter, they had to stop. It was a regretful outcome, for it meant that what he had accomplished was all in vain. But regret was useless. Besides, it wasn't the first time he'd run up against a higher power. He'd just consider the case closed and go after other strangers.

43

The Monkey King

Xing thought he was done with the case, but Liu Yuejin would not let him off that easily, and went to see him every day. Solving the case with Jia might not have served any real purpose, but it was all because of the USB drive. After finally learning Xing's true identity, Liu wanted a deal with him before going to the toilet to retrieve the drive. He would turn over the drive, but Xing had to help him find the pack that had been stolen twenty days earlier.

"It's been all about you and your police work. Now it's my turn," Liu said.

Yang Zhi, who had first unburdened Liu of the pack, was already in custody, though he hadn't been caught at the shed; he was still recovering from broken ribs at the Tangshan gang's residence when the police kicked the door open. With the injury, he could not flee through the window, as he would have done before. As for the Gansu gang, Xing had seen them before, and did not think it would be hard to find them again, at least not as hard as finding the drive. When he was finished with the case, Xing started looking for the gang, checking all the places Yang mentioned, but came up empty after five days. In the meantime, the chief assigned him to another life-and-death case, believing him to be the best man for the job. He began to pay less attention to Liu's problem because of the new case, and changed his tone when Liu went to see him.

"I looked all over the city, and nothing." He added, "They might have left Beijing and gone to another city."

The deal with Xing turned out to be a lost cause and Liu felt he'd been deceived, while the deadline specified on the IOU was only ten days away.

"Fine, if you can't find the thieves, you have to go to Henan as my witness so I can get my money."

"You need evidence to solve a case. What good would a word from me do if you don't have the IOU?" Xing didn't know whether to laugh or cry. "Besides, Henan is outside my jurisdiction."

Xing began avoiding Liu and refused to take his calls. Liu was disappointed, but could do nothing to a police sergeant, so he went out looking for the thieves again. He had no luck after a week of searching, yet he did not want to quit. He kept his job at the site, where a new owner had taken over the construction as if nothing had happened. The new boss, a heavyset man with a square face and a jovial personality, came to inspect the dining hall. Ren Baoliang told Liu the boss's name, Sui Yi, but the pack was too important to pay Sui much attention; he continued searching for another week whenever he could find time.

After living in Beijing for six years, Liu had known little about the city, but since losing his pack, he'd spent more than a month looking for it, and could now boast intimate knowledge of every major thoroughfare and small lane, though still with no results. One day he learned that his search was wasted effort. Li Gengsheng had paid up even without the IOU, and Liu's son, Liu Pengju, got the whole sixty thousand yuan. When he and his girlfriend were kidnapped, they'd been beaten; their captors had burned their chests and legs with cigarettes. Pengju was outraged that his father had hidden the truth about the purse and caused them such pain and suffering, but through the incident he also got the story behind the kidnapping and, in particular, the IOU. Concluding that he needed to be compensated for his suffering, instead of pestering his father, he went back to Henan to demand sixty thousand yuan from his stepfather.

Telling Li he would not let him off the hook now that he knew what had happened six years earlier, he wanted Li to give him the money or he'd seek revenge on his father's behalf. His father might have been a coward, but not him, he threatened. When Li heard that the IOU was lost, he refused to pay by claiming there had been no such agreement.

"Liu Yuejin was such a liar." Li feigned anger. "Next time I see him, I'm going to give him another thrashing so he'll know not to lie like that."

The setback inspired Pengju's girlfriend, Mai Dangna, to suggest that they go see his mother, who had to know what had happened. Li was his stepfather, so it was natural that he would not honor the agreement, but Huang Xiaoqing was his birth mother, who had to be on his side.

But Pengju did not go to see his mother directly. Instead, he kidnapped his half-brother the next day around noon when his mother went to get her hair done. The baby brother was not even three months old, but luckily was fast asleep when Pengju took him to Luoyang, where he checked into a hotel and called Li Gengsheng. Pay up in three days and he could have his son back; if not, he would strangle Li's bastard son, he said. Stunned, Li was about to call the police when Huang stopped him and began to wail, complaining that it was all Li's fault that her family had fallen to this state. Li had to kick himself for being so careless. A worldly man who had been through so much, he nevertheless was had by a youngster. He had no choice but to give Pengju sixty thousand yuan.

Liu Yuejin was still out looking for his pack when the money changed hands. One day, after another fruitless search, he happened to pass by Weigong Village and decided to take a break at Lao Gao's noodle shop and unload what had been troubling him. He'd lost a pack and found a purse, which had led to a harrowing experience, but in the end he'd come up empty-handed. Lao Gao, who had just returned from a visit back home, did not wait for Liu to finish his complaint before telling him about the money, a news event that had rocked the whole town. It stunned Liu, who could not have imagined such an outcome.

Wordlessly, he left Gao's shop and went directly to West Station, where he bought a ticket for Henan. After getting off at Luoyang, he switched to a long distance bus to Luoshui, fuming all along the way. Li should have given the money to him, not his son Pengju. It was a sum that would determine how the second half of his life and his relationship with Manli would turn out. After what she'd gone through, Manli blamed Liu for her near-death experience and refused to talk to him. On the other hand, the episode also changed the tenor of their relationship, and it was unimportant that she would not talk to him now. Once he had the money to open a restaurant and became a rich man, she'd change her tune. It was precisely this plan that had motivated his search over the past two weeks.

Liu had changed after his recent brush with death. In the past he'd have thought first of suicide if he ran up against a problem, which was why he'd thought of killing himself when he first lost his pack. Yet when people began coming after him for the purse, the thought of suicide never occurred to him, not once. As he thought back to all that had happened, he realized that in the past he'd been alone and usually backed himself into a corner thinking about his problems. Now, with someone after him, survival was critical, so he had no time to do that. Or maybe his earlier problems were insignificant compared to what the USB drive entailed.

More importantly, his world had been so small that he was unable to see the big picture until the drive threw him into a tumultuous ocean, where he learned not to take things too seriously. He finally understood what people meant when they said one does not drown easily in the ocean, but can capsize a dinghy in a ditch. With his old habit of muttering to himself, he said, "Fuck it."

He had learned to curse instead of ruing what had happened, as he used to do.

But he could not really tell the sixty thousand yuan to go fuck itself. His dream for the second half of his life was shattered by none other than his own son, the real thief.

By the time he got back to Luoshui, Liu had heard that his son had gone to Shanghai, telling people that he and his girlfriend would make a name for themselves with the money. They had thought of going to Beijing, but the nation's capital disappointed them so much they'd changed their minds. Liu nearly fainted. He knew his son too well; instead of striking out for himself, the no-good young man would simply squander the money. He left Luoshui to go to Shanghai for fear that the money would be gone if he did not show up in time; it was a large sum to him, but would not go far in either Beijing or Shanghai. The situation was dire, so he did not go to see his ex-wife or her current husband; besides, what good would it have done to see them now?

Liu first went to see Pengju's classmate to get his son's new phone number. In order not to alert him, Liu did not call right away; he wanted to wait until he arrived in Shanghai. Backtracking his earlier journey, he traveled from Luoshui to Luoyang, where he bought a ticket for Shanghai. The train would not be in the station for two hours, so as he waited, he realized how hungry he was after not eating for twenty-four hours. How many times had he forgotten to eat over the past month or so? Walking out of the station, he crossed the street to a shop and ordered a bowl of noodles with stewed mutton. As he ate without really tasting the food, he thought about how to get the money from his son. Reasoning with him would not work; Liu knew he needed to ensnare Pengju, but how?

He racked his brain trying to come up with an idea when a woman sat down across from him and ordered a bowl of noodles. Engrossed in his own thoughts, Liu did not pay her much attention until he paid and was ready to leave; a casual glance made him freeze on the spot. It was Qu Li, Yan Ge's widow. He recognized her from when he'd played a corn vendor over a month before, and later, when he'd seen her from a distance when he and Yang Zhi tried to extort money from her. She had changed; she was now slender and well tanned. Recovering from his shock, Liu wondered if this was a chance encounter or if she had been looking for him.

"What . . . what are you doing here?" he stammered.

"It's the perfect place to run into you." She looked him in the eye.

"How did you know I was here?" He was frightened to know that she'd been looking for him and yet could not suppress his curiosity.

"You recall how Han Shengli got away during the raid?" Qu smiled.

Obviously, she'd found him through Han, who had been in the toilet when Xing showed up with the police to arrest Cao and his gang. Han had taken off at the sight of the police cars surrounding the shed. He must have gotten Liu's information from old Gao. Liu looked around and saw Han standing outside the shop gesturing at him, still asking for his money back.

"I didn't want to go see you in Beijing, where you could have betrayed me."

So she had been following him for all that time. The more he knew, the scarier the situation felt to him. Qu could not be after him for Han's money, and Liu had nothing to do with the traffic accident that killed her husband, though when he thought about it, he was not completely in the clear.

"That wasn't my idea." He added, "Mr. Yan wasn't a bad person."

"That has nothing to do with you." Qu Li dismissed him with a wave.

"Then it's because of that corrupt official who got Mr. Yan into trouble."

"It's not his fault either. It's no big deal for someone that high to accept bribes. Just like a cook who takes a few bites of the food he's cooking. Am I right?"

Liu gave the analogy some thought and shook his head. "What then?"

"It's what else he wanted," she said with a sigh.

Liu was confused, but dared not ask any more. She took out a cigarette and lit it.

"The matter should have been wrapped up, but when people are in prison, they're scared, and when they're scared they talk. They'll say anything, whether they should or not, and that leads to something else."

Liu knew she was referring to the corrupt official, the fat man on the video, but what did that have to do with him, Liu Yuejin? He wasn't a corrupt official; all he wanted was to get his money back. It had been six days since his son had gone to Shanghai, which likely meant there was only forty thousand yuan left.

"There were some cards in the purse you found."

There had been, but they were all bankcards, useless without a pass code. Besides, he wouldn't have dared using them, even if he'd known the codes. Too risky. After hearing his explanation, she said:

"I don't mean those. There was another card, smaller than the ATM cards, with a picture of the Monkey King. Where is it?"

So that was what she was after. He had seen that one, which was indeed smaller than the ATM cards. One side was golden yellow with the picture of a bauhinia flower while the other side had an image of the Monkey King wielding a club in front of a multicolored background. A dainty little thing, it had seemed unusual, so he'd kept it, but it had later escaped his attention, since everyone was focused on the drive. Then, after seeing the contents of the drive, he was worried that the card, like the drive, would bring him trouble, so he panicked and threw it away. He hadn't mentioned it to Ma Manli. Why was this woman after that? He was going to play dumb, but she stopped him.

"Please don't say you didn't take it. I've spent over a month checking on the other items in the purse, and everything but the card has been accounted for."

"I saw it but was afraid it would bring me more trouble so I threw it away."

"It wasn't a bankcard. It had even more on it, involving several lives." She added, "I've been looking for you to see if you could help me find it."

Liu jumped up from the bench. It had been over a month since he'd tossed the card into a trashcan in Bawangfen, in the eastern outskirt of Beijing. Where was he going to find it now? Besides, he had to go to Shanghai to find his son.

"I'm just a cook," he railed. "Don't come to me for the Monkey King, all right?"

"I didn't want to." She sighed. "But without it, people will still be looking for us."

Liu sat back down, with his hands around his head, when a loud train whistle sounded in the station, announcing the arrival of the train for Shanghai.